THE
FRENCH VAQUERO

The Story of a Cajun Gunfighters Journey

D1601460

JOHN "BLUE" BUNCH

outskirts
press

Acknowledgements

I want to thank all my history and cultural anthropology professors for their patience and instruction over the years. I learned that culture, the learned ways of a group of people, is paramount for most societies. I drew heavily on their lectures and writings.

A special thanks to my friend, Mimi, for endlessly editing my scribblings to make this manuscript readable and coherent. A special thanks to Dawn for her exquisite photography, practicing 'a picture is worth a thousand words'.

My wife was unbelievable, putting up with all my request to re-read a flawed manuscript. I promise to do the dishes tonight.

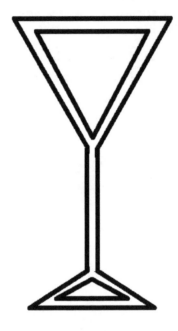

Champagne Brand

Foreword

John Alvarado could have been the most infamous gun fight-er of the old west. But he chose to ignore the pleadings of all the dime novelist who wanted to embellish his fights to sell paper-backs. He wanted to always be remembered as the defender of the less fortunate and protecting himself. That didn't fit the dime novelist collective narrative, so they instead sought to denigrate and then ignore what he had done. His story presented here, is the true history of John Alvarado the French Vaquero.

Chapter 1
Exploration

John's eyes were bloodshot, and his throat was parched, as he peered out from his tent flaps into the Iraqi morning desert. He knew this was going to be another scorcher. New Orleans could be hot, but not like this, and not this early in the morning. He had pulled an all-nighter for the battalion commander and now he had to get his boys ready for the mission. John would give anything for a cold shower and a cool mint julep right about now.

He had just graduated from college and he figured the Army National Guard was just about the right amount of military for him. After graduation, he had broken up with his girlfriend and decided a European vacation was a great way to clear his mind. Iraq was not John's idea of a vacation.

"Room, ten -hut!"

"At ease, take your seats, and listen up."

"I'm Lieutenant Alvarado, 199th Support Battalion, Company A, First Platoon leader. For those of you who are not normally part of this unit we have a unique mission that the "Louisiana Tigers" are undertaking. We have five generators we need to get to the Green Zone in Bagdad to support a hospital. We leave tomorrow at zero six hundred from the docks where the generators will be loaded on our duces and we'll drive straight through. There will be fuel stops at X-ray and Bravo, otherwise, four-hour watches for each driver and pedal to the metal the rest of the time. Everyone pack your duffels because I don't know when we'll return. Those of you not part of the 199th are now effectively reassigned to me."

"Master Sergeant Alvarado will be your den mother on this trip. I want full ammo loads for every soldier, two jerry cans of diesel per truck, and food and water for four days. Two soldiers per truck, one scout motorcycle, one soldier as a tail guard and a driver and turret gunner with me in my Hum-V."

"Sergeant Alvarado has an intel briefing for you, Master Sergeant."

"Perk your ears, boys and girls! I don't wanna write a letter to your mommas about how dumb her kid was. Right now the rag heads have a unique..."

"Sergeant!" the lieutenant warned him.

With just a hint of sarcasm the sergeant responded, "Sorry, sir, I didn't know I had to be politically correct in a war zone."

"Continue, Sergeant."

Facing the room, Master Sergeant Alvarado proceeded with his briefing "What the insurgents have been doing is loading a donkey's saddle bags with improvised explosive devices known as IED's, herding it into the middle of a convoy, then remotely detonating it. If you see that scenario take out the donkey!"

"But Sergeant, them donkeys never done nothing to me. I can't kill a dumb donkey, I'd rather kill the son-of-a-bitch with the remote," retorted Lance Corporal Scott.

"Understood, Corporal, but you won't be able to see the perp. Take out the donkey before it gets into the convoy, got it?"

"Yes, Sergeant Alvarado."

At this point, Lieutenant Alvarado joined in, "Sergeant Alvarado, I also want tarps covering the generators. I don't want some insurgent spraying them with his AK-47 just because he can see what they are. We will also be on Tac-2 radio convoy frequency."

"Ok, sir. I'll also add a can of gasoline for the scout motorcycle."

"No need, Sergeant, the motorcycle runs on diesel. Put Corporal Stéphane Bossar on the scout cycle."

"Why does the girl get to ride the crotch rocket?" said Corporal Scott.

With a withering glare, Cpl. Bossar warned, "If you don't back off Scotty, I'll stick a cold bayonet up your butt and let you figure out how to get it out."

"If you do, that'll be the coolest I've been since arriving in country," said Lance Corporal Scott.

"Both of you, knock it off," an irritated Sergeant Alvarado spat out.

"Questions? Good. Remember what Napoleon said: an army travels on its stomach, but logistics gets it there on time."

"Radio check on Tac -2, lead 1."

"Scout,two,three, four, five."

"Ok, make sure you maintain radio discipline, standard intervals, and keep your eyes open."

"Roger Scout, Roger two, Roger three, Rodney four, Roger five."

"No, smart ass, four. Do it right!"

"Yes, sir, Lead… Roger four."

"Corporal Scott, if you would, take us to Baghdad," ordered Lieutenant Alvarado.

"Well, sir, it's a four-day drive to that famous flying carpet center of the Middle East, so might as well get comfortable in this Hum-V. Darn, don't see a CD player, sir."

Corporal Scott was one of those troops who stayed just inside the boundaries of discipline, barely keeping him out of trouble with his superiors. But he was a good marksman and equally good driver.

"Sir, can I ask you a question or two?"

"Go for it, what's on your mind, Corporal?"

"Are you and Sergeant Alvarado related in any way?"

"No, Corporal, not that I know of. Obviously, you don't know much about New Orleans. There's twenty separate Alvarado families living in New Orleans that aren't related by blood."

Perplexed, the corporal blurted out, "How the heck can that be, sir? With that many families in the same town, seems almost impossible."

"Well, Corporal, it's a long story, but I'll be glad to tell you about the Alvarados of New Orleans."

"Got four days, sir; I'm all ears, but I have a question first. Is it true your great grandfather was a gunfighter?"

"Yep, but most people don't know that. How do you know about that, Corporal Scott?"

"Before I joined the Army, after nine eleven, I was in junior college in Texas studying history. Once I heard that you were the new detachment commander, I just looked you up."

"Well, let's see, where shall I start? I think Havana, Cuba, in 1538 is a good place."

"Are you kidding me, sir? Havana, Cuba, that shit hole of a communist paradise, is where your grandfather was a gunfighter?"

"Keep it shut, Scotty, and just listen, you might learn something.

"Ok, where was I before you interrupted? Oh, yeah, Havana, Cuba, 1538. It was fall, just after all the hurricanes had spent themselves. Governor's palace, evening, sometime."

"Well, son, what is your name?"

"They call me Juan, Senor."

"What, no last name… just Juan?"

"Yes, Senor. I don't even know how old I am. I think about thirteen, Senor General."

"Well, Juan of unknown age, I am looking for a cabin boy to take care of my horse and all my accoutrements on the expedition to the North American continent. Do you think you can discharge those duties without stealing from me, son?"

"Si, General De Soto, this I can do for you, and I don't steal, sir!" Juan adamantly declared.

Juan's head was spinning now. He was leaving the streets of Havana, where he was a nobody, to care for the captain-general of the new Spanish conquest of the southeast portion of the North American continent. Heady stuff to be sure, but all that really mattered to Juan was that he would, for the first time in his life, be eating three meals a day. For a scrawny, underweight thirteen-year-old this was all that really mattered in life. He easily turned his back on all his homeless street friends in Havana and changed his life instantly.

The Spanish Empire feared the incursion from the north by the British in Canada who were ever-expanding southward, and wanted to establish a buffer to protect their possessions in Florida. The king of Spain had ordered the governor of Cuba to organize an expedition to plant the Spanish flag north of Florida, and west toward Texas, to thwart the ever-aggressive English marauders. His choice to lead the expedition was Hernando de Soto, who had helped to conquer Peru in South America. He chose Luis de Moscoso Alvarado to be the second in command. He was a nephew of a Peruvian conquistador with some expeditionary experience of his own. Of course, the cost of the expedition would be recovered with the acquisition of slaves and gold that the conquistadors would surely bring back. The king would get a fifth of all proceeds, and the Governor of Cuba would not go unrewarded.

On May 25, 1538, the expedition landed at what is now Tampa Bay, Florida, with 220 horses and 620 men. Nine ships would keep pace along the Gulf coast and resupply the expedition as necessary. For almost three years, the expedition would explore the southeast of the future United Sates.

Essentially, de Soto had two regiments of men; not an inconsiderable sum, but not an overwhelming force either. But, one thing the white man would learn about the North American Indian, was their inability to unite to fight a common foe. Many of the smaller tribes would even help the Spanish to defeat a neighboring Indian nation that had harassed and diminished their own small band. They scouted, guided and even joined forces with the Spanish to defeat the major tribal groups. Captain-General de Soto capitalized on the native's inability to organize a united front. He encouraged fractionalization amongst the tribes to get what he wanted: safe passage, slaves and gold.

Although every man was considered a soldier, only about half of the expedition were real fighting men. The other half could be counted on in a fight, but they were generally employed keeping the soldiers fed, watered and in good condition to repel any attack. There were also women and priests along; the latter to convert natives to the Catholic faith even if they were unwilling though a surprising number listened to the brown robes and became obedient servants. But Juan knew that he wanted to be with a woman when he got older and the celibacy oath the priests took would not fit Juan's desires.

The number of domestic animals brought along for subsistence was staggering; however, the supply did not last long. But once the expedition found a way to harvest the forest buffalo, meat supply was not an issue for the expedition. The native allies were increasingly employed as hunters and fishermen to feed the many mouths. But it was the constant search for gold that really drove the expedition forward; even to the point of razing a village because they would not reveal the meager source of the gold nuggets that they possessed. The Spanish did not believe the marginal supply of gold was the result of simply panning a stream. There had to be a big mine somewhere.

The natives soon learned that they could avoid the wrath of the Spanish if they pointed to the west and its setting sun as to the true source of all the gold the Spanish desired. That correlated with the myths that the Conquistadores believed about the "Seven Cities of Cibola."

Juan marveled at how well the expedition was handled, and being only a tent flap away from overhearing all the decisions that were made, he gained an appreciation of the reason. Usually, the officers were well intentioned and made sound decisions, but it was the subordinates that impressed Juan the most.

The rank of sergeant carried the most influence in the camp. Once an order was given, it fell to these mid-level leaders to execute the instructions of the well-bred and educated officers. They generally were natural leaders, but without the family heritage and connection, nor an extensive education. Most were creole, of Spanish descent, born in the new world. They made all the difference in a well-run, well-directed and efficient expedition. The sergeants were in tune with the men's morale and needs. When Juan grew up and got to choose his profession, he wanted to be a sergeant.

It fell to the sergeants to arrange the most effective fighting formation in the Spanish army, the fighting square. It had served Spain tactically for over a century and was just as effective on the frontier. Once the fighting square was formed with two ranks of musketeers it was virtually impregnable. Not until massive artillery formations could be brought to bear did it fall out of favor. But during the conquest in the new world the native tribes never could defeat it. Why they continued to assault the square Juan never could understand. Once the first rank discharged its muskets, the second rank withheld fire until the first rank reloaded and then they volley fired. If the natives timed their charge between volleys, they were met by helmeted and body armored soldiers who welded the finest steel blades in Europe. Technology, as much as anything, helped conquer the new world.

The expedition was never well received by the native population mostly because of the slaving incentive of the Spanish. As far as Juan could recollect, only one group of twenty native slaves were ever transported to the coast and embarked to Cuba. Most died in route or escaped. The tension was palpable between the southeast American Indians and the conquistadors. The latter always frustrated at not finding a Mexico City laden with gold staircases, and the former resentful of the Spanish incursions.

It all came to a head at the battle of Tuscaloosa.

Once the Spanish square was formed, the Choctaw kept assaulting it to no avail. Juan was essentially a bystander; his only duty was to relay messages to the various units from General de Soto. On one of his runs, Juan encountered a Cherokee boy probably doing the same for his tribesman. Neither were armed and they just stared at each other. He did not hate the Indian boy and they just simply went about their respective errands.

The battle was devastating for the Indian village. All the residents were scattered, and about half the village was burned to the ground. The smell of burning wood, thatch and flesh permeated the air. The expedition did not escape unscathed, almost one hundred of its members were dead or wounded, and Juan thought to himself, "for what reason was this done?"

After the battle, General de Soto decided to break off contact with the coastal supply ships and strike out toward the interior of the continent. The tangle of thorn and thick forest made things difficult going for the expedition, but they managed to find several native trails to follow. He crossed the Mississippi and patrolled the mountainous region of the present-day area of Arkansas. The expedition was slowly being whittled down by disease, constant ambushes and copper colored snakes. Even the great leader of the expedition succumbed to a fever in 1542. As a result, Luis de Moscoso Alvarado, became the "maestro de campo" or field commander. Unfortunately, due to his mishandling of an engagement with the Chickasaw Indians, the expedition lost a further dozen men and numerous horses. Morale plummeted.

The new commander tried to salvage something of the expedition and decided to take a circuitous route back to Cuba via Texas. He elected to go back to the Mississippi River, build seven brigantines and pinnaces, load the remainder of the 322 survivors on them and sail down river.

"Come here, scout," said General Alvarado. "What is that monument on the shore of the Mississippi River over there?"

"It is Red Stick. Indians north of it are mean; Indians south of it not so mean."

Moscoso Alvarado knew his sick and severely wounded would not be able to traverse the Texas route and further the expedition goals. He needed to deposit them someplace safe and retrieve them later. He selected the last great bend in the Mississippi River, on higher ground, just before it spills into the Gulf of Mexico.

"You men are elected to care for these wounded and sick. I will make every effort, as soon as possible, to come back and take you to Cuba after completing the exploration in Texas. You can select the tools you need to build sufficient protection for yourselves. I have been assured that the natives here are not hostile."

With that, General Alvarado disappeared down the Mississippi in the brigantines, leaving 21 members of his expedition to fend for themselves. Juan had lost his sponsor when General de Soto died and, therefore, was of little value for the remainder of the expedition, and was subsequently dropped from the rolls. He was left with the other men on the banks of the muddy river, to survive as best they could, with the added burden of caring for seven severely wounded among them.

Captain Herndon Barbarossa was a rather short, intimidating fellow who was a former Spanish pirate that preyed on English merchant shipping in the Caribbean. He had fiery red hair, a black beard and bushy eyebrows. He acquired his merchant ship from the right honorable English gentleman, Sir North, during his pirating days. Barbarossa maintained his pirate persona to keep his crew in line.

The outlaw soon found it was safer to become a merchant man himself, rather than a pirate. Boisterous, self-centered and always looking for a way to make a "piece of eight," he hired out to General Alvarado to retrieve the 21 men the general had left on the shores of the Mississippi, near present day New Orleans.

Captain Barbarossa's ship, the "Raven," was well past where he thought the Alvarado settlement would be. He saw the "big red stick" on the shore of the Mississippi River and knew he must turn around and go back downriver. He had obviously missed the Alvarado settlement somehow, that is, if it still existed. Three days later he saw a single line of smoke on the eastern horizon and chose to heave to, set an anchor and go ashore. But before he did, he ordered three cannon shots to be fired, just in case the smoke came from an Indian camp fire.

It took over an hour before anyone showed themselves on the scant beach. Unbelievably, there were 20 rag tag men that slowly gathered at the captain's landing site. Amazed that anyone was alive after eighteen months in the wilderness, Captain Barbarossa approached the Alvarado expedition survivors with a certain trepidation. His six well-armed sailors were nervous and prepared for anything the survivors might attempt to do.

"Gather around and hear me. I'm Captain Barbarossa, sent by the governor of Cuba for your relief. General Alvarado could not be here himself because of his wounds. I will take you back to Havana. Get yourselves ready to depart."

"Why should we go back and be peasants under the general's thumb?" said one irritated survivor. Another loudly protested the captain's order with the same reasoning, "He left us here for eighteen months without any regard for us and now he wants us back to work us like dogs!" The rest of the crowd voiced the same opinion and the crescendo of voices increased to a unanimous "No, we will not go!"

The captain knew that with a slight wave of his hand, his six sailors could easily wade into the throng of men and deal them a punishing blow, but he held off for the moment. He also noticed that at the back of the crowd one young boy left the scene and headed back into the wooded shore.

"The general owns your contract for the expedition until he sees fit to discharge you. I must show a profit for my troubles to retrieve you from this place. I assure you; you will return with me!"

The situation was growing very tense. Captain Barbarossa knew he could not let this throng of subordinates' scatter without some control being exerted over them. He also knew they had survived for eighteen months in a hostile environment and now felt they owed nothing to anyone. Their self-declared independence was mostly bravado and defiance, but could turn more forceful should he push them. At the back of the crowd of men he could see the same boy, who had moments before left the group, struggling with a broken-down wheelbarrow piled high with three sacks of grain. As the boy pushed through the crowd he stopped and rested the wheelbarrow in front of Captain Barbarossa.

"Senor, Captain," said Juan, "I have collected these three bags of wild rice and wish to sell them to you."

In an instant, Captain Barbarossa saw the solution to the situation. He could make a profit on this trip, establish a colony for the Spanish Empire, and leave these troublesome men where they wanted to stay.

"Do the rest of you have goods to trade or sell for my efforts to retrieve you from this place?" inquired the captain.

"I have dried fish," said one survivor.

Another intoned, "Cypress wood by the board foot."

"Good," said Captain Barbarossa, "I will buy and sell and trade to settle your debt with General Alvarado. I can come back about every six to eight weeks if you can continue to supply me with these items of trade."

The men on the shore were slightly stunned that a simple deal was going to alleviate their condition and they would be free to do as they pleased. The fruits of their labor would determine their futures, not some distant general. Once Juan was paid a silver coin for the three bags of wild rice, the general feeling among the survivors was euphoric at the change in their circumstances.

Captain Barbarossa was satisfied with the deal and admonished the small band of men, "I will hold all of you Alvarado's accountable for our contract. I am not to be trifled with. I will return on a regular basis and I expect you to be here to trade with me exclusively, do you understand?" There was a general consensus among the survivors.

Chapter 2
"Sannd"

No one knew the date Sannd (pronounced Sand) was born, and none of his Apache family really cared. Suffice it to say, his mother gave birth to him in the spring which gave him the best chance to survive to his first birthday. Sannd was raised as a true Apache by his father and grandfather. He learned the Apache way, which was the right way to learn to be a man, and later a warrior.

Sannd's culture was based on the extended nuclear family, including grandparents. They traveled together, hunted together and made war together. They would occasionally group and camp with other Apache families uniting in a loose tribal confederation based on a strong leader; but family groups and bachelor groups only followed who they chose to follow. There was no hierarchy or structure to the tribe. At best they were splintered groups of nomadic tribes, and at worst considered by civilized societies as totally disorganized. But they did not care what others thought and simply wanted to be left alone to live the Apache way, the right way.

Apaches were avid raiders and merciless killers, often warring among themselves. It was Apache country as defined by Apache bands and to territorial invaders they were ruthless. No one would encroach upon their land, and no one would take it, as the Apache knew how to fight for their beautiful and bountiful land. It had all they needed or wanted. It rained when they needed rain; it was dry when it needed to be dry. It was a perfect land for the Apache way of life. Only the Apache could appreciate what others would call a barren land.

The Apache was well suited to the country he inhabited. He was more of a long-distance runner, shorter in stature rarely growing over five and half feet tall. Built for endurance, he was muscular with sinews of iron, had a strong heart and a darker complexion to survive the harsh sun of their homeland. He rarely showed any sensitivity to hunger and pain. The Apache thrived in the American southwest where others feared to travel. Those that came to their country were obviously inferior simply because they could not survive there, and because they were not Apache "*the people.*" Apaches were the true people of the earth, and their way was the right way; all others were beneath any Apache.

Sannd enjoyed evenings sitting around the family campfire listening to his grandfather and great grandfather tell stories of his people. How they survived one calamity or another including how his grandfather killed a black bear, thus feeding the family for a week. Many times, the stories consisted of how both his father and grandfather bested the enemy of the Apaches' and made the enemy look like fools. It was the duty of every Apache to protect his family and then his territory. Sannd could only hope to uphold these sacred duties for his own family in the future.

His father trained him to learn everything about his enemy's culture, tactics, social customs, and superstitions; these were as important as learning wood craft and traveling in hostile terrain. Predicting how an enemy would react was as important as knowing how to use one's weapons.

But his most important and greatest weapon was his own mind. Sannd had to understand that if he was captured by an enemy, Apaches may not be able to rescue him. He had to find a way to get himself free on his own. He must use his mind in ways that he never thought possible to plan and execute whatever he needed to do. His psychological strength was his best trait for survival.

For the Apache the power of observation paid huge dividends to a warrior or hunter's survival. He had to be self-reliant, always looking to the sky instead of his feet. He had to learn to build a small fire and sit close to it, not a large fire and sit back from it, particularly in enemy country. To conserve what he had in case he needed it later, and above all else, look outward not inward. Don't feel sorry for yourself but look for a way to turn a calamity into an advantage. If you accustomed yourself to being prey, you would be more alert to the dangers of your surroundings. Learn to endure solitude, for if you don't it will lead to lapses, missed clues, and lack of patience.

Sannd's father taught him to run long distances with a mouth full of water without swallowing it. He learned to forage on plentiful yucca which had fruit and edible flowers, as well as to find wild potatoes, wild berries and various squash. The tasty rattlesnake and the peccary, a pig-like animal, as well as an assortment of small birds abounded in Apache land. No one should starve in his country. He also learned to use the dried intestines of various animals to carry fresh water, or to hollow out a gourd for the same purpose. He learned to never gorge on food when it was plentiful for it would make his stomach big and require more to fill it. Instead he would always eat sparingly so his stomach remained small and would not feel hunger as readily. And he learned to locate flint deposits for knife and arrow making. Apache land had everything a man could ever need to survive. Truly his father and grandfather were great men to pass all this on to him.

Although a long-distance runner, he knew how to ride the 'big dog' that the early Spaniard's brought into his country. But foot travel was preferred over horseback as the animal needed to forage for food periodically and only slowed a warrior down. It was also easier to hide in enemy country when traveling on foot.

One thing that never made sense to Sannd is when the white tribes started to come to Apache country. They were called by various names: Spaniard, Missourian, Mexican and Texan. He could not remember so many tribes looking the same and behaving the same and having so many different names. They were all dishonorable and extremely difficult to get along with. You could not trust any of them and they all had an odor about them that fouled the Apache nose. What rankled Sannd the most was that they all wanted to claim the land and put up fences. How can you own the land? It belongs to all men. And how do you fence it so others cannot travel, why a boundary? Apaches had no boundaries and had wandered for generations. His father and grandfather could not understand this either. The white tribes were not true human beings.

Sannd's grandfather told stories of the first white tribe to come into Apache lands. They were feeble and were initially few and the Apache paid little attention to them. Grandfather did mention the big dogs that they had; which would later benefit the Apache. The numbers of white tribesmen increased over the years and they travelled all over Apache land without permission. It was getting to the point a 'true human being' could not relieve himself without fouling a white man's dignity. They were always looking for someone else to do their work for them, enslaving everyone they met. The Zuni and Navajo were better suited to be slaves, but not an Apache. If an Apache was enslaved, he only stayed that way for a few days, escaping with nothing more than the clothes on his back. This confounded the

Spaniard tribesmen the most. They would not believe a person could survive in the wilderness with so little and continue to reject civilization. Truly the white tribes were the oddest of all people in Apache country.

The one white tribesman that fascinated Sannd was the brown robes. They had a penchant for creating some of the finest "orchards" as they called them. Those fruits were exquisite and Sannd and his friends could not steal enough of them. Sannd never killed a brown robe since they had a similar early morning chant that started their respective days. But he never fathomed the respect they showed to two crossed sticks, even to the point of dying for those crossed sticks. White tribesmen were indeed crazy.

His family always avoided the whites whenever they could, only trading with them when absolutely necessary. The idea that Sannd had to avoid the white tribesmen irritated him to no end since it was Apache land the trespassers were on. One evening his grandfather told him a story about the time the Spaniard tribe ceased to exist. Initially, Sannd thought they left Apache country, but according to grandfather's story they simply no longer wanted to be called Spaniards and changed their name to Mexicans. He never understood. How could an Apache simply no longer want to be called an Apache when the moon rose on a given day? Sannds confusion about the white tribes only deepened.

Sannd knew his own mind. He would grow up to be a good Apache. One day he asked his grandfather to negotiate a bride for him.

"But grandson, you are far too young to take on a wife and then a child. You must wait till you are older and ready for these responsibilities."

Sannd stood firm in front of his grandfather, feet spread

apart, fists clenched, head erect and chest out.

"I see you are not going to take no for an answer, grandson. I will negotiate for you. But you must be ready with a fine gift for your bride's father, so the loss of his daughter will not be so great. Who is the woman you have chosen?"

"Coyotes' daughter, Yellow Flower. She is named after the cactus spring flower blossom. It suits her well, Grandfather. She is the most beautiful woman in the world. Her hair is shiny black and she moves just so."

"And the gift, grandson?"

"I wanted to give a horse but if I stole one from the Mexicans, they would try to take it back. I have decided to give Coyote a fine black bear hide I prepared myself."

"Well put, grandson, that will keep Coyote warm in the winter and keep his heart warm at the loss of his daughter."

One day his family travelled to a new canyon and set up camp. His wife and one-year-old son, as well as the extended family, were all enjoying the bounty of the land. They expected to stay, as all Apache did, till the canyon had nothing else to offer. Once settled, Sannd chose to go for deer meat; it would take him about three days to stalk and kill a buck large enough to feed everyone.

As usual, Sannd preferred to travel alone and on foot. He was a successful hunter and this trip was no exception. On his return, he was carrying the buck on his shoulders, approaching the camp in a zig zag fashion so as not to alarm anyone. Normally if there was a danger in the area Sannd would approach in a straight line letting everyone in camp know to prepare to flee.

During his approach, he noticed the campfire was irregular, like someone had forgotten to tend it and it was faltering and dying out. Then, to his horror, his eyes saw something unspeakable! The entire family was massacred; everyone was dead and some were mutilated. The worst of it was his baby son was roasting in the flames over the dying embers of the central campfire!

Sannd stood dumbfound not knowing what to do or what to think. He wanted to yell out, scream at the phantom responsible for this disaster but he knew he could not. Like a wounded animal on the prairie, the sound would allow a predator to know its whereabouts and finish it off. He could not be an Apache husband, father or son mourning his tremendous loss, not just yet anyway. All he could do for now was bury his emotions along with his family. Of course, this was the worst day of his life!

He dropped the buck and started to look for clues as to the perpetrators of this horrendous crime. It did not take long to discover a single boot print with a long straight line behind it. It was the clear mark of a Spaniard who wore big roweled spurs. That was all he needed to know.

It took three days for Sannd to bury his family in the Apache way. Mourning them would take a lifetime and the anxiety, loneliness and despair would never heal. He had to avenge them. In the Apache way, he sought his vision as to what to do next. The vision was not long in coming and his reasoning was clear. Apache country had been violated by the white tribes who came here uninvited. It was a white tribe that massacred his family. They kept coming from the direction of the rising sun and their numbers were increasing every year; he must stop them any way he could. He had to prevent them from hurting any more Apache the way they had hurt him. He now had a mission to walk toward the rising sun and kill as many members of the various white tribes as he could. It became a singular goal to avenge the death of his family, especially the future warrior his son would have become. This would be how he mourned the loss of his family, by killing.

It wasn't long before he had an opportunity to begin his revenge on the white tribesmen. He happened on a single wagon pulled by two yokes of oxen. He knew the whites would always try to hunt for meat whenever they could, so he used his blanket to cover himself and bleated like a sheep. In the distance, he must have been very convincing as the two white men grabbed their guns and proceeded to stalk him. He simply disappeared around a bluff, jogged to the other side, and then came up behind the wagon as silently as falling pine needles.

The woman was gazing in the distance, hoping her men would soon shoot a sheep for supper. The four children were in the wagon watching their father and uncle when Sannd struck. He walked silently up behind the woman, and stuck his knife point in her neck at the base of the skull. She fell silently to the ground. Without alarming the children, he reached into the wagon, took the dried buffalo pouch, known as a parfleche, containing dried meat and left just as silently as he had come. He had jogged a hundred yards when he heard a commotion behind him. The two men had returned to the wagon, discovered the dead woman and were now firing at him. They did not come close to hitting him and he half smiled, turned away and was gone into the neighboring canyon.

Sannd never learned to use the white man's rifles. They required too much feeding and when they barked everyone knew where you were located. He would carry out his solo mission with his traditional tools; his lance, a bow and arrow and his belt knife. He would steal what he needed and keep going east, trying to terrorize all the white men he could with his stealthy attacks. He would make them think there was more than just his army of one. Make them all pay for massacring his family. There were many opportunities for Sannd to kill these white trespassers and he would exact his revenge tenfold before he was done.

Sannd did not know it but he was fighting the same fight that many other civilizations and societies had been fighting for millennia. The same fight the Chinese fought when the Mongols attacked, the same fight when the Toltecs were pushed out by the Mayans and they in turn were pushed out by the Aztecs. It was the inevitable outgrowth of overpopulation of one culture, or envy of other societies' resources that caused these migrations and resulted in the rise of an oppressed societies' freedom fighters. He was experiencing the same thing the Sioux in Minnesota had when the Fox tribe pushed them out onto the plains. They in turn pushed the Blackfeet and the Crow further west, resulting in deadly enemies on both sides. But Sannd knew nothing of this history, nor did he care. He only wanted to rid his country of these white tribesman that came uninvited and took what was rightfully Apache.

He understood that the weakness of the Indian was their inability to unite. All the tribes he knew of always fought each other for one reason or another. Sannd could see that if all the tribes united, they could keep the four encroaching white tribes from gaining a toehold in any red man's land, but the Apache never had any allies. In fact, the Apaches were notorious raiders of their neighbors, and, unfortunately, Sannd was no great orator that could go to his neighboring tribes and seek common ground to fight the incursion. He was a simple Apache warrior, seeking revenge on those that had hurt him. He was engaged in singular battle to terrify as many white tribesmen as he could, to get them to turn back and go to their homeland. It was his life mission.

One day Sannd and a friend happened upon a wagon in the middle of the prairie that had a wheel stuck in a deep rut. The team of six oxen could not pull the wagon out and they could see that the white man was laboring at the wheel trying to help free it. Suddenly his wife stood up in the wagon and pointed at the two Apaches. The white man grabbed his gun and began firing, but they rushed him before he could reload and Sannd's friend arrowed him through the heart. The woman sat still on the wagon seat and tried to be invisible to the two Apache. Sannd scalped the white man and laid the hairpiece next to the corpse. While the wife remained rigidly silent on the wagon seat, the Apaches went through the wagon and took what they wanted. Sannd butchered the small family pet dog so they would have fresh meat for supper that evening. As they walked away, they knew the white woman and oxen would be dead within two days.

Why did such weak people come into this country?

By now Sannd's reputation had spread far and wide. He was responsible for at least thirty white men's deaths on the frontier, probably more. Once he had a reputation for killing, other deaths that were unexplained were attributed to him. The White Mountain, Lipan and Jicarilla Apache families would sit around campfires and tell stories to their children about the great warrior Sannd and his singular quest.

He was now entering the Comancheria. If there was any other tribe that could equal an Apache in ferocity and cunning it would be a Comanche. Although Sannd was told that they approved of his quest to kill as many whites as he could, in no way did they want any of those deaths associated with the Comanche. He was welcome to cross the Comancheria, but the Comanche had an agreement with the Texans and they kept their agreements. Sannd knew if he violated the Comanche rule, they would send twenty warriors after him. That would be a challenge and a distraction for Sannd in his quest, so he needed a signature to let everyone know it was him. He told the

Comanche that he would scalp his victims and leave the scalp next to the corpse as his signature. They agreed.

Sannd was not hard to please. He sought solace in his own company and needed very few items to survive. He would find a half carved out sandstone cave in a rock cliff, make a fire and cook a meadow lark for his supper; adding some roots, and a single corn bread tortilla. That was a feast for him.

He would think of his family at these times. It would be about time to teach his son to use a bow and arrow had the boy survived. Sannd would have liked that … but he could not dwell on such thoughts for long because of the constant need to be vigilant. After his meal, he would heat some rocks, dig a shallow hole in the sand and cover them. Then placing his single blanket over the spot, it would give him a warm bed for the night.

As he traveled eastward his targets became more numerous and more frequent. One day in the openness of the plains Sannd saw a single ox-drawn wagon approaching. He simply lay down in the tall grass and let them pass. They came within twenty-five yards of his position, paying no attention to their dogs when they barked in his direction. As they passed, Sannd saw nineteen in number with only three rifles among them. He did not molest these people, as they were heading in a direction that had no water. He knew that in three or four days he would cut their track again and all would be dead of thirst.

On the fourth day, he approached the buzzard-covered carcasses of the sole wagon in the middle of the prairie. The stench offended Sannd, but he had need of a new belt knife and thought this was an opportunity to recover one. As he rummaged through the wagon, he heard a small cry come from under some blankets. He gave some thought to building a fire and throwing the surviving baby into it but thought it would be too much trouble.

Why do such weak people come into this land?

Further east he happened onto a lone settler's family home-stead. It was a substantial place, looking like it had been in operation for several years. Sannd noted the three enormous hay stakes that were set aside so the white farmer could feed his livestock throughout the winter. That night Sannd snuck up to each stake of hay and set it on fire, the three blazes could be seen for miles. The next morning, from his hidden vantage point, he saw the white man hitch his wagon with his mules and load his precious belongings and family into it. The white man's last act was to go to the corral and free all his livestock. Sannd noted a nice sorrel bald face with flaxen mane and tail. It was a pony with four white knee-high legs running free. He would have coveted the animal under other circumstances, but to his delight the farmer turned his wagon east and left the homestead. Sannd looked up to the sky and simply said *"han"* (yes). A moment of glee filled his heart.

Sannd did not necessarily avoid the small settlements and towns he came across in his sojourn moving eastward. Many times, he would enter them at dark and create mischief. Things like untying the hitched horses in front of a saloon and turning them loose onto the plains or setting unexplained fires. Other times he would find a drunk passed out in a dark alley and slit his throat. His body would only be discovered because of the decaying corpse that alerted the townsfolk. Once when he was caught mutilating a passed out drunk, a general alarm went out and Sannd had to steal a horse and make for the nearest canyon. He rode into it and found a large rock on which to dismount, then spooked the horse up into the back end of the canyon. The posse rode by and eventually caught the frightened animal, never suspecting how Sannd had evaded them. But his favorite terror tactic was harassing the small wagon trains that kept coming west.

When a small wagon train would fort up for the evening, they would put all the livestock in the center of the circled wagons. That way they could protect them throughout the night with just a few guards. But in the morning the people in the wagon train needed to leave it and go to the bush to get rid of the poisons from the lower body. That's when Sannd would strike. Once the white bottom was exposed, he simply stuck the man or woman with his knife in the back of the neck at the base of the skull.

The terror it created among the travelers was immediate. It got so bad that the immigrants began sending two people out to do their business. Sannd simply arrowed the guard and then dispatched the indisposed settler before they could react. To counter Sannds uncivilized war on them, the travelers soon had to foul their camping sites just to be safe in the area in which Sannd was rumored to be.

Sannd was often beseeched by other renegades to form a war party and raid all the western settlements. But he knew once he formed a raiding party of the most notorious fighters, the Texans and other whites would pursue him with the Army and Texas Rangers, with a determination like no other in history. For now, Sannd preferred to carry out his mission by himself. He would entertain the war party idea at a later date.

For the time being, he was content to enter settlements at dark, dispatch drunks by pushing their faces into mud holes and suffocating them or setting mercantile stores ablaze. Once one of the supply stores he set on fire erupted in a dangerous, loud explosion when the fire torched the powder magazine. The fireball could be seen for miles, bright as the rising sun.

Sannd also enjoyed raiding a settler's chicken coop for his dinner. When he left, as an afterthought he opened the latch on the farmer's corral and let the animals wander out onto the prairie. The next day Sannd encountered the farmer pursuing his animals. The farmer unwisely took a shot at him, but before he could reload, Sannd rushed him and ran his lance through his mid-section. Sannd laid his scalp near the body.

Why do such weak people come into Apache country, he would ask himself again and again?

By his own recollection Sannd had more than amply avenged his family. He calculated killing upward of seventy-three people in retaliation for what the white man had done to him. Mexicans figured the number was twice that. But Sannd did not feel he could quit and go home to his tribe. If he did, the whites would follow and subject the Apaches of his homeland to more privations. Sannd's life now was to go east and try to eradicate as many whites as he could, stopping them from coming into Apache land. He continued to walk east into the sun following his vision.

Chapter 3
"Warf Rats"

Captain Barbarossa continued to serve the twenty Alvarado families for some fifteen years in an exclusive arrangement benefiting all concerned. But it came to an end when the red-headed captain was engulfed in a hurricane and lost his ship, his crew and his life. By then other merchants were aware of the settlement on the Mississippi River and were establishing lucrative mercantile franchises. The crossroad of a river junction and the ocean has always been a geographical intersection that humans have tended to inhabit creating towns and cities.

New Orleans is no exception. It grew over the centuries into a thriving metropolis. It was eclectic in nature with multiple cultures asserting their will at various times, New Orleans was ruled by one super power after another, not really caring which powerful state was "the boss" at any given time. Spain and France would, depending on international intrigues, transfer Louisiana several times. Even when it became part of the United States, the residents fully expected Louisiana would change governmental hands again. New Orleans residents tended to be loyal to New Orleans first.

Creole influences of Spanish descendants, plus the African characters of the slave trade and the French exiles from the Grand Derangement, made up the early cultural mix of New Orleans. American dominance would come later. Meanwhile, each culture tried to keep its identity, each insisted its way was the right way, but ultimately, they succumbed to the inevitability of melding together. It was unavoidable; once a culture met another both were changed forever. New Orleans formed a distinctly New Orleans culture from the various combinations.

John Alvarado was the descendant of Juan "with no last name," and was the progeny of almost three hundred years of Louisiana history. He knew about his ancestors' early struggles to survive the Desoto expedition and Captain Alvarado's decision to leave twenty-one members of the expedition on the shores of the Mississippi. It was a great source of pride for his branch of the Alvarado's that Juan survived and ultimately prospered in the New World.

John's parents were prosperous middle-class merchants. They owned a mercantile business in New Orleans, a freight line and two warehouses on the cities' wharf. The unique thing about their warehouse business was the service the Alvarado's offered. They employed only family members and provided a night watchman to guard the respective warehouse; ensuring the safety and security of their customers' transited goods. No other merchant provided this type of additional service to their customers.

John's father and uncle were the primary owners of the Alvarado Mercantile of New Orleans. They both believed in honor, respect and family first, with their Catholic faith grounding them in everyday life. Pique, John's father, was married to Joanna, a Cajun beauty, and he had one older sister, Julia. He was born and raised a Creole/Cajun, inheriting his blue eyes from his grandfather Aristotle Alvarado. His branch of the Alvarado family was well respected in New Orleans. As a French Creole, his father had the good taste to speak English without lisping when conducting business with the Anglos.

John's early years were spent helping his father and uncle with the business. But in his free time, he was always running with his cohort of "wharf rats," a gang of young boys who constantly sought to help the sailors and riverboat men with necessities when they came ashore. Running errands for the dock workers and sailors, the boys would often fetch pails of beer or run letters to the post office. They would be compensated a penny for their services--a fortune for eight to ten-year-old's. John would always take the "rats" to his mother's store to spend their wealth on candy and his personal favorite, peppermint sticks. Joanna would often provide lunch for the throng of five or six boys, afterward enjoying the sound of their play in the family quadrangle home. Many of the other parents did the same on occasion. John's only rule was to be home before dark.

Even as a young boy, John exhibited adult traits. He was scrupulous, honest, polite, calm, obliging, with the ability to listen to people. He had the gift of a soft bright smile with kind blue eyes prompting people to trust him. He was loyal and devoted to his family. John was quick with a quip and apt to tell a joke to disarm any tense situation. He did not like confrontations, but he never ran from them. Every person who spent any time with John was sure to leave charmed. He always assumed the role of protector, for in his young mind he was a sort of gallant knight, fending off evil and shielding those he cared for.

He was the leader of the wharf rats and they looked to him for guidance. He was slow to anger but when he was forced to fight, he was a hurricane in combat. In fact, his temper was uncontrollable at times. He punished his opponent without mercy once he had him down, often having to be pulled off the unfortunate miscreant before serious harm ensued. Protecting his "gang" made John feel useful, a point of satisfaction for him.

John's best friend was a light complexioned black boy named Pasqual Toussaint. Pasqual's father, Samson, had emigrated from Jamaica when Pasqual was a toddler. He had a farm just outside town and provided John's family store with fresh vegetables for resale to the public. Samson was a freed black man and rumors about how he got his freedom always swirled around him but nothing was ever confirmed. Pasqual wasn't bitter about the rumors, only the fact that they never stopped. Knowing that best friends kept each other's secrets, he decided to confide in John what he thought he knew about his father's freed status.

Samson was born a slave on a Jamaican plantation, destined to live and die there in slavery. But his white master had gotten a slave girl pregnant and needed a way out of the socially debilitating situation. Samson saw an opportunity to gain a wife and negotiate his own freedom in return for marrying her and keeping all quiet. The plantation owner readily agreed but insisted Samson leave Jamaica. Samson thought it was an easy price for freedom. The former slave did not deny his identity; he knew he had no legal standing. Once he left with his wife and toddler and arrived in New Orleans his young bride succumbed to one of the numerous yellow fever epidemics that plagued the region. Pasqual never knew his mother, but John's mother, Joanna, served as a surrogate for the boy since she was his best friend's mother.

Samson's farm prospered with the aid of two of his own slaves to work the grounds. He rarely frequented town, but when he did, it was mostly to trade with the Alvarado family. Sometimes he would be accosted by wealthy plantation owners about his slaves. Samson simply told the other plantation owners that his two slaves could out work any ten of their slaves on any given day except Sunday. That usually shut them up.

John's early life consisted of school till noon, running with the wharf rats when ships docked, and visiting with Pasqual on his family farm. Sometimes they went into the swamp and exuberantly hunted all sorts of creatures, thereby helping to supplement both families' meals. One day, as he carelessly stalked a deer, John ran across a ten-foot alligator that almost took his foot off. Luckily, he was quick enough to avoid the death grab roll and even managed to put a rifle ball in the dragon's head. Pasqual thought the affair was funny, and couldn't stop laughing until John threatened to hit him on the head with his rifle butt.

When Pasqual stopped laughing, he thought, "You know some French sea captain might want the hide for a souvenir or something. He might want to hang it in the captain's cabin to frighten his crew members." John considered for a moment and suggested they skin and tan the hide and see if they could sell the alligator for a profit.

Unbelievably, the boys found a French sea captain who was looking for a "New World" souvenir. The tanned alligator hide was just what he wanted and he happily paid the boys the unheard-of sum of ten dollars for the swamp dragon. Pasqual and John could not believe their good fortune. Five dollars each was a fortune at their age! They considered going into the alligator tanning business, but later found the market was extremely small.

When John was not with the wharf rats or hunting in the swamp with Pasqual he was usually daydreaming. There was a cypress tree on the edge of Pasqual's family farm and the adjoining swamp. The giant tree had a series of large round branches that served as a perch for John and Pasqual. Sitting some twenty feet above the ground, on hot days the boys would sit in the shade of the branches, letting the breeze cool them while they tried to solve the world's mysteries. War, politics, family matters were all subjects that fascinated them both.

An added advantage of being up so high was the ability to observe their surroundings with a greater range. They heard and saw nature at its best and worst. John could even shoot a deer at an estimated 150 yards from his perch with a second-hand cutdown Mississippi rifle his uncle had given him. Their roost in the tree taught both boys to be consummate observers. They learned to tell by the softly moving grass the direction and size of a snake moving in the marsh.

When they went to town, they would always play a game. Picking out a subject or person they would try to discover the most unique thing about it or him/her. Often, they would select a new traveler in New Orleans and observe him or her. John noted that one French client of his father's had his sideburns unevenly trimmed; while Pasqual noted that the same gentleman was missing his left cuff link and that the other link was not real silver. The boys further noted that the man was escorting a lady whose shade umbrella did not have a lace tip on the top; it was bare metal. The boys decided it obviously had been put in the ground and used as a cane and the tip had come off. Those games were fascinating to the boys. They loved their detective work, always trying to see something in their environment the other missed. Sometimes it was hilarious what they could notice about the world around them.

Occasionally the wharf rats would have fights with other wharf gangs. Since John was the leader of his wharf rats, he usually wound up defending their turf from other gangs. He always tried to negotiate the issue with the other gangs but it generally devolved into some sort of short-term scuffle. Invariably before a fight broke out John would become very quiet. He would hold his temper, focusing on his intended target, but the other boy often missed John's simple warning sign. John being slightly bigger would strike quickly and the struggle would be over in an instant. John's gang never sought to take anyone else's turf but they never surrendered any of their turf either.

Sometimes the wharf rats were hanging around the docks

and riverine system when bodies were discovered. They were either the victims of accidental drownings or foul play and often unrecognizable. The boys were often the first to find them and would simply report to the local magistrate, in hopes that the body was not one of the seaman or riverboat boys to whom they had provided a service. Making these discoveries was upsetting to the wharf rats but being constantly in the area increased the likelihood of finding them. The boys remembered hearing that the city council was tired of footing the bills to bury these itinerants. But what was to be done if the city did not?

One evening as John was hurrying home to beat his curfew, he was a witness to a struggle between two men. The glare of the setting sun prevented John from getting a clear picture of the combatants and distance made it impossible to make out what each was saying. He remained at a safe distance absorbing the fight, hopefully being able to identify someone so he could report it to the town sheriff later. But the combatants' struggle always had John facing the setting sun, and he could only make out silhouettes.

The struggle was titanic in John's mind, two grown men fighting to the death. Suddenly, the shorter man raised his arm, and holding a knife, stabbed the taller one. The taller man collapsed, raising his own arm belatedly to defend himself and then ceased to move.

John was dumbfounded at what he had just witnessed. He could not believe it. He stood there with his mouth open in a state of shock. All he saw was the silhouette of the shorter man as he was turning to head back into town toward John's own housing district. But there was something about the silhouetted figure that seemed familiar to John. He had seen that shadow somewhere before.

John followed at a distance still not able to identify the figure and lost him in the growing darkness close to John's home. It was dark now and John had violated his curfew. Fearing what his mother's punishment would be for the violation John decided to wait until morning to talk to his parents about the incident. He did not sleep that night anticipating the early morning conversation with his mother and father. He knew he had to frame last nights' events to appear that he arrived home before his curfew.

In the morning, just as the sun rose, John was up and ascending the staircase to his parent's room. Normally knocking before entering, he instead was so excited he burst into their room ready to detail the events of the night before. But as he entered the room, he caught his breath and instantly froze. There silhouetted against the early morning sun was his father's figure standing on the balcony—unmistakably the same silhouette he had seen the night before.

"Yes, young man?" his mother smiled.

For the longest moment John stood speechless, having nothing to say. But he quickly regained his composure and blurted out, "I'm going to hunt deer with Pasqual for a day or two."

With that John turned on his heel and ran all the way to Pasqual's farm.

It was a full two days before Pasqual could get a word out of him, but finally John blurted out,

"Pasqual, can you keep a family secret?"

"Yes, I can," Pasqual assured him, "you've kept my family secret all these years, haven't you?"

"Yes, of course!" That's what best friends are for," said John.

Chapter 4
"Big Dallas"

"Hey Big Dallas, where are you?"

"Down here, Johnny. Climb up on the fence and look down. I'm squattin' on my spurs. What can I do for you, son?"

Curious, John asked, "What're you doin' down there, Big Dallas?"

"Well, Little Johnny Alvarado, I'm figurin' what to do with all these cayuses right now." Johnny knew the cayuse was a type of pony used by a few Native American tribes and, as he watched Big Dallas, he commented, "My father said I could buy a horse this year."

"What kinda horse you lookin' for?"

"Well, I need something that's steady and can keep up with a mule team all day."

Big Dallas' family had emigrated from North Carolina when he was a young child. His father hit the mercantile trade just right when all the wagon trains were heading to Santa Fe, New Mexico, from Freeport, Missouri. His father's skills were in high demand and a good teamster was worth his weight in gold. When Big Dallas was old enough to travel, he accompanied his father on several trips on the profitable overland passage. He knew his Pittsburg and Murphy wagons and knew how to handle them before he was twelve years old.

Unfortunately, his father was killed in the Indian raid of 1847 that almost cost him his life too. Only a handful of teamsters managed to walk back to civilization after that catastrophic battle. Tragically, Dallas's mother could not face the fact that her

husband had perished so violently and subsequently abandoned
Dallas to return east to her family. Alone and destitute, he hired
out as a young teamster going back out on the Santa Fe run.

Big Dallas was a talker with a wide knowledge base, especially regarding the wagons, and he particularly liked Ford
wagons and Pittsburg freighters. He was very competent with
horses and a fair pistol shot, but his specialty was talking. If you
asked him a question, you'd need to pull up a chair because you
were going to get an earful.

One thing Dallas noticed on his trips to Santa Fe was the
abundance of horse herds running wild on the plains. He
thought it might be a good enterprise to round them up and sell
the finer ones back East; he knew many would make excellent
mounts in places like St. Louis and New Orleans. And he was
right, it was a profitable trade. The market was always there if
he could supply it.

"Why do they call you Big Dallas anyway?" asked Johnny.

"There's a pimp up in Kansas that's known as Little Dallas,
and I don't wanna be confused with his reputation if you don't
mind." Raising an eyebrow and peering at John, Big Dallas asked,
"So, you want a horse that can keep up with a mule team?"

"I'm looking for a steady horse to use as an outrider on a
freight wagon train," explained Johnny. "My father and uncle
deliver supplies to Fort Jessup and some other settlements in
east Texas and this year I can ride my own horse instead of the
wheel mule of one of our Pittsburg wagons."

"I can imagine ridin' a wheel mule ain't much fun for a strap-
pin' boy like you," said Dallas.

"No sir, not one bit!" said John.

"Well, there're seventy-eight horses in the corral, and you
can have your choice. They'll all make ya a fine animal for your
purposes."

As John and Big Dallas sat in the corral one of the ponies walked over to them. "Looky here, Johnny, that bald face sorrel horse is just about to step into your shirt pocket," laughed Big Dallas.

One of the horses, a strapping one about fifteen hands tall, four white knee-high stockings, stouter looking than the rest of the herd, just sauntered over to John and put his nose in his lap. John reached up and stroked him between the eyes, creating an instant bond.

Shaking his head, Big Dallas remarked, "I never seen such a thing, little Johnny."

"Me neither, Dallas. Would you look at that, he has a blue eye!"

"Come over here on this side of him and you'll see he has another blue eye," said Dallas with a grin. "It looks like he's picked you out of the human herd instead of you picking him out the horse herd!"

"I like him, Big Dallas, what can you tell me about him?"

"Not much, Johnny. As you know we round up these animals on the prairie and bring'em into New Orleans for sale. This one was running wild with them, but you can tell he has some eastern breedin' in him, probably some coach horse judgin' from his stoutness. Best I can figure he escaped from a frontier settler or something and banded up with the wild horses we captured. Has a nice handle on 'im, really a good horse that oughta be a top seller at the auction tomorrow."

After gazing at the horse for a moment, John inquired, "What would you take for him right now, sir?"

Dallas raised his hat slightly, scratching his forehead as if to start the thinking process and said, "He'll probably bring 'bout twelve-dollar fifty cent at the sale, being well broke as he is, Johnny."

"My gosh, Big Dallas, that says a lot about the sale tomorrow, doesn't it? I'll tell you what, I'll give you twelve dollars right here and now and you won't have to worry about the auctioneer fee and the extras involved, what do you say, sir?"

Lowering his hat down to where it normally sat, Dallas appeared to stop thinking about the matter and said, "Twelve dollars gold or silver, no paper money. I remember that St. Louis bank failure a couple years ago so I don't appreciate paper money."

"Done, sir!" John reached into his pocket and produced twelve dollars in silver coin as well as a bill of sale for Big Dallas to sign. Handing back the signed bill of sale, Big Dallas confided, "There's one peculiar thing 'bout that horse I can't put my finger on."

"He's not a bronc or something, is he?" asked John.

"No, nothin' like that, but it's just somethin' I can't explain 'bout him. It's probably nothin' anyway. You have yourself a good horse so treat him well and he'll do some good service for you. In fact, if you do what the Army does, he'll last you quite a while."

Puzzled, John inquired as to what Dallas was talking about, "How so, sir?"

"Well, the Army only issues one horse to each trooper. They grain those animals every day and can get lots more outta them cause of it. In fact, cause they grain their horses regularly, one Army unit marched eighty miles in one day!" exclaimed Big Dallas. "That's somethin' even the Apache can't claim to have done."

Dallas continued, "You ever wonder why Indian pony herds are so large? It's cause those horses have ta eat the poor fodder they have on the plains, makin' it so an Indian gotta have a dozen or so just for one day's work. Why, an Apache will ride a horse for twenty miles till it collapses, then light a fire under its belly and get it up and ride it another twenty miles. When it collapses again, he'll butcher and eat it." John nodded his understanding.

"Well, Johnny, what are you gonna call him?"

"Blue eyes won't get it, Big Dallas, but he has a patch of sorrel over that one eye, so I think Patch is a good name," said John.

"Fine name, Little Johnny. Might as well get you a new saddle for that new horse too," suggested Big Dallas.

"I intend to sir, so I'm going right to Quewannoceii Saddlery this very minute. I got some ideas as to what I want too."

"He's a good saddle maker for sure, Johnny. Rough sort but his work speaks for itself. Say hi to 'im for me, would ya? And good luck with your new mount Johnny. Have a good day, son!"

As John left the corrals he turned and saw his sister and her friends coming in his direction. John cringed. Girls! What an irritant they were! God must have put them on earth just to bother boys in general.

"What you got there, Johnny? A bronco nobody can ride?" asked one of the girls sarcastically.

"He's cute," teased another.

"Must have cost a pretty penny," said a third.

Defiantly, John shot back, "He'll still be running long after your daddy's ponies are all winded and gone for sure." John could not wait to be rid of these girls; they were so irritating.

As he departed, leading Patch down the road toward the saddle maker, one of his sister's friends who hadn't participated in the general teasing, admired his handsome form and blue eyes. Nancy stared far too long at John to be considered a polite young lady.

"Mr. Quewannoceii, are you about?" inquired John.

"I am, young man, and I'm ready to do you any service you need of a good saddle maker. I see you have a fine pony and I assume you want a special saddle for him?"

"I do indeed, sir. If you're ready we can get down to business this very minute," John announced.

"Well son, first things first. If you want to get down to business this very minute, you'll have to wait till I get my quill and paper. If this is a special order it will be cash on the barrel head, and that means gold or silver. Like almost any craftsman these days, I no longer trust that paper stuff."

"That's the same thing Big Dallas said just ten minutes ago. No paper money. It must have been really bad when the banks failed."

"It was bad indeed! I lost my underwear in that failure and I don't wear underwear, you see?" offered the saddle maker with a smirk.

John didn't quite understand the bank failure issue, but he knew his uncle and father only used the banking system when it expedited their business. They both made sure they only kept enough money in their respective accounts to keep the mercantile and freighting business functioning. At the end of the month they would withdraw the profits and do what most New Orleans residents had done since General Alvarado abandoned them on the banks of the Mississippi. They put the gold and silver coins in clay jars and buried them in the yards of their homes.

John had no idea how much of the family fortune was buried in the quadrangle of their home, but he knew his father always admonished him never to be ostentatious about their well-being. Never flaunt it, as it may raise the envy of those who covet wealth. The Alvarados had been in New Orleans for over 300 years and had, through frugality in their business, achieved a tidy sum. They never wanted for anything these days and lived well within their means.

"Well sir, I'd like a unique saddle; something that suits my needs on the long supply runs to Ft. Jessup that I take with my father and uncle. I need something stout enough to assist an outrider to lasso a struggling wagon stuck in a muddy bog and assist the mules trying to free it."

Referring to the fork in the saddle that holds the horn, and the raised back of the saddle, John continued, "Something with swells and a cantle that'll protect my legs if I have to shift my angle to assist the pull. I don't want the lariat to pin my leg to the saddle."

"I can make it so you have a set of squaw tits that you screw onto the saddle when you need them and a high-backed cantle that should do the trick." Mr. Q's sarcasm couldn't be missed and John bristled internally at the derogatory comment, but said nothing.

"No sir, I want permanent swells, so I'm ready at a moment's notice to use my lasso to assist."

"I see, a permanent set of tits, high cantle, double rope horn and I better double bullhide wrap the tree too. Best bet is rounded skirts so the rope doesn't get under the saddle at odd angles. Let me get some copper wire so I can measure the withers and flanks of your pony for a proper fit.

As Mr. Q finished his measurements John could hear him mumbling some numbers under his breath. He figured ordering a unique saddle would be expensive, especially given Patch's wider girth and stouter foundation, but he blanched at the amount Mr. Q blurted out.

"Young Johnny that'll have to be twenty-five dollars. It's all special built you see. Take a good month to boot."

In less than an hour John Alvarado had spent thirty-seven

dollars on a horse and a new saddle. That was more money than some men would make in six months working on the shipping docks. It would take the biggest part of his savings, but he was committed to the purchase, otherwise his reputation would suffer if he backed out now. John's reputation was everything to him and he would not renege on a deal.

With a hard swallow, John raised his palmed hand to Mr. Q and said, "It's a deal sir, and can you throw in a set of good tapaderos too?" John fully expected Mr. Q would want more money for the addition of the hooded stirrups, but was relieved when the saddle maker assumed the request was part of the negotiations.

"Sure Johnny. See you at the end of the month." As John turned to go, Mr. Q commented, "Say Johnny, you know there's something peculiar about your pony, don't you? Don't rightly know what, but you can see it from here. Never seen a horse stand so quiet this long. Anyway, good day to you."

Leaving the saddle maker, John was satisfied with the deal he was able to negotiate, but he kept staring at Patch as he led him away to the family stables. He could not see what Big Dallas and Mr. Q were talking about.

"Come on Patch, let's go."

Chapter 5
"College"

"Howdy Sergeant Thompson, how are you?"

"Well, hello Johnny, how's the best outrider in all of New Orleans doing?" asked Sergeant John "Mac" Thompson.

Sergeant Thompson was the First Sergeant of Company A, First Dragoons, quartered at Ft. Jessup. He had joined the unit as a bugler and reenlisted at every opportunity. He was an orphaned boy with no direction in his life and found a career with the Army, letting the service decide his fate. He'd earned his stripes with the Dragoons in the Florida Seminole Wars where he fought as a foot soldier in the swamps and captured three renegades, bringing them back for justice. His commanding officer was impressed and cited him in dispatches back to the War Department. Sergeant John Thompson was an unusually young sergeant to oversee a troop of Dragoons, but the reward for his deeds came with early responsibilities. No one knows where the "Mac" moniker came from but it stuck with him his entire life.

"Fine, sir," answered Johnny, "what brings you to New Orleans today?" John had heard of the sergeant's accomplishments and was a dedicated admirer of him.

"I'm here with Major Michie recruiting a company of New Orleans finest. We need new recruits to fill out the ranks of the First Dragoons in order to get ready for anything the President of Mexico might do. He seems to want a little more of Texas than the Texans are willing to give up."

John, at his youthful age, was certainly enamored with the prospects of martial glory. Not thinking of the hardships, but only of the parades and celebrations, as well as the honor of wearing the smart Dragoon uniform, he was intrigued with the thought of enlisting. He could see himself in the striking uniform, with the orange piping of the Dragoons, marching off to defend the territory against the villainous Mexican dictator. He could not imagine the painful reality of war; he only envisioned the martial songs the bands played and the cheers of the crowds. It all played a one-note tune in John's mind.

"We need drummers, buglers and messengers right now and I think you might fit the bill, Johnny. Can't ask for a better opportunity to strike out on your own, son. Sign up and you'll be with me through the whole campaign. What do you say?" said the smiling sergeant.

John, emboldened by the encouragement of an older man he respected immensely, was eager to join on the spot. "I have my own Colt model '39 and I also have my own horse. I'm ready to go!" said Johnny.

Trying not to disappoint a possible new recruit, the sergeant responded, "Well, Johnny, only officers bring their own weapons and horses. If you show up and enlist, they become the property of the Army. The Army generally issues you everything you need for all your duties. If you join company K of the Second Dragoons, you'll be with all New Orleans boys, most of them you already know. I know you Creole New Orleans boys have no great love for Santa Anna, right?" said Sergeant Thompson.

Frowning, Johnny stated, "Well Sergeant Mac, I'm half French and that half has no love for Santa Anna either, not after what he did to the Texans some years ago."

"Half this, half that, don't matter much, we're all American now and Santa Anna wants the Mexican border up around the Nueces River instead of the Rio Grande. He just decided on his own to chop off a hunk of Texas for his own ranchero without asking!" confided the sergeant.

John's young mind was churning. A dictator wanted someone else's land and decided to take it. That defied any sort of decency in his mind. It angered his sensibilities that someone could be a bully like that and John knew how to deal with bullies. You stopped them in their tracks with a swift punch in the nose.

"Well, sir, I need to see my parents about this. Give me a day or two; I'm sure they'll be agreeable." With enthusiasm bubbling over, John said, "I'm going to be your best bugler to boot!"

"Ok, Johnny, I won't be hard to find; I'll be in the city till the end of the week. Look forward to your musical skills as Company K goes south to set things right with that dictator."

With growing excitement for this new chapter in his life, John watched the sergeant walk down the street to find other potential recruits for the military endeavor.

As John was riding Patch back toward the family stables he was filled with thoughts of martial glory and the commitment he'd just made to the U.S. Army. Rather proudly, he could see himself riding up a contested hill against the hated Mexican army, blowing Army commands as Major Michie and Sergeant Thompson directed him to do. It all made sense to him; he even stiffened in the saddle pushing his chest out and straightening his back as he fantasized about the coming war. He would be the best bugler in the whole of the expeditionary Army to Mexico.

As he rode along, he saw a young lady waiting to cross the busy street and he recognized her as one of his sister's friends. He realized she was with the group that had teased him about purchasing Patch, but she was the only girl in the group that didn't join in the fun at John's expense. He slowly approached her and greeted her with a confident, "Good day, miss."

Nancy looked up to see the very boy she had admired and returned the amicable greeting. In her genteel French manner Nancy replied, "Good day to you sir, how are you?" The respect in her voice was noticeable and he also noted that she was gorgeous — tall, lithe with curly brunette hair that caught the sunlight. John was charmed by her beautiful smile.

Nancy de Coleville was the daughter of the current charge d'affaires in which her father represented the French government in New Orleans. They had previously been posted on the island of Jamaica where her mother had died in one of the yellow fever epidemics. With her mother gone, and traveling the world with her diplomat father, Nancy acquired a more circumspect view of life in general. Although just seventeen years old, she was much more mature than her contemporaries; being less inclined to frivolity and more down to earth. She tended to be private, socializing when necessary, but did not suffer fools lightly.

Nancy was the main reason her father was as successful as he was since she assumed the social and secretarial duties for him once her mother had passed. She kept a diary about her frank views of life, mostly about the frustration of always being in the public eye. She loved to write and often fantasized being an author of a famous novel. Being realistic, Nancy knew she would have to write under a nom de plume as it wasn't proper for young women to venture into that gentlemanly realm. She was always aware of a woman's place in society and especially of her own special circumstances as her father's representative.

As John edged closer to the sidewalk so he could talk more easily to Nancy, she reached up and petted Patch between the eyes. John could feel Patch relax beneath him and the more she stroked the horse the more relaxed Patch became. John felt a momentary jealousy at the attention she showered on Patch.

"Mr. Alvarado, this is a very nice horse you have; he must be the envy of all of New Orleans, sir." John took note that Nancy was the first one to call Patch a horse, everyone else called him a pony.

"Most people marvel at his blue eyes and make predictions about the good luck he'll bring me. He's as gentle as the day is long and has a very good handle on him to boot," he said, repeating Big Dallas' opinion.

Just then a large wagon traversing the street had an axle break directly behind the young couple. The sound was as loud as a cannon shot and the general commotion it created on the busy street was hard to ignore. Everyone hoped no one was hurt as the contents of the wagon spilled onto the ground, creating a huge mess. After the momentary excitement, John returned to his conversation with Nancy, amazed that the axle was so fragile, but knowing regular maintenance would have prevented the problem.

"Well, Mr. Alvarado, that was interesting," she said. "I noticed that your horse did not even flinch at the loud noise as the axle snapped. That is peculiar for a horse indeed, sir."

John paused for a moment. Both Big Dallas and Mr. Quewannoceii had said that there was something peculiar about Patch. Now a total stranger said the same thing. But John simply thought that Patch was well broken in and said so.

"Miss, he's just well trained, and I think it's his discipline that makes him so steady," said John even as doubt crept into his mind.

Nancy retorted, "Sir, there might be another possibility," she paused, then blurted out, "he could be deaf!"

A deaf horse? John could not comprehend the possibility. Patch had been captured on the prairie by Big Dallas. How could a horse survive on the plains if he was deaf? Surely the predators would have taken him by now. John had to process this for a long moment.

"Well miss, you might indeed be right. I'll have to check it out. Thank you for noticing something crucial that I might be missing. You and others have mentioned he was peculiar and now it forces me to consider the matter more closely. I must thank you again, but you have the advantage as I don't know your name."

"I am Nancy de Coleville. My father is the charge d' affaires, representing the French government in New Orleans. I believe I may live only ten minutes from your home."

"Well, Miss Nancy, I have to be on my way, but let me say our meeting has been most pleasant and I wish you a good day!" said John as he rode on with an unfamiliar sense of happiness.

As Nancy crossed the street she was light-footed remembering something she had read some years before about Queen Victoria and Prince Albert: *"Albert is extremely handsome, delightful exterior appearance, makes me perfectly happy: he is kind and amiable and very good natured. His eyes are large and blue, a sweet mouth with a well perfected nose. He suites me very well."* Nancy thought to herself, "John is my Prince Albert!"

"I said *NO* Papa; he is not joining the Army. I will not be signing him over to them. I will not Pique!" screamed Joanna.

With a scowl on his face, John faced Joanna, "But Mother, it's my decision, not yours. I said I'd join as a bugler. You can't stop me."

John's father stood between the two, frowning at them. "Both of you calm down, get your emotions under control, I will not have a screaming match under this roof," warned Pique. The three of them paused as they realized the discussion had spun out of control.

"He is not going into the Army, Pique, and that is final. I will

not sign him over under any circumstances. He is too young."
Joanna's anger was building again. It was not a pleasant sight to
see a mother and son fight.

John was equally headstrong. "What about grandfather, he
fought for General Jackson at the battle of New Orleans. He gave
all the gunpowder from our family business to the U.S. Army
so they could repel the 'lobster-backs' from taking our homes."

Joanna's Cajun temper was evident and her patience with
her son was wearing thin, "Your grandfather was old enough to
join, you are not. Now go to the sitting room and practice your
violin scales. Go right now!" ordered Joanna.

Glaring at his mother, John brushed past her in a disrespectful manner. As he did, she cuffed him on the back of the neck.
Now he looked back at her in defiance, ready to fight. Seeing this
uncharacteristic display from his son, Pique blurted out, "Don't
you ever do that to your mother again! Do you understand?"

John shot a challenging look at his father and Pique met it.
John immediately looked away.

"To the sitting room and do your violin scales *now*!" directed Pique. John sullenly slid the pocket doors to the sitting room
shut.

"That ill temper comes from the Spanish side of the family,"
Joanna fumed.

"And the disrespectful attitude comes from the French side
of the family, Joanna," said Pique.

Joanna was not finished. "I will not let the Army have him,
Pique. Remember his grandfather took a rifle ball in the foot at
the battle of New Orleans and what did the Army do for him?
Nothing, not even a thank you; nothing, absolutely nothing. He
is not going into the Army and that is final."

Pique gave a big sigh and paused for several minutes. Joanna
could see by the furrow in his brow he needed to say something

he did not want to. But she also knew that they had to deal with their recalcitrant son or they might lose him altogether.

John's parents could hear the sour violin notes emanating from the sitting room and Pique shouted at the door, "Play the scales properly, John, do you hear me?"

A meek, shallow "Yes, sir" came from behind the door.

Pique led his wife to a seat at the kitchen table. "Joanna, Sergeant Mac said that officers bring their own horses and firearms when they join the Army, correct?"

"Yes, but I am still not going to let...."

Pique cut her off. "Hear me out, Mother."

Joanna knew now was not the time to interrupt her husband. Creole men were very mindful of their position as family patriarch and expected others to respect that; including their wives.

"Mother, what if we could get John to agree to go to college? That would be a four-year educational stint that would give time for all this war talk to blow over. Unfortunately, I don't have any connections in the legislature to get John an appointment to West Point. What if we got him into a university up north where he could get an education and later could apply to the Louisiana Militia for a commission? He'd be the first Alvarado to go to college and the first to be commissioned into the Army. The war will probably be over in four years, John would get what he wants, which we won't be able to stop anyway, and he would be preparing himself to take over the family business. I hate the compromises we'll have to make, but there you have it."

Joanna hated the option but she had to admit that time away from all this war talk might change the dynamics with her son. He was very good at his schooling and would probably excel at college, but would John accept his parent's decision that would alter his future?

"John, put your violin down and come in here. Your mother

and I have decided something," Pique called.

John did not like that last portion of his father's statement. They decided on something without his input. It was his life not theirs and he should have the final say. But both his mother's Cajun lineage and Pique's Creole ancestry were known for stubbornness. They may have forgotten John was the progeny of both cultures and was therefore doubly headstrong.

"Son," Pique began, "your mother and I have decided to send you to a university up north. One that will equip you to lead the family business. Mother will not under any circumstances let you join the army."

John simmered and did not say a word. He was still underage and at the whim of his parents. His only option was to leave their protection and strike out on his own as Sargent Thompson suggested. At this point in his life he was still impulsive, but not illogical. In reality, he didn't have any significant longing for a change in his life, but the actions of his parents made him want to join the army just as a token of defiance. John listened but he was tense and had his fists involuntarily clenched in resistance.

Pique continued, "John, you're good with numbers and your education so far has left you well grounded in the humanities. You will do just fine at college. We need you to learn about business law and future government regulation in order for the family mercantile and freighting business to survive the next several decades. Change is coming to Louisiana and we need to get ahead of the changes. After four years at university you can apply for a commission with the Louisiana militia if you so desire."

John's long pause was nerve racking to his parents, but he had a lot of thinking to do. He would be leaving the *"wharf rats"* of his youth and moving to an entirely new part of the country. He would be the first in his family to compete for a university degree, maybe even the first in New Orleans. It would be cold up north and he wondered if the Yankees would accept a south-ern gentleman in their midst. Right now, all he wanted to do was get away from his parents who were dictating his life choices for him. Without thinking about it first, John simply blurted out, "I want to take Patch with me."

Pique knew John needed some small victory right now in order to feel he had some semblance of control. With a nod of his head Pique acquiesced to John's minor demand.

It was settled. John would leave for the next semester en-rollment at Hillsdale College in Michigan. John did not hug his mother nor shake his father's hand. The battle between the three would take time to heal. Hopefully, it would heal.

Chapter 6
"Scholar"

The trip to Michigan was mostly uneventful for John. But if Joanna had known how dangerous it could be, she may very well have let John join the Army. The route was notorious for roadmen and scammers, but John knew how to handle himself and had learned survival techniques from his numerous trips to Ft. Jessup and St Louis with his father and uncle. John took passage on riverboats up the Mississippi as far as he could then he rode the rest of the way on Patch.

The riverboat captain who took him up to St. Louis knew the Alvarado name and gave John every courtesy, but past that bustling port the captains were more mindful of the need for every inch of cargo space. Knowing this, John monitored every stop to make sure an overzealous captain did not try to put Patch ashore for some more profitable freight. Such were the scams to separate a man from his money both above deck and below. These were some of the early lessons for John during his travels for the family freighting business.

During the journey, he was absolutely amazed at the amount of riverboat traffic on the Mississippi, and was further enthralled at the amount of railroad traffic he observed from the boat. Nothing like it existed in the south.

At the final stop John decided to ship his baggage the rest of the way to his new home at Hillsdale College. Patch and John would then enjoy a leisurely fall ride to the school, stopping for the night at inns along the way. The evenings were balmy this time of year and the people for the most part were friendly. But some did hold back once they realized he was a southern gentle-man–the slavery issue being the sole barrier to a cordial evening.

One thing John noticed at the roadhouses was the blandness of the food. It was nothing like the tang of delicacies like boiled meat, potatoes and vegetables New Orleans style. Spices were lacking, and fish was rarely found on the menu. There was no joy at the meals and he realized early on how much he would miss his mother's crawfish pies, gumbo and jambalaya. But there was a saving grace. The cheeses that were provided were exqui-site. John had none better and, once settled at school, he would write his father about importing these Michigan cheeses to New Orleans; they would sell well.

During the final leg of the trip, about a mile from the school, Patch eyed two men walking down the road toward them. He came to a stop and raised his head, alerting John. Patch's ears were up and facing forward, causing John to suspect something was amiss. As the two vagabonds approached, John hailed them with a polite, "good day."

The two thugs seemed to be trying to encircle John, but he saw the scheme immediately and remembered his uncle telling him how it worked. One man would engage the victim in con-versation, while the other would lunge at the horse's bridle and attempt to drag the rider off his mount.

As predicted, the taller one, a scarecrow of a man, took his hat off and tried to draw John into nonsensical conversation. At the same time, John kept one eye cocked on the short man to his left and as that one took a step forward, John backed Patch up one step. The second time the short man took a step forward John moved Patch back another step, so that he quartered the two men. John unbuttoned his light jacket and lifted the keep-er thong, a simple leather loop, off the hammer of his Colt '39 which was resting in a cross-draw holster, and laid his palm lightly on the grip.

The two robbers glanced at each other and then the taller one abruptly said "Good day," put his hat on his head and took off down the road. As the short one passed by, Patch pinned his ears back, bared his teeth and took a lunge at him. The miscreant barely missed being bitten and mumbled under his breath, "smart ass horse." John almost lost his balance in the saddle when Patch went after the short man, but regained it quickly. He put Patch into a trot and thought to himself that horses were much smarter than they let on.

The bond between Patch and John grew deeper that evening.

On John's first day at the university there was a general air of excitement for all thirteen boys in his class that would matriculate with him for the next four years. With some interest, John could see that two of the boys were still drunk and hung over from an impromptu party the night before and he suspected both were chronic alcoholics even at their young age. John wasn't sure if the professor noticed, but he guessed the state of the boys' condition would not go undetected for long.

Professor Arnold slowly appraised his new class and decided the first order of business was introductions. "Gentlemen, I am Dr. Arnold, headmaster, and I'd like to welcome you to Hillsdale College. I would like each of you to introduce yourself and let us know a bit about your heritage and from where you currently hail."

Nodding toward John, the instructor directed, "Sir, please stand and deliver your introduction." Standing, John addressed the professor and the class, "I'm John Alvarado, descendant of Juan Alvarado of the DeSoto expedition that discovered and claimed the southwestern part of the United States for the King of Spain. My family have lived in the New Orleans area for over three hundred years. We have a mercantile store and a freighting business."

One of the more inebriated boys made a barely audible remark about being a Creole, but no one reacted; leaving the impression that he seemed to have little credibility with his classmates. John noted his remarks but said nothing.

Glaring at the errant student, Professor Arnold directed, "Anything more, Mr. Alvarado?"

"My mother is of Cajun ancestry, part of the dislocation forced on the French of Canada, and relocated to Louisiana in 1757." This time the hungover boy was a bit louder and the whole class heard his comments.

"Cajun married to a Creole, like a monkey jumping on the back of a dog!" snorted the boy.

Professor Arnold left the podium, walked directly over to the offensive boy, leaned into his face and made it clear he had crossed a line.

"You, sir, are drunk! If you so persist in imbibing, you will be unwelcome at this institution and especially this class. Furthermore, you will refrain from disparaging other students, or you will be out. *Is that clear?*"

Completely taken aback by the professor's rebuke he mumbled, "yes, sir," but did not lower his challenging stare. The professor then grabbed him by the collar and stood him on his feet.

"I do not repeat myself to people like you, young man! No more of your impudence or I will be forced to have you expelled from this school. You will tell your father to come speak to me forthwith. Do you understand?" With the threat of his father being brought into the fray the boy immediately knew his future was in jeopardy.

"Yes sir, I understand," replied the chastened youth.

"Then sit in your seat and be polite for the rest of your tenure here," warned Professor Arnold.

John knew he had just made an enemy of the chastened student, for no other reason than he had caused him to be admonished by the professor in public. He also knew a conflict was brewing from that moment forward, but felt confident that when it exploded, he could handle it. All his life he had been challenged by these types of bullies. John would be polite if he could, deferring to the person hoping kindness would assuage the aggressiveness. But he knew it probably would not and he would have to resort to fisticuffs or a wrestling match. John had always been an inch taller and a little heavier than his age group but his most advantageous feature was his speed. But older boys tended to resort to weapons when they could not win a physical contest and that could change everything in the future.

John did not fare much better the second day of class. He had started to wonder if he really was destined to finish his higher education in a satisfactory manner.

"Gentleman, our focus today is the Missouri Compromise that is presently before Congress. I will choose three students to deliver their thoughts and opinions about the subject. After hearing their presentations, each of you will have one week to prepare a paper either agreeing or disagreeing with their stands. I want cogent arguments, not emotional ones. Logic is your friend in this classroom. No grandstanding, no beating your self-righteous chest, but only a logical conclusion to your point of view."

Glancing around the room the professor's gaze fell upon a student in the second row. "Mr. Sherer, you're from the southern state of Maryland, you are up first. Your arguments and assessment of the debate in Congress, sir."

"Class, Professor, as you know, the negro is in need of

guidance and solicitude in order to make his way in the world. Since the negro is unequal, the races must be kept separate and the darkies cared for by their betters so as to not lose their way. It is the duty of Christians to own them when their means permit, as negros generally don't have souls."

Robert Sherer continued, "Representative Pinckney of South Carolina, one of the framers of the Constitution noted that there is not a single line in the New or Old Testament censuring or forbidding slavery."

"Mr. Sherer, the Missouri Compromise if you would," said Dr. Arnold patiently.

"Sir, the Compromise limiting the expansion of slavery into any new states but allowing it to exist in the current slave-holding states is the best that can be expected. But if the Compromise, in my opinion, is expanded to divest the slave-holding states of their slaves then there might be a conflagration of huge proportions between the north and the south."

"Hear, hear," intoned several students in the room.

Professor Arnold was quick to admonish the students, "Class, there will be no cheering section. This is to be a logical, unemotional and objective presentation. Now let's hear from another gentleman."

"Mr. Alvarado, you're up next, to the front of the class please."

John, still incensed by the confrontation yesterday with the bully student, was ill prepared to face his cohorts at this moment. But he knew the spotlight was on him and he dare not falter. He proceeded smartly to the podium, paused and looked the other students in the eye.

"Gentlemen, I see the Compromise as the beginning of the end of the institution of slavery. If you look at slavery in its totality it's not economically viable. If a slave owner must feed, clothe, and house a man versus hiring him for daily wages, it's cheaper to do the latter than the former. The Compromise has no real bearing on the institution itself as it's slowly dying out. It may take several generations, but it is dying out." John returned to his seat not knowing what effect his statement was having on his classmates.

The class was stunned. They did not expect such utterances from a southern gentleman hailing from a city hosting the second largest slave market in the country. Now, John had made enemies of an additional number of students. He felt slightly sick at heart, because, like all boys his age, he wanted to be well liked. But he knew what he knew and said so. John accepted that his college years might be difficult.

Professor Arnold was slightly surprised at John's pronouncements but made no outward sign of approval or disapproval; he simply tapped the floor with his cane and arbitrarily chose another student to come to the podium.

"Thank you, Mr. Alvarado. Mr. Windsor to the front of the class, please."

As Edward Windsor of Madison, Wisconsin, approached the podium he began speaking to the class, but Professor Arnold interrupted him. "Mr. Windsor, do not talk to the class with your back to them. Wait until you have gained the podium, face your audience, pause momentarily, and then commence your presentation if you please." Edward, slightly embarrassed at forgetting communication etiquette, did as requested.

"Gentlemen, the actions of slavery are an abomination to humanity. They need to be and will be swept away from this continent and it will, indeed, be a conflagration to do so. Mr. Frederick Douglass points out how the slave has toiled over the soil of America under a burning sun and the driver's lash, plowing, planting, and reaping. The institution of slavery will be forced to cease through the Missouri Compromise and following legislation and I will fight for that change." Edward left the podium abruptly, red-faced, assured of his righteous position and proceeded to his seat.

Retaking the podium, Professor Arnold declared, "Well then, gentlemen, we have here three differing positions on the Missouri Compromise which is pending in Congress. You all have much to think about for your papers due this Friday. I want a logical approach, no bravado about any of your positions. Answer the question as to why or why not the legislation should be passed."

Professor Arnold got a roomful of blank stares except from the three boys who had come to the front of the class to enlighten the others regarding their respective positions on the issue. The professor was inwardly pleased with himself because he had randomly picked three different boys and had gotten the three prevailing reasons for or against the second Missouri Compromise. The rest of the class had plenty of food for thought. Although his ambition was to jolt the boys to consciousness about the national debate on slavery, he felt they missed the major point of the current issue. It appeared that the vagaries of a minority of outspoken activists were going to cause disunion and that fact would be his major task in educating these boys.

Hillsdale College was going to be a different school than the ones back east. Places like Brown, Harvard and Princeton emphasized rhetoric and memorization of the classics rather than critical thinking. But Professor Arnold planned to make intellectuals of his students; individuals who could problem solve by reasoned argument and logic, avoiding dogma. By employing the Socratic method of instruction Hillsdale would be more in line with the rigorous approach of the German academies. Professor Arnold wanted to show his boys a way to utilize objective, verifiable and clearly communicable truths. Their endeavors would use a fact-driven approach grounded in evidence with no reliance on ideology or any sort of bias. Objectivity, not romanticism, was the goal.

"By the way, gentlemen, in the coming weeks we will be going on a field trip to hear a debate with the esteemed Senator Douglas, one of the foremost authors of the Compromise bills, on the issue of union and disunion, and the efficacy of slavery. We will be traveling by train to the event, and for those of you who feel you cannot afford the trip, the school will make arrangements as all students must attend."

John was absolutely thrilled to be traveling by train! He had always been mesmerized by the so-called "iron horse" and wanted to learn more about its workings. He could not wait to begin the journey and was excited at the prospect of visiting with a key senator in the national debate about slavery.

"Gentlemen, you have your studies, and a major paper to write. I shall not hold you any longer from your work. With that, Professor Arnold dismissed the class.

John thoroughly enjoyed his trip to Chicago, delighted by the train ride more than anything else. He liked his side excursion to the rail yards and engaged the engineers in endless questioning about their professions.

At the debate, the presentation given by Senator Douglas seemed to be well reasoned. The esteemed Senator was more for the Union than John had thought; favoring the Missouri Compromise that was designed to satisfy all parties. Of course, John knew it would never satisfy anybody, just delay the outcome.

What was patently apparent was the passion people were displaying about the issue of slavery. They wore their emotions on their respective sleeves and would engage each other vociferously at the drop of a hat. Thus, things were very heated at the senator's presentation. John neither condemned the senator's position nor rejoiced in it. He still felt that slavery was a dying institution.

John's education proceeded as planned. Like all boys his age he excelled at topics he was interested in and tolerated those courses he had to complete for the degree program. His French and Spanish classes came easily, but he was constantly corrected by his professor for pronunciation. Being a product of Creole and Cajun influenced speech patterns, languages were a challenge for John. Latin was passable but the conjugation bothered him tremendously. Greek confounded him the most and he never excelled at any linguistic endeavor.

Despite finding geography of great interest, the class he enjoyed the most, and in which he excelled, was history. World history utterly fascinated John. He could not help comparing ancient classical history about slavery to his own country's current dilemma. Every society he read about had slaves, but not one of them ever set them free. He marveled at the Muslim culture that instituted slavery for non-believers and he was aware that most North and South American New World Indian tribes had slaves. His own family never saw the need for slaves, only employing family members in their business. But his best friend's father, a Jamaican black man, had slaves of his own.

It seemed to John there was an abundance of hypocrisy to spread around, but his country was twisting and turning itself inside out about states' rights and whether to keep people in bondage. It would be unique for American society if people like Edward Windsor, his friend and fellow student, had their way; willing to die to rid the country of the abomination of slavery. The whole topic was confusing.

Throughout John's stay at Hillsdale College he made sure Patch's care was a priority and managed to check on him daily in the stables adjacent to the college. John frequently rode Patch on the trails that were carved out in the nearby woods and he loved these times of quiet and solitude with his horse. John wasn't sure if the rides were more cathartic for Patch or himself, but they did take his mind off his strenuous studies and gave him a chance to get back to nature. Patch's rhythmic gait as they paced through the dappled shade of the trees was pleasant and relaxing. John knew these arboreal forests were certainly different than the swamps of his home, or the dryer climate of east Texas and he liked exploring the new terrain.

On one occasion, he heard the distinct sound of gunfire and being more curious than cautious, approached the source. As he watched from a distance, he saw some of his cohorts from the college engaging in sporting target practice. With their respective revolvers, they were trying to hit a sawed-off stump placed horizontal with a painted bull's eye in the center. Several of the boys drew aim in the classic duelist fashion and struck very close to center.

John decided to break cover, riding into the ring of target shooters offering a hearty, "Hello boys," and was eagerly greeted by the throng of shooters. "Step down from your horse, John, and try your luck. The winner gets the 'penny pot' of money we've put up," said one of the boys.

"O.K., I'll post my penny, but I'll shoot from horseback and try my luck," stated a confident John as he prepared to take his turn at the target. The rest of the target shooters stared at John in amazement that he would risk his money by shooting from such an unsteady platform. Surely his horse would spook at the report of the pistol!

As he turned Patch sideways to the target, one of the boys handed John a Colt '39 with a longer barrel than he was used to. At twenty paces John carefully aimed the borrowed pistol. Meanwhile, one the other fellows in the throng thought it cute to try and spook Patch just as John shot. Patch ignored the noise and was steady for John's aim. John fired and hit dead center and the band of target shooters let out a general cheer for John's marksmanship.

"Good job! A well-placed shot from an unsteady seat is no easy feat, but of course, you do have a knack, John."

To his surprise, it was Edward Windsor complimenting his achievement. With acclamation from the other boys, and Edward's compliments, John finally felt accepted by his class-mates. A deep relief came over him as he no longer felt like an outsider.

"I have an idea, boys," said Edward. "It's simple to hit a stump from the offhand position, but I wager, and I mean wager substantially, that we can all compete shooting at these stumps from a moving horse. We all have our own mounts and there are sufficient trails in these woods where we can create numerous courses that will challenge us to show off our best marksman-ship. The winner takes the purse but then must stand the rest of us a round of drinks at the Yesterday Tavern down the road. What do you say, boys?"

There was general mulling over of the proposition, but in a moment, there was a consensus agreement to what Edward had suggested. It had all the elements college boys craved, gam-bling, danger, competition and alcohol consumption. Working together as a team for a common goal, not to mention concealing something from the headmaster of the school, was enticing to the boys.

"Why not?" came an enthusiastic response.

"Definitely count me in." said another. And with that, John was the first to put up a dollar for the undertaking.

For the next three years John's classmates had an escape from the drudgery of class. A release that brought comradery and pleasure for all who participated. It was a sport that honed skills that each one of the boys could use as they grew into men. Setting up courses in the forest and galloping while discharging their pistols at twelve-inch tree stumps, placed three feet off the ground horizontally, was a difficult task. But with time and self-training the boys managed to excel at it.

Sometimes the winner of the weekly contest would only have one hit out of five shots fired. Later, with much more practice, three or four stumps hit would be the weekly winner. John was the first of the boys to hit all five stumps. He won the purse but the boys did not make him pay for the drinks at the tavern that evening. That night John wrote a letter to Nancy about his small victory, and included a lame poem he had composed. Nancy loved reading John's letter and was amused at his poetic efforts.

The issue of slavery was a constant shadow over the country and in academia especially, a highly controversial topic of much heated debate. Although most Marylanders were split on the issues, James Sherer, the outspoken classmate of John's, insisted on trying to convert the rest of the class into some sort of consensus about the issue of slavery. He was always confronting those that disagreed with his conviction that slavery should continue as it was in the South. James and his counterpart, Edward Windsor, seemed no different as they embraced opposite poles about slavery and would constantly bicker on campus and in class about it. They both tried to enlist the other boys to their respective sides, but John stayed out of the fray.

Things came to a head when the arguments at one of the weekly mounted target shoots were changed from good natured ribbing to the inevitable issue of new states being admitted to the Union as slave or non-slave states. Bloody Kansas was the case in point.

"I believe we should ride to Kansas and help the population initiate slavery," said James.

Edward challenged him right away, "No sir, it should be free and we should not interfere, let the local population decide."

John could see this was going to get out of hand, and sought to intervene and stop both boys before something happened; after all, they both were carrying pistols. He put himself physically between them trying to force a barrier and calm them both down.

James immediately resented John's imposition, pushed him away and glared at him as he slowly reached under his coat. Squaring his body, John faced James, but James missed John's subtle warning signs.

Approaching John, James continued reaching under his coat where his belted pistol would be. He got within an arm's length of John, spat on him and said, "Nigger loving, Cajun whoreee…"

He never finished his epithet. John hit James squarely on the tip of his nose sending him backwards, landing him on his backside in the dirt. As James sat there, he grabbed his face, blood flowing from his nose and glared up at John. John stared right back. Both boys knew this was not the end of their fight, but Jame's injury was severe enough that he would need a doctor's attention. They knew they would meet later to finally settle things.

John did not like confrontation, but as he demonstrated earlier in life, he did not run from it. He was irritated by the name-calling James hurled at him, and it bothered him that James thought so little of John that he felt free to disrespect him. John internalized James's aggression, wondering if it was somehow his fault that James reacted in this manner. It took some time, but ultimately, John realized James had a serious character flaw. John did not want another enemy, but this time he knew he would have one for life.

Meanwhile, Professor Arnold was determined to make social gentlemen of the boys. It was not sufficient for them to be great thinkers; they must also be graceful functionaries in a civilized society. Therefore, the school periodically hosted socials and cotillions that taught the boys the finer points of civil conduct including ballroom dance. John was a gifted dancer and he, along with the others, enjoyed these chaperoned evenings with the local girls. During these events, he would fantasize that the young lady he was dancing with was the beautiful Nancy.

One day, shortly after starting at the university, the professor was dismissing class when he stopped John. "Mr. Alvarado, would you spare me a moment, please?" Several boys had smirks on their faces as they assumed John was possibly in trouble with the professor. One chuckled under his breath that John was not long for this university if he kept up his frequent visits with the headmaster. As John approached, he noted that Professor Arnold had a bemused smile on his face.

"Young man, if you are to remain here you must frequent the post office on campus and periodically collect your mail." As Professor Arnold handed John a letter, John was shocked that he would have singled him out for a routine task a clerk could have performed.

"Remember Mr. Alvarado, if someone goes to the trouble of

writing you a letter it would be a common courtesy to return the favor." With a wink, the professor dismissed John. Thanking Professor Arnold, he hurried to his dormitory room to unravel the mystery of the slender document. He did not recognize the writing on it, but the return address was New Orleans. John noted the penmanship was exquisitely formed and perfectly shaped indicating the author had taken extreme care in writing it.

Mr. Alvarado,

I hope this letter finds you well. I trust your journey was safe and you are deep into your studies by now. I wanted to convey our collective support for your University endeavors, as you are the first from New Orleans to attempt a degree. Congratulations, sir! I look forward to hearing from you.

Your friend,
Ms. Nancy de Coleville

As John read the signature a small electrical charge surged through his body. He had hoped to hear from Nancy but never really expected to do so. And now here was the chance he craved to establish a relationship between them. He would respond immediately. He thought so often of her and, indeed, needed a good friend, especially now. Neither John nor Nancy knew it yet, but their monthly correspondence would turn into love letters that would cement their relationship. For now, John knew that communication between them was based, first and foremost, on friendship.

However, Nancy had made her mind up about John. She had associated with eligible young men in the diplomatic corps and was generally unimpressed. By its nature diplomacy often requires a certain lack of genuineness, and though a necessity of the job, Nancy did not like it. She preferred people like John who seemed honest to a fault, willing to protect the innocent and weak, and who avoided liars.

It also helped that Nancy liked horses and adored John's horse, Patch. He was as kind an animal as one could imagine and was beautiful with his four-white stockings, bald face and two blue eyes. And, of course, since Patch belonged to John, she liked him even more. She longed for the day when she might own one too, but the constant work she had to do for her father kept her too busy to attend to the needs of a mount. Needless to say, Patch was often one of the subjects in their letters.

Unfortunately, John visited New Orléans only twice during the three years he was away at college and both of those times were over the Christmas break. On one of his visits Nancy was away with her father so they missed each other. But the one time they did see each other it was enough to confirm their love; and the letters between them helped to keep that spark alive.

Chapter 7
"Responsibility"

Graduation for John was not as thrilling as it might have been. Many of the other boys in his class had their families and friends attend the modest ceremony. John's family trek would have been very arduous and would have left the family business too vulnerable to competitors if left unattended. Instead the family chose to celebrate his graduation when he arrived back in New Orleans.

John never really aspired to achieve any academic awards. He was not that dedicated to his studies, but was satisfied that he had learned new information which would be beneficial to him later in life. However, there was one thing that did impress him at the graduation ceremony. Professor Arnold took John aside and wished him a successful post collegial life, stating that if John ever needed any advice that he would respond immediately to John's letters. He appreciated being singled out by his mentor.

John had been homesick during his time at school and his loneliness was palpable as graduation finally arrived. He could not wait to get home to more familiar surroundings and hopefully an embrace from Nancy. He missed her and only hoped she liked him as much as he liked her. John was infatuated with her light auburn hair and the small curls she so painstakingly put in it. He could smell her perfume even now after such a long separation. In his mind's eye, he would visualize her beautiful face; fantasizing about kissing her. His anticipation grew by the day at the prospect of seeing her again.

For the past three and half years he had wanted to be with Nancy, but had only managed two short visits over that time. He wondered if her father interfered on purpose to cut those visits short. But the memories were the elixir that carried John's thoughts, and the letters they exchanged held John and Nancy together over their long separation. John became very comfortable with sharing his innermost thoughts with her; hoping she could see decency in his character. It was so heartening that she promptly responded to every one of his letters; the postmaster being the only delay in the process.

John could not wait to see the city of his birth. Although Nancy was away with her father again, hopefully she would be back in time for the family levee, a reception held to honor a particular person. It was to happen on the fourteenth of June. All the notables in the "Big Easy" would be there to congratulate John upon his graduation. Hopefully, Pasqual, John's best friend, was not too busy and would show up with his great big grin that John had dearly missed.

The riverboat trip back to New Orleans was uneventful; however, John still had to be vigilant at every riverboat landing to ensure Patch didn't end up left behind for more valuable cargo. Since John's last river cruise, the Mississippi traffic seemed to have tripled in its intensity. The "Big Muddy" seemed to team with economic enterprise all the way to New Orleans. He was pleased to see the increased railroad traffic along the river course and planned, in the future, to invest in this logistical method of transportation.

The long voyage home gave John plenty of time to contemplate his future. College was an exhausting but fruitful endeavor; he loved what he'd learned and knew it would be useful at some point. But he was adrift as to what would become of him. He still had an inkling of joining the Army, but there were no glorious wars at hand. What career path would he choose? He was still unsure if Nancy was really in love with him after their long separation. The only way he'd know was when he could look into her eyes.

John did not like being unsure of anything and wanted more certainty in his life. Sometimes he would sneak down to the makeshift corral on the lower deck of the riverboat and engage in a one-way conversation with Patch. At least Patch would not object to the self-indulgence John would allow himself. But when John brought up Nancy's name, he could have sworn Patch seemed to behave positively, perking up his head. Not bad for a deaf animal.

On one of John's clandestine trips to watch over Patch he was greeted by the captain of the White Cloud. "You seem to be protecting that horse. Is there a problem with the way the crew takes care of him, young man?" As John rose from his seat and turned to face the captain, he noticed the man step back a pace and squarely look John in the eye.

"A lot of artillery on your belt, son, is it necessary?"

"I hope not, sir. I come down to the corral at every stop to make sure some over-aggressive steward doesn't put my horse ashore for more lucrative cargo."

"Not on my boat, son. I won't have it. You paid for a service and we'll deliver the both of you to New Orleans. Anyone gives you any worry about the matter tell them to see me. Captain Sam Clemens at your service."

"Thank you, sir. I will if I need to."

"So, sir, quote me something from Plato, if you would. I want to measure your great thinker's capacity," said Pasqual with a playful smirk.

"You're an alligator's butt without measure," retorted John.

"I dare say that classical scholar may have been politer in his assessment of my anatomy, but nevertheless direct," said Pasqual.

"Plato simply didn't lie. Which still makes you an alligator's butt," retorted John.

They embraced like best friends and the room erupted in general laughter at the two of them. They pretended serious-ness, but joked with each other the way only true friends can do, and even the ladies excused the near vulgarity of the boy's conversation.

John's Uncle, Cezanne, interrupted the merriment with an invitation for everyone to try the new Spanish sherry he had imported for the occasion. Then Pique called for the visitors to gather around as there were to be gifts handed out.

John went to the center of the room and asked an aide to bring up the gaily wrapped gift he had for his mother. Joanna, slightly embarrassed, stood at the center of the room while John made his modest speech.

"I want to thank you, ladies and gentlemen of New Orleans for attending this levee at our quadrangle. You've filled our house with gaiety and merriment, and made my homecoming very special. Now, I would like to present my mother with a spe-cial gift. If it was not for her, I would not be standing here today receiving your accolades."

John turned to his mother and beseeched her to unwrap the gift. She was unusually quiet, and reluctantly snipped the bow and delicately took the wrapping off the box. Opening the pack-age, she hesitated, and then looked at John questioningly. As she pulled the item out of the box, she was flush with pride as it was a framed parchment of John's diploma from Hillsdale College.

John simply said to all present. "Had it not been for Mother I would not have earned this degree."

The guests were pleasantly surprised and agreed it was a very appropriate thing for a son to do for his mother. Many were aware of the argument she had with John several years earlier about going to college.

"May I have your attention please?" piped Cezanne. "As John's uncle, I'm pleased at my nephew's success and hope he will become a permanent part of the family business. As a token for his past success and his bright future, I would like to present …. Well, John, you open it and see for yourself!"

With that, John opened a mahogany box the size of a bible. It held one of the newest Colt 1851 handguns with all the accoutrements needed. It was lightly engraved. John could not believe what he saw. It was exquisite, perfect in every detail. He knew its reputation as the finest firearm of them all. It would give him some fine service. He embraced his uncle and shook his hand, forgetting to shut his lower jaw that he kept open in amazement.

Pasqual sidled up to John to congratulate him on his fine prize. "Well done, friend, that's a fine firearm."

"Thank you, Pasqual. I'd like to gift you my old Colt model '39, if you'll accept it." replied John.

"You're too kind. I know that '39 has been your favorite for a long time. I'll take care of it forever. Thank you," said Pasqual.

John's father now stepped to the center of the room. "Please indulge one more presentation, ladies and gentlemen."

John, smiling self-consciously at the attention, stood motionless as his father held the audience.

"My only son has been a joy to me over the years. Rambunctious as boys are!" laughed Pique. "But now his college graduation has ushered him into the world of manhood. I think he needs a true representation of that manhood… Here son, open this."

The light oak colored box weighed very little in John's hands. As he opened it the red velvet lining gave way to an exquisitely engraved four-inch drop blade knife with whale bone handle, with a carved design known as scrimshaw engraving. It read *"John"*, on one side of the handle and, *"Alvarado"* on the other side. Remarkable workmanship and exceptional engraving, something any man would delight in.

But John blanched at the present, remembering a long-ago knife fight he had witnessed. He hesitated to take the knife from the case until his father prompted him to show it to the assembled guests. John was slightly ashen faced as he liberated the beautiful tool from its well-appointed cradle. The audience was very impressed with the workmanship of such a beautiful instrument. John, still unsure if he wanted it, was eager to hand it off for the visitors to handle and admire.

"That is a fantastic gift! You should be proud of yourself, Johnny!" exclaimed Pasqual.

Keeping his voice down, John replied, "I am, 'P', but the knife bothers me, and you know why."

"Yes, but that was a long a time ago. You need to just enjoy the party in your honor. By the way, that young lady over there seems to be very interested in General Clark's grandson. Do you know her?" teased John's friend.

John glanced in the direction Pasqual had pointed and saw that Nancy was engaged in conversation with the grandson of General Clark of Lewis and Clark expedition fame. John had not seen her arrive, but was now obviously excited with her presence. He shot a furtive glare at Pasqual and under his breath said to him, "alligator butt!"

Just as John was headed over to greet Nancy there was a commotion at the front door. A slight scream and a man groaning in pain were heard. John saw several guests carry his uncle back to the sitting room and place him in the large overstuffed chair, elevating his leg onto the adjoining foot stool. "O' mon Dieu!" cried out Joanna. What has happened, Uncle?"

"Quickly John, bring some sherry to ease the pain and find Dr. Peters forthwith," painfully ordered Cezanne. John went to summon the doctor as directed.

Doctor Peters was there almost immediately and ordered the stricken man, "Let me remove the shoe and sock, sir." After a long pause and examination, the doctor announced, "I'm afraid it's broken; the discoloration indicates rather severely. I shall use a scarf to bind your ankle for now and suggest bed rest for at least six weeks. Do you understand, sir?" Dr. Peters inquired.

"Yes, yes, I understand," said a very impatient Cezanne. "More sherry, John, more sherry, please. The pain!"

"But Uncle, how did this happen?"

"My fault, Nephew. I was answering the door and forgot the stoop was six inches lower than the door jamb. I took a step and awkwardly landed in the street. My fault completely. More sherry, please. Fill my glass."

Pique glanced at Joanna and she responded to his cue by asking the ladies to remove from the sitting room to the anteroom. At the same time, she fetched the box of good imported cigars and brought them to Pique.

"Well, Cezanne, this throws a wrench into the trip that leaves on the morrow." Pique gravely remarked to his brother. Several of the men in the room were investors in the Alvarado caravan that was headed into east Texas to sell goods on the frontier, and they wondered what effect this would have on the venture.

Pique was the first to speak, "I must depart in the morning for St. Louis and meet our bankers. I will not be able to lead the caravan, Cezanne. Your three boys are ready I know, but we will need a fourth."

John remained perfectly still. He would love to take on the adventure, using certain college acumen and also previous knowledge gained on the trips to Ft. Jessup to further the family fortune. He wanted desperately to prove himself.

Pique continued, "Cezanne, we need to go further than Ft. Jessup this time. We need to tap the markets deeper into Texas. As long as the ports of Corpus Christi and Houston remain underdeveloped New Orleans is the key to east Texas." The New Orleans investors pressed closer to absorb all the information they could about the economics of the expedition.

Cezanne mused for a moment then blurted out his opinion of the situation, "Brother, the only one able to do our bidding is my nephew, your son, John. He would make the fourth."

The assembled financiers and family looked toward John. He nodded his acquiescence, accepting the position of expedition leader; leaving the details to his father and uncle to work out. Inside, John was totally elated at this boon to his prestige.

"Well, nephew, you have a daunting task to resupply Ft. Jessup per our contract, and then take trading goods further west, maybe even to San Antonio, to make a profit for all concerned."

John simply said, "I shall do my best, Uncle."

With that, a conversation broke out among several of the expedition backers who started to offer suggestions about certain river crossings, the types of goods to be carried, timetables for departures and return, Indian activity and anything else that could be useful to the caravan. Pique marveled that people who had never ventured into the sketchy world of hauling freight always seemed to have opinions about how things should be done. While mentally forming his own agenda, he decided to let them think the plans were all their idea.

John was eager to turn his attention to the one who had occupied his heart for so long, and whom he had not seen in over a year. The ladies had withdrawn to the anteroom while the men smoked cigars and drank sherry in the sitting room. John knew Nancy had joined the women, so he made his excuses to the gentlemen, pretending to want to talk to his mother.

He approached Nancy and spoke softly, "Miss Nancy, you look exquisite tonight."

"Thank you, sir, but I must say you look a little pale, Mr. Alvarado. There is not much sun in the northern climes, so I am glad you returned to a more favorable and healthier atmosphere than those north woods."

The knowing glance exchanged between them made the encounter all the more humorous in the crowded room. No one else was aware of the correspondence between them; they had taken effort to ensure it remained a secret.

"As you point out, miss, it is a better climate here in New Orleans. In fact, this evening is the most beautiful time of year. An evening that justifies a lazy promenade."

"Well, sir, I accept your invitation for a walk in the park if you will then escort me back to my father's apartments. The party seems to be winding down."

"It will be my pleasure, Ms. Nancy." As they left the main room John shouted over his shoulder to his mother. "I'll be back shortly, Mother."

Just as John was closing the door, he reached back to the umbrella rack and grabbed a cane sword. John knew it was better to have it and not need it, than to need it and not have it. With the national tension growing over slavery one never knew how safe the streets were, especially in a city as large as New Orleans. John believed in being ready for anything, anytime.

As they began their leisurely stroll, Nancy regretted being dressed in an evening gown instead of a more suitable walking frock. Appropriate attire was an important element of etiquette for a lady, but Nancy gave it only a fleeting thought, her mind glued to someone special.

Just as John had predicted, the New Orleans evening was balmy and beautiful, a young couple could not have asked for anything better. They talked about everything in general and nothing specific. The banter was light and they both totally enjoyed each other's company. They revisited the subjects of their three years of letter writing and still found them interesting.

Nancy enjoyed being with John as he was her Prince Albert; and John totally enjoyed the sound of Nancy's voice and could have listened to her talk all night. The promenade lasted almost an hour and a half and they had no idea where they had walked; they were just happy to be with each other. Somewhere during their walk Nancy slowly slid her hand from John's socially acceptable elbow to his hand and squeezed it. Reciprocating, John intertwined his fingers with hers. After all these years they were adding touch to their relationship and both were ecstatic.

Finally, Nancy proclaimed, "Well, John, here we are at my father's apartments."

There was a long pause as John and Nancy faced each other holding hands in front of the apartment door. Nancy lifted her closed fan to her lips. John was familiar enough with the etiquette of fan language to know what that meant. Just as they leaned forward to kiss each other good night, the door flew open....

"What are you children doing? My... my...!" exclaimed Miss Trumay, the de Coleville's rather rotund house maid. In a huff, she edged between them as she kept talking and staring at John. While intending her words for Nancy, she continued to stare at him. "The apartments are clean, ready for your father's return on Monday from St. Louis." With a very obvious meaning, Miss Trumay proclaimed, *Good Night, sir!*" Then she waddled down the street and around the corner.

John looked at Nancy, Nancy looked at John and a mischie-vous smile came over both. John closed the door to the apart-ment very gently behind them.

The sunlight from the eastern sky was just barely making its appearance into Nancy's bedroom. John was already wide awake and wondered if Nancy was as well. He rolled over on his side, elevating himself on his elbows. He saw that she, too, was awake so he gently reached down and kissed the tip of her nose.

"Well, my lady, we're going to have to make some more per-manent plans," John crooned.

Smiling broadly as she met John's eyes, Nancy asked, "Is that a proposal, sir?"

"It is, unless you decide not to accept it."

"I do most assuredly accept, sir, but you know we have a problem, don't you?"

John was confused. He thought for a moment. "You mean your father's best friend? If I remember right, you told me he proposed to you when you were thirteen."

"Yes, he did, but thankfully my father intervened and told him I was too young." Nancy continued, "The problem is my fa-ther is a Francophile and the purity of the French people is very important to him. Above all he wants me to marry a Frenchman. I am sure it is a holdover from the Napoleonic era or something. But he is adamant I remain a French woman."

John jokingly said, "You were a very French woman last night."

Unsure of his meaning and how to respond, Nancy said nothing, but looked at him blankly.

Attempting to lighten the conversation, John quipped, "You

know I'm half Cajun; doesn't that qualify me as somewhat French?"

Again, Nancy missed John's attempt at humor. She decided to move on and laid out the options for the two of them.

"We may have to elope to some exotic place like San Antonio to be together," said Nancy.

"Nonsense, my love. Once I come back from the frontier expedition, having made a fortune for the family business, your father will see that I can provide for you and make you very happy. That'll change his mind, for sure," stated John.

Nancy considered John's beautiful blue eyes, and holding his face gently, in a strained voice, said, "John, I don't think you know how strong my father feels about the matter. I will have to work on Papa while you are gone, and convince him of your worthiness."

The sunlight gained momentum into the apartment bedroom as Nancy and John made love for the fourth time.

Chapter 8
"Massacre"

The sun was well into the morning sky and John's three cousins, Dufilho, Quinin, and Napoleon were wondering where he was. They finally spied him running toward them carrying his travel gear; they assumed his late show was due to the short notification of the early departure, never suspecting his romantic interlude. John hustled past them, tossing his valise, rifle and jacket into the last wagon and headed into the stables to saddle his horse. He made a vague apology as he came out of the barn riding Patch. "Waiting long, boys?"

His parents were standing behind the last wagon waiting to wish all the boy's luck on their adventure. Joanna had a box of sugared beignets for the boys and John reached down from his perch on Patch and gratefully accepted the box of desserts. "Thanks Mother, we'll enjoy these tonight."

As he settled back in the saddle he looked up and saw Nancy standing some twenty yards behind his parents. She was the picture of a lovely young lady in a plain dress with her hands crossed in front of her holding her purse. As she lifted one hand and gave a graceful wave to John, he smiled and winked at her. She reciprocated with a knowing grin.

Napoleon had already put the two Pittsburg wagons in motion heading down the street. John wheeled Patch around and urged him into a trot to catch up to the caravan. As they rounded a corner leaving the main street, John looked back one more time to wave to his parents and to the lady of his dreams.

Nancy turned to head home to her apartment. As she did,

she had a terrible premonition, but she dismissed the bad feeling as quickly as it came. She automatically assumed it was the fact that she would have to deal with her father, convincing him that John was the man with whom she wanted to spend her life.

The trip to Ft. Jessup was relatively uneventful as some of the backers of the expedition had given some good advice about the state of some of the rivers they would have to ford. The caravan made some sales to local farmers and villages on the way, but the bulk of the goods they carried was for the far west trade.

As they rode into Ft. Jessup on schedule, a familiar voice greeted them. "Well, I'll be if it isn't little Johnny, or should I say, not so little Johnny? How are you, son?" bellowed Sergeant Thompson.

"Fine, sir, and you, Sergeant?"

"Great, young man! Sergeant Major of the whole regiment now. Lieutenant Colonel Miche is the assistant regimental commander."

"Well, it seems the war has been good to both of you. Punishing dictators down in Mexico appears a good business, sir."

"You should have seen the Second Dragoons, son. They were magnificent! You know Johnny, you could have been our bugler, but you had to run off to college up north didn't you, son?" teased the sergeant.

"Not entirely my idea, Sergeant Thompson, but what matters most is you and the boys are back safe and sound."

"Well, Johnny, not all of the New Orleans Company made it back. Lost more boys to disease than anything else, but the ones that did fight, fought like Louisiana Tigers." Sergeant Thompson was obviously proud of his troops.

"Sounds like I missed a chance to make history with you, Sergeant," said John with a hint of regret in his voice.

"Well, yes, you did, Johnny."

Sergeant Thompson continued, "You need to put the supplies for the army into warehouse number one at the end of the north part of the parade grounds. I'll get some boys to help you. We need to have a talk about the future of our resupply mission, Johnny."

"How so, sir?"

"Well, seems some changes are coming. The Second Dragoons will become the Second Cavalry Regiment shortly and we're moving to the Texas frontier. That means there'll be fresh negotiations for the resupply contracts way out West to a new post, Fort Worth. But no one knows about this yet, so not a word to anyone, son."

John knew this tidbit of information gave the Alvarado Freight and Mercantile Co. a leg up on the other freighters and he had to get the information back to his father in New Orleans fast. But first things first. They needed to get the wagons situated and the freight transferred. When that was done, they'd have to find a wagon train to join up with for the caravan to San Antonio. It was only after those tasks were completed that he could solve the dilemma of getting critical business information to his father and uncle. As John and his cousins were unloading the contracted Army supplies at warehouse number one a stranger approached John and inquired about his last name.

"May I introduce myself? I'm Captain Buerke, grandson of General Jackson. Would you happen to be related to Aristotle Alvarado of New Orleans by chance?"

"Indeed, sir, my grandfather. He passed some three years ago. Can I be of assistance?" inquired John.

"The general talked about your grandfather in the warmest of terms; particularly his service during the battle of New Orleans. General Jackson was always thankful that your grandfather provided the army with all the gunpowder and ball that his family stores had. Appears the two had a fond friendship."

"I've heard the same from my family. Grandfather hated the British since the Great Derangement and wanted to kill as many lobster-backs as he could. Unfortunately, he took a rifle ball to the foot that shortened his fighting in the trench line."

With hesitation, Captain Buerke remarked, "Mr. Alvarado, the way the general tells it, that rifle ball was your grandfather's own doing. Seems your grandfather kept shooting at the red-coats even after being told to cease fire. One of the regular army officers had to bring down the broad side of his sword on the old gentleman's shoulder which spun him around, causing him to lose his rifle, accidently shooting himself in the foot."

John chuckled, "I heard rumors of something like that, but had not had it confirmed till now. Grandfather would still be shooting at red coats if there were any left in the country. Hated 'em, flat hated 'em."

"Your grandfather also made an impression on the freight business. He was the first to import those big Pittsburg wagons from Pennsylvania just for hauling. Not only that, he managed to convince the Missouri breeders to raise those mammoth mules for towing his freight wagons. Great combination. He also pioneered the six-up team, even bringing a spare mule along to keep the whole shebang moving. He even had a motto, 'Ten miles a day and get out of my way', if I remember right."

John was extremely flattered that Captain Buerke knew so much about his grandfather's contributions to freighting. He was certainly competent and knowledgeable about captaining a wagon train and John was impressed so far. He wondered about the captain's destination and inquired about it.

"Well, we're headed to San Antonio. We only have four wagons now, but I'd rather have at least five."

John was delighted. "Sir, my cousins and I are headed to the same destination. Might like to sign on with you if that's okay?"

With a smile the captain shook John's hand and said, "Excellent, once you're unloaded here come over to our camp west of the Fort and we'll get you all signed up. Need to have a contract you know. Got to obey all sorts of rules, sir."

John knew exactly what Captain Buerke was talking about and parted with a confident, "Be along directly."

The next morning John was riding back to the wagon train camp site after finishing his business with the army supply officer. As he rode up to the campfire his cousin Dufilho was kneeling over the fire cooking breakfast. He reached behind him to get another piece of firewood when the worst thing happened. Instead of a piece of wood he absentmindedly grabbed a rattlesnake hidden in the pile of wood. It gave no warning and struck Dufilho on the web of his right hand. As Dufilho fell back, John drew his pistol, while still sitting on Patch, and instinctively shot the reptile in half, saving his cousin further injury from a second bite. The gunshot aroused the rest of the camp and they soon gathered around the Alvarado campfire to see about the commotion. Dufilho was in a slight panic, moaning and cursing at the same time. John intended to administer the suggested remedy for snake bites. He dismounted, drew his knife and attempted to cut the typical two "X's" on top of the fang marks to rid the wound of the poison. Just as he started the incisions Captain Buerke's Navajo woman burst from the crowd.

"No white boy, don't cut!" she exclaimed in broken English. "You wrong. Use Indian poultice. No kill snakes. Snake good luck. Put knife down!" she screamed into John's face.

Grabbing Dufilho's wrist and pinching it at the back of the

thumb, she simultaneously took John's knife and threw it to the ground. Dufilho was showing signs of shock, his face turning a sickly white, but he remained conscious. She reached into her waist pouch and produced a white powder that she sprinkled onto the bite marks. Within minutes Dufilho's face relaxed, color returning to his cheeks. The inaudible chant that she performed completed her triage of Dufilho.

John was dumbfounded, but the admonishment that was coming was even more startling.

"No kill snake, white boy. Snake good luck. No use knife, bad for snake bite. You not so smart, learn Navajo ways, better for cousin!"

John was totally taken aback by the Navajo woman's rebuke. As the crowd started to clear he helped his cousin to the back of the wagon, all the time just shaking his head. "Crazy Indian woman," John kept muttering to himself. Dufilho told John not to be too hasty, as he was feeling much better, woozy but better than he had expected after the snake bite treatment the Indian woman gave him.

No one noticed that Hatten Willoughby, Captain Buerke's head teamster, was cautiously walking away from the campfire with something hidden in his coat pocket. He protected it with his hand, while avoiding the gaze of anyone nearby.

As the four cousins gathered at the back of the wagon to discuss the future of their expedition, Napoleon looked at Dufilho, who was still pale, and stated, "Well, he's mangled and may not be of much use for the trek to San Antonio." Looking at John, he continued, "Well, cousin, any ideas on how to proceed?"

Dufilho just sat there and let his cousins talk. He did not feel like saying or doing anything, steadily feeling sick to his stomach. John was deep in thought; he knew this was the first challenge to his leadership of the family expedition and he wanted to make the best decision for the four of them. Quinin, the least assertive of the four, was silent.

Napoleon resumed his thought, "The way I see it boys, Dufilho needs to recover from the snakebite and we need to get the information about the army moving to Ft. Worth back to our fathers. John, we should change the wagon loads around so that the most valuable items go onto San Antonio and let the least saleable goods go back to New Orleans. I mean, the kegs of nails, gunpowder, spirits and bolts of cloth go west, and the pots and pans and the like go back east. We can sell as much as possible to the farmers and small villages and towns on the way back, while getting the information to father about negotiating with the army for the new supply contract for Ft. Worth."

John knew Napoleon was being logical about the situation and his idea was well thought out. He liked it when he didn't have to make all the decisions, and allowing for a consensus to be reached among his cousins was a welcome relief.

"I agree, Napoleon, you and I should continue west and Dufilho and Quinin should take the second wagon back to New Orleans." John tried to sound as authoritative as he could, but his cousins were already on board and knew this was the best solution to the unexpected turn of events. Without any further conversation three of the boys started to make the wagon transfers, adjusting the ton of goods while Dufilho languished in a stupor. He was actually feeling worse now than he did just a few minutes before. He knew he needed rest and he was eager to do just that.

"Damn it all to hell!" John shrieked to no one in particular, as he pawed at the supplies in the back of the wagon. "Damn, damn, and all that crap!"

"What is it, John? Why all the cussing? Another rattlesnake?" asked Napoleon warily.

John was clearly frustrated and replied, "No, I can't find it, damn it all to hell. I can't find it!"

"Find what? Calm down, John, your cursing is putting the family in a bad light and you, of anyone, know how important our reputation is to our fathers. Now, what have you lost, cousin?"

"My knife, Napoleon, my knife, the one father gave me for graduation."

"O', mon Dieu. The one with your name engraved on it?"

"Yes, the very one. I can't believe it's gone. It's like it just walked off. I can't see it anywhere at all!"

"That's unfortunate, John. A gift like that has to be guarded with the utmost caution. This isn't good, not good at all. You mustn't say a word to anyone until it turns up. Don't tell a soul until we find it," advised John's cousin.

"Agreed, Napoleon, not a soul. I'm sure it'll turn up, but I just can't believe I misplaced it. I'm searching my mind about where I may have left it. I won't sleep till I find it," a very shaken John said.

Captain Buerke was turning out to be a very capable wagon train leader. He sought out the best river crossings for his five charges, and settled around noon at some of the better campsites so the animals had adequate fodder to eat. The travel was actually very pleasant. Each wagon had its duties and all seemed to cooperate for the good of the group.

However, Hatten Willoughby seemed to always be at odds with the other drivers. Though not an easy task, Captain Buerke was able to keep him in line. Hatten's reputation as a difficult man was playing itself out during this journey.

During the trek, John's status as a marksman was further

enhanced when he managed to dispatch two Lobo wolves that kept pestering the livestock. The first wolf sat approximately one hundred fifty yards out and John took only one shot to finish him. The second wolf was on the run at about fifty yards when John was able to eliminate him with his paper cartridge Sharps carbine.

Finally arriving in the small burg of Crocket, Texas, Captain Buerke made camp on the west side of town near a small grove of trees with good water and pasture. During the evening meal another wagon team, with a pair of brothers on board, came into camp and asked if they could join the caravan on their way to San Antonio. The brothers said they missed, by four days, a caravan that passed through Crocket headed to the same destination. That caravan was a supply train of eight wagons with all sorts of trade goods for which San Antonio residents were desperate. John and Napoleon absorbed that information with disappointment as their own trek to San Antonio now seemed less profitable if the eight wagons preceding them were equally loaded for mercantile trade.

"Well, John, those ahead of us will beat us to the market. Our goods will be worth much less if we go on to San Antonio." admitted Napoleon.

"I see that, so I'm thinking we might be able to kill two birds with one stone. If we change course and go to Ft. Worth, we can get a lay of the fort for future contracting with the army and be the first mercantile wagon there. I'm pretty sure our goods would be more valuable there than in San Antonio," submitted John.

"Agreed cousin, that's the best we can do for our company. We need to tell the captain that we're headed northwest in the morning, maybe catch up to the migrant wagon train for the trek to Ft. Worth. Saw one leaving yesterday out of Crocket."

With regrets, Captain Buerke bade farewell to John and Napoleon as they departed early the next morning. Their goal was to overtake the Crocket immigrants' ox drawn wagons that had departed the previous morning. With their well-trained large mules pulling the Alvarado wagon, the captain had no doubt they could catch up to the Crocket group. Besides, there was no current report of banditry in the area and John and Napoleon could take care of themselves. Fine boys, thought Captain Buerke as he headed his group toward San Antonio.

Capitan Buerke's five wagons pulled into a small meadow about noon, just in time to relax for their normal high noon break in the daily itinerary. The wagons made a very loose circle and the stock was unhitched and let loose to graze on the fine grass adjacent to a trickling stream. Only one guard was placed on them. It was not long before cook fires were going, and the men relaxed with a good meal before they needed to hitch up and travel till dusk.

Seventy-five yards away, hidden in a grove of trees, concealed and out of sight, was Sannd and his raiding party. Sannd had finally acquiesced to leading a war party of likeminded renegades to exact a blood revenge on whites immigrating west. He reluctantly did so. Sannd always fought by himself, but these thirteen warriors wanted a big raid to cleanse this part of Texas of the hated white man. Sannd's father had talked about one he put together of twenty-seven warriors to raid into Mexico, but this was the largest one of which Sannd had been a member.

It was made up of several Kaw, Arapaho, and Pawnee, plus a Cheyenne, a Delaware and two Watonka brothers. All had grievances against the white man except the two Watonkas, who seemed too young to have any bad memories, but they had insisted on coming on the raid. The surprise to Sannd was the Delaware, since their tribe was known to be friendly to the whites.

Just as Sannd was about to rise and start the attack on the relaxed teamsters, the Delaware touched him on the elbow and motioned him to look up to the eastern sky. He saw the same thing as the Delaware, a single line of dust headed toward the camped wagon train. Sannd suspected it to be another wagon and knew patience was the warrior's friend. He settled back into his hiding position and observed.

Meanwhile, Captain Buerke called Hatten over to him. "See that dust in the distance? Pass the word to the boys to stand close to their rifles."

"Yes, sir, Captain."

It didn't take long for the single wagon to come into view. It was pulled by a hitch of six mules and seemed to be unencumbered and very light judging by the ease the animals could pull it. Although the dust was substantial in the area, Captain Buerke noted that the five outriders didn't remove their bandanas as they approached the camp. This was cause for concern.

Captain Buerke looked around his campsite, turned to Hatten and tersely addressed him. "I thought I told you to pass the word to the boys to have their guns ready."

"Sorry, Captain, must've forgot," Willoughby casually replied.

Captain Buerke glared at Hatten and the man glared back.

Captain Buerke could not believe what happened next. As the five outriders started to surround the camp, Hatten walked over to the driver and passenger on the wagon and shook hands with them. One of the outriders left the group to go find the lone livestock guard. All the outriders drew their pistols.

Hatten ordered the teamsters and immigrants to be quiet and sit still. This was just a hold up, nothing more. It was obvious the teamster was part of the outlaw band and Captain Buerke could only watch with deep disgust and disappointment at the actions of the man he had hired.

The bandits proceeded to go through the wagons and transfer the most valuable goods from the wagon train to the single bandit's wagon. The action took less than a half hour. The valuables would sell very well on the frontier and would be untraceable. Captain Buerke watched with contempt as his chief teamster joined the bandit team.

Sannd's observation simply brought a smile to his face. He could not believe his war party would have an easier raid now that the bandits had totally disarmed the immigrants. They were now just sitting around the campfire, no livestock, no weapons and no hope, and at least ten miles from any town. Once the bandits left, Sannd would spring his raid on the disarmed teamsters.

With the receding dust cloud of the bandit wagon dissipating into the eastern sky, Sannd knew it was time. Since none of his warriors had firearms the raid would not bring back the robbers with the report of rifle shot. The raiders proceeded from their hiding spot in single file using one of the wagons as a blind, allowing them to get within feet of the disheartened immigrants. Half the warriors went around the left side of the wagon and the other half around the right. In an instant, with total surprise, they were upon the unsuspecting white men. They had no weapons so their hands were their only defense, and only one of the immigrants was able to punch a Kaw warrior in the throat before a tomahawk split his skull. The immigrants were all dead in seconds, and then the mutilations started. Sannd was surprised that none of the immigrants begged for mercy, but the raid had been swift, and the surprise complete.

Clearly the grievance the raiders had against all whites manifested itself in the decapitation, dismemberment and disemboweling of these hated whites. It was brutal, and it was total. Literally the ground around the campfire was red with the white man's blood. The glee with which these raiders proceeded was unmatched by any other massacre in Texas history. Hands, feet and heads were separated and tossed into the campfire. Stomachs were opened, and the contents spread over the central camping area. No one would ever recognize the whites and they could never be put back together to travel to their heavens to see their respective makers. It was a joyous time for Sannd. He smiled at his success as he laid the second scalp near a Navajo woman's body. He thought to himself that was deserving for her since she was far too fond of the whites. It was a just end to her life at Sannd's hand.

The Delaware raider touched Sannd on the elbow again and pointed to the western sky, "Many horses come."

Sannd could see the large dust cloud and assumed the worst. A Second Dragoon patrol was approaching. He whistled to the raiders and they all looked to him except the Watonka brothers. Knowing their best chance of survival was to scatter to the four winds, Sannd signaled them to go back to the horses tied in the grove of trees. He had to physically stop the Watonkas from their grisly task to get them to leave the scene, and then Sannd set fire to all he could before he left.

Big Dallas's head wrangler saw the black smoke in the distance and thought it prudent to investigate. He did not need a wild prairie fire stampeding the cavy of two hundred head of horses they were herding to New Orleans. As he approached the smoking ring of wagons his horse seemed reluctant to move any further forward, forcing the wrangler to use his spurs liberally to urge his mount closer. Once he saw why his horse was so reluctant to advance, he understood. He could see the ground was still red with the blood of the victims; it had not had time to dry black in the sun. The wrangler saw the massacre in its totality and physically got sick, retching on the spot. After he recuperated, wiping his mouth with his bandana, he quickly surveyed the surrounding area for any sign of the raiders. He knew he must report back to Big Dallas immediately so they would not, in turn, be raided.

Having now gotten the report from his head wrangler, Big Dallas ordered the horse herd to be held at the creek bottom. Then he had his pack string brought up and the shovels unlimbered. As Dallas walked into the ring of wagons, with the smoldering flames fading, he too got sick to his stomach.

He turned to his wranglers and ordered them to start digging a large common grave.

"It's the Christian thing to do. I know it's horrible to see but it must be done. I'll rummage in the wagons and see if I can identify these victims. When all the body parts are in the hole, set a bonfire on top of the covered bodies so the wolves won't dig them up. Alright boys, get to work! I want to be out of here quick. These raiders are still close by."

Pique heard the soft knock at the door and thought it a very pleasant day to have guests. As he opened it, he saw his brother, Cezanne, his nephews Dufilho and Quinin, and Big Dallas.

"Come in, boys, and have a seat," he said with a smile, calling out to Joanna, "Mother, we have company, refreshments, please." Happily, Pique escorted his guests to the sitting room and offered chairs, but they all remained standing. Pique instantly knew something was wrong.

As Joanna arrived in the sitting room, Cezanne said, "Brother, Joanna, please take a seat."

Only then did Joanna see the grave look on her guests' faces.

"Pique, Joanna, there is no simple way to say this, except to just tell you.... Uh, there's been a massacre." The pain in

Cezanne's voice was evident. Joanna's face turned instantly pale and Pique braced his back in his chair and sat very rigid.

"Dallas came upon a massacre on his way back from the frontier, delivering horses to New Orleans. There is no doubt that John and Napoleon were massacred, and in the worst way, at a place just west of Crockett, Texas."

"Proof! Is there any proof, brother?" Pique exclaimed in a strained voice.

Big Dallas stepped forward. "Dufilho and Quinin have verified that John and Napoleon signed on with a Captain Buerke leading a caravan headed to San Antonio. Here's the contract that I managed to pull out of a smoldering wagon. There were two Pittsburgh wagons that were partially burnt when we arrived on scene. I also found the remains of the body of an Indian woman, who worked for the captain. And there is this," Big Dallas held out an oil-stained cloth to Pique, letting him unfold it and display the contents.

Joanna leaned over her husband's shoulder and watched him unwrap the cloth.

Seeing the contents, she jumped up with her hands over her ears, made the sign of the cross, screamed "No!" and ran upstairs to her bedroom. Pique sat where he was, tears welling in his eyes. He would not cry in front of the men. He gripped the knife with his son's name engraved on it. Nothing else was said.

Dallas politely closed the door behind them when they left.

Chapter 9
"Damaged Reputation"

When John arrived at the campground of the Ft.-Worth-bound wagon train, there was a lot of commotion. They had just been hit by an Indian raid and they were taking cover thinking a second assault wave was coming. But the arrival of John and his cousin seemed to have driven off the renegades. As John rode up to the lead wagon he heard and saw a young woman sobbing and mourning. One of the settlers explained to John that she had lost her husband during the attack and even more tragically the couple had married only the evening before the raid.

As John was speaking to him, he felt Patch stiffen, throwing his head up, pointing his ears forward while looking at something in the distance. John automatically looked outward too and noticed what had captured Patch's attention.

A figure, about one hundred and fifty yards out, had broken cover and was moving to a grove of tangled trees trying to evade the gaze of the people in the wagon train. The figure stopped and stared back at John. At the same time, several of the immigrants also saw the figure and began to panic.

Instinctively, John removed his Sharps rifle from the saddle scabbard, levered it open, slid a paper cartridge into the chamber, closed it, shearing off the end and capped it in an instant. As he raised the rifle to his shoulder, with his left thumb he smoothly pushed the ladder rear sight up and elevated it to the distance where the figure lurked. John stood up in the stirrups, leaning forward to support his body on the saddle swells while Patch froze, giving John a solid platform from which to shoot.

Even at this range, the figure resembled that of a renegade Indian. Although he wasn't sure, John thought he saw a smile cross the rogue's face as if he was thinking, "Go ahead, shoot if you dare, but you can't hit me from this range anyway."

John's senses were alive. His palms were sweaty, his mouth dry, breathing measured, eyes focused to the point he could see the small polka-dots of Sannd's cotton shirt. John closed his left eye and focused the gun sight on the bottom talon of Sannd's bear claw necklace; visible despite the distance. At that moment John had a conflicting thought, "*Thou shall not kill*"; but he knew the reality of the dangers posed by Indian raiders. The immigrants were in fear and he could hear them urging him to take action.

The figure turned ever so slightly toward the cover of the trees when John fired. The bullet caught the rogue Indian just under the breastbone, killing him instantly once the 400-grain bullet hit his body.

Sannd dropped silently to the ground. His eyes were open, turned up to the sky as if to say, "Did I do enough to avenge my family?" Although his eyes never closed, he would sleep forever.

A tremendous cheer went up among the wagon train immigrants. "Hurrah to the French Vaquero for the amazing shot!" Another traveler chimed in, "I bet you got Sannd at three hundred yards!"

"I'm going to find out if it really is Sannd," said a teamster. Once the captain of the wagon train verified that it was, indeed, the notorious Apache raider, a general relief spread among the immigrants.

Sannd's almost ten-year reign of terror was over, but John's self-doubt was just beginning. Had he done the right thing? He had been urged to shoot by the terrified immigrants, but he was a reluctant assassin.

John felt anguish. The moment the hammer of his carbine fell striking the cap, igniting the powder, sending the bullet down the barrel toward the target, doubt crept into John's mind. He wasn't sure he had done the right thing. He shot the renegade as if he were a mere lobo wolf that had bothered his livestock. If it hadn't been for the cheers of the crowd approving of John's action, he didn't know how he would have felt. But they did approve knowing this young man's action freed them from a possible massacre along their journey. John tried to assuage his conscience with their obvious gratitude.

That evening John was talking with the young widowed bride from the wagon train. She was lovely, chatty, and had been traumatized at the prospect of another Indian attack. She and John were discussing the demise of Sannd when a familiar individual accosted them. Hatten Willoughby approached in a menacing fashion and in a loud voice demanded to know why John had shot someone at that range when he could not identify the person.

"Aren't you Hatten Willoughby? Captain Buerke's head teamster? What are you doing here a full day's ride away from his wagon train?" John demanded.

"None of ya business!" Hatten retorted, "none ya damned business, half breed! I said wha' right did ya have to shoot someone at that range? Didn't even know who it was, did ya?" Hatten's voice and actions were becoming unreasonable now.

Stephanie Dawn Bossar wasn't going to let her new friend be abused by this filthy, bearded loudmouth. From her perch in the wagon, she leaned over the edge, and just as loudly as Hatten was in his attack on John, she challenged the man.

Glaring at Hatten, she launched into her defense of John. "Mr. Willoughby, and I use the word mister very loosely, Mr.

Alvarado saved us from a fate worse than death at the hands of the notorious raider, Sannd. And you, *sir*, should be grateful he did so!" declared Stephanie Dawn.

"Wa does some silly fourteen-year-old gal know 'bout matters of life and death? Go play with your dolls, little girl, before I have to smack ya! Now, git!" threatened a sneering Hatten.

Hatten Willoughby missed John's warning sign.

"I'll have you know I'm fifteen and will tell you anything I choose regardless of your uncivilized manner!" With that admonition, Stephanie Dawn swung a wet dish towel at Hatten, and as he tried to block it with his left arm, he hit her in the head with his hand. John's rage was instantaneous. Simultaneous with his attack on the girl, John grabbed Hatten's ample beard and slammed his head into the metal wagon wheel rim.

Hatten staggered backward grabbing his face as he fell to the ground, moaning and rolling left and right. He was still holding his face in his hands as John stepped over and straddled him. Reaching down and taking Hatten's Colt '51 from his belt, John stated, "I'll just take this so there won't be any mischief tonight." Hatten didn't say anything, he just continued to lie on the ground and moan softly. John didn't see him again during his brief stay at the encampment.

That same evening a young lady bearing a remarkable resemblance to John's beloved Nancy came to the Alvarado wagon. She was impressed with the brave young man who had come to the defense of the wagon train. She enjoyed the company of Napoleon and his reassuring ways. The next morning when she departed, nothing was said at all.

There is a story of a young maiden who immigrated to a small town on the Trinity River after her husband had been killed in an Indian raid by the notorious Apache Sannd. Eight months later she gave birth to a baby boy. The citizens of the small burg noted his ever so slightly darker complexion, but he had the bluest of eyes. Those blue eyes were the boy's passport to Dallas society. They say he grew up to be a fine young man and prospered in dry goods.

Unbeknownst to John, three weeks after his altercation with Hatten Willoughby, Hatten died in his mother's arms of a fractured skull. Two days after Hatten's funeral his brother, Joshua, convinced a crooked judge in Livingston County to swear out a warrant for Hatten's murderer.

It then fell to Hatten's cousin, Sheriff Kalvin T. Knapp, to advertise "Wanted Dead or Alive" posters for the "French Vaquero," alias John Alvarado. The family of Hatten Willoughby would pay 126 pieces of silver for Alvarado's capture or his demise.

Sheriff Kalvin T. Knapp enlisted some of the vilest hombres and villains in East Texas to pursue John Alvarado. It is rumored that the "T" in Sherriff Knapp's middle name stood for "Terrible."

After leaving the encampment, the rest of the trip to the Ft. Worth army post was uneventful. Arriving in the evening, John and Napoleon started the process of looking for quarters to house their new venture mercantile store. Before they could secure lodging, Gunter Berquist, a buffalo hunter, wanted to make their acquaintance. He had 78 tanned buffalo hides, but no place to sell them. He was wondering if he could enter into an agreement with the Alvarado boys to take them back to New Orleans and get the best price for them. John was more than agreeable to the deal.

Berquist was happy to know his goods were finally on their way to market. "I know you merchants hate to have an empty freight wagon, so if'n we could draw up a contract to send these hides back to yer father for sale it'd be beneficial for the both of us. Hides er goin' fer nearly ten dollars apiece." John could easily see the advantage to both parties and said, "I'll draw up a contract, sir, and we'll enter into a short-term partnership."

"One other thing, Mr. Alvarado, are ya the man who shot that savage, Sannd, at three hunert yards 'bout three weeks ago?" Without relish, John acknowledged that it was, indeed, he who killed the Apache. "The same, sir, a nasty task that had to be done, but it was only one hundred fifty yards to be accurate."

"Then, sir, lemme shake yer hand in thanks. He was the one responsible for killin' my mother a number a years ago. My brothers and me were watchin' our father hunt sheep on the prairie when that savage snuck up behind our wagon, stuck her in the neck with his knife and escaped as she died. I'd be happy to stand ya a drink at the cantina if'n you don't mind bein' seen in public with me."

John chuckled at Gunter's offer but said, "Well, sir, I would accept your offer, but I don't drink. Would it suit you if my cousin here, Napoleon, could go in my stead? I would then be most grateful for your kind offer."

All the dry goods that John and Napoleon brought from New Orleans were sold within the first week of their arrival. John had secured a rough building with a lease that would start in six months. Everything was going according to plan, including the tidy fortune the goods had brought. John could not believe the acute need for mercantile goods, nor how quickly they had sold. They were now ready to leave for New Orleans on the morrow and Napoleon wanted to visit the cantina one last time.

Seeing Napoleon's soon return, almost out of breath, John

inquired, "What's the trouble, cousin?"

"You won't believe it, John. There's a wanted poster out for you!" Napoleon informed his cousin with urgency.

"What are you talking about, cousin? I've done nothing wrong!"

"But I saw it, John, wanted dead or alive for the murder of a certain Hatten Willoughby. The family's offering one hundred twenty-six pieces of silver for the death or capture of one John Alvarado, alias the French Vaquero."

"I don't understand it. I didn't kill Hatten! I pushed his face into a wagon wheel, but I didn't kill him!" John grasped his cousin's shoulders and beseeched him, "Napoleon, remember the girl, Stephanie Dawn Bossar? She was a witness to the whole thing and I've got to find her so she can clear the Alvarado name."

John's only choice now was to change his plans and stay on the frontier rather than returning to New Orleans. It was imperative that he find Stephanie Dawn Bossar. He knew she had decided to stay with the family of her dead husband, but John had no idea where the Bossars had been heading. He needed her to testify in a federal court to clear his name, but John would be on the run for the next two and half years searching for Stephanie Dawn, and avoiding Sheriff Knapp.

As Napoleon was talking to his cousin, he looked over John's shoulder and told him trouble was coming down the street. Turning slowly, John lifted the leather thong off the hammer of his Colt '51 and tucked his thumb gently into his gun belt. When he looked closer, he saw that it was Gunter ambling toward them. He had his buffalo rifle in the crook of his arm, and John noticed it was not capped; John relaxed slightly.

"Hey, John, heard some bad news," offered Gunter with a grimace. John was somewhat wary of Gunter and shot back defensively, "It's all a misunderstanding as far as I know."

"Slow down, John, I jes came over to give some advice. I've had dealin's with the Willoughbys and that Sheriff Knapp. They're a nasty bunch in my estimation. Even the women of the clan are downright horrible."

John relaxed a little more.

Gunter continued, "I still need to get my hides to market, and you'll need a friend to confront the Willoughbys. I wanna ensure yer survival so my hides get to market, don't I?"

Considering the proposal Gunter just offered, John replied, "Okay, Napoleon will leave tomorrow and take the load to New Orleans to sell your hides as planned. I need to stay on the frontier and find Stephanie Dawn Bossar, who witnessed my confrontation with Hatten Willoughby."

Napoleon objected immediately, "I want to stay and help, cousin."

"No, Napoleon, I'll write a letter to my father explaining everything. You need to get back to him with all the money we've made here in Ft. Worth, plus the contract for the building. Explain that this is a worthwhile venture and will be very lucrative for the family business. You must *not* tell anyone on your way back that you're an Alvarado. Your goal is to get Gunter's hides to market and let my father know what's happened. Gunter will help me survive this disaster; do you understand?"

In the morning as Napoleon was hitching the last mule to the Pittsburg, John approached him with the promised letter to his father. "Napoleon, God speed! Get this letter to my father; it explains everything. And would you also take this bundle of letters to a certain Nancy de Coleville for me?" Napoleon nodded with a shrug of his shoulder. He looked at his cousin with some trepidation, not knowing whether he would see him again. After grasping John's shoulder in a reluctant farewell, Napoleon shook Gunter's hand and climbed onto the wagon. Long before the morning sun broke over the horizon, he would be well along on the trying journey home to complete their mission.

John had changed, and he did not like it. Just a dozen weeks out of college and he was a wanted man. His plans for the future were thrown to the wind and he couldn't believe the turn of events that might sabotage his ambition. He thought of himself as a scholar looking to take his family business into the future with the aid of the love of his life; but look at him now, a killer on the run, no future except survival.

He knew searching for the witness was destined to be like looking for the proverbial needle in a haystack, but there was no choice if he wanted to see his family. He was also tormented with the possibility of never seeing Nancy again.

John's self-image was shattered, unrecognizable; a villain hiding from everyone and everything. He hated himself for what was an unintended action that now threatened to change his life forever. How had this happened, and why?

His only hope was his faith; he had to believe in something bigger than himself. He had to believe he was a good person and that he would triumph in the end. It was all he had now.

Chapter 10
"Fresh Breezes"

The news of John's and Napoleon's deaths spread through New Orleans society quickly. People were stunned at the loss of such young members of this old, well established merchant family, and saddened for the parents of both men. Understandably, Nancy was overwhelmed as she saw her world shatter around her. Making the matter even more devastating was the fact that she couldn't seek comfort for her pain because her relationship with John had been largely unknown.

"I don't understand, daughter. Just a few days ago you were trying to get me to let you stay in New Orleans, even asking for help to find a governess job. What has changed?" She turned her back to her father as tears welled up in her eyes and said, "I think it is time for me to see my own country." Her father did not understand her at all. Perplexed, he told her, "I must hurry down to the wharf and book a second passage for you back to France, I hope I am not too late."

As Pierre turned to leave, Nancy muttered under her breath, "There is nothing in New Orleans for me now."

Her father claimed his coat from the foyer closet as he called over his shoulder, "Miss TeAunna, Miss TeAunna, pack all of Ms. Nancy's belongings, we leave for France in the morning!" With that, Pierre left in a hurry and headed toward the dock to secure Nancy's passage.

Miss TeAunna Trumay, the de Coleville's housemaid for many years, hurriedly commenced preparing Nancy's things for the voyage, but she did so with a heavy heart. She would miss

Nancy tremendously as she had grown close to the motherless girl; watching her grow from a child to a woman.

They were three days out from New Orleans and Nancy had not said a word; alternately weeping and staring out into the emptiness of the ocean. She kept trying to suppress the idea of John's gruesome death at the hands of an Indian savage. Did his last thought before he died include her? What a horrible death! She also felt guilty that she was selfish enough to hope her beloved would think of her before he died.

One of the male passengers, not knowing of Nancy's turmoil, tried to cheer her by pointing out that "dying and going to heaven and living in New Orleans was one in the same thing." His wife didn't think he was humorous and jabbed her elbow into his ribs.

"It will be fine, young lady, New Orleans has that kind of effect on people. You will return." Nancy thanked her for her kind thoughts, but assured her fellow passenger that she would not entertain thoughts of venturing back to that beautiful city again.

Shortly before leaving New Orleans, Nancy had felt the unmistakable changes in her body and knew she had to do something about it. The very next evening the captain invited all the passengers to "sup" with him in the captain's cabin. Nancy made a point to be seated next to Pierre Tillie, her father's best friend. This was the very same man who had asked for her hand in marriage when Nancy was just thirteen. The conversation was friendly and all had a good time with the captain as host. Nancy and Pierre got along famously.

Pierre Tillie was her father's lifelong friend. He was only slightly younger than her father and was gentlemanly. Competent and well read, he had accompanied her father throughout his tenure as charge de affaires in Jamaica and New Orleans, working in conjunction with the French foreign office.

He would be posted to the Court of St. James along with her father, a boon to both gentlemen. Political turmoil would delay Pierre de Coleville's posting to the Court of St. James. But the foreign ministry had plenty of work for him as the international intrigues settled down.

While in the captain's cabin, Nancy noticed the alligator skin tacked to the cabin wall and wondered if it was the same one John had talked about when he and his best friend had sold a hide to a sea captain. No, it couldn't possibly be.

For the most part, the voyage to France was a pleasant journey; the passengers could not have asked for better weather or company. One of the more pleasant tasks a sea captain has is to exercise his function of overseeing marriage vows. Some three days out from docking his "*White Snow*" brig, the captain got to do just that.

"Do you Nancy, Nicolle, Marie de Coleville take Pierre Tillie to be your lawful wedded husband?"

Nancy responded with a quiet "I do."

"Do you, Pierre Tillie, take Nancy de Coleville to be your lawful wedded wife?" "I do," said a happy Pierre.

"Then place the ring upon her finger," instructed the captain. A beaming Pierre slipped the beautiful ring onto Nancy's slender finger and the captain continued, "You may kiss the bride, sir."

The nuptial celebration was as enthusiastic as the circumstances on board the small ship could be. Nancy's father was brimming with joy. It seemed truly the best of all worlds; his daughter married to a true Frenchman and his best friend to boot. And now the hope for a grandson occupied his thoughts.

It wasn't long before Nancy informed the two Pierres that she was pregnant. They jostled for opportunities to select a name for the child long before it was born, never consulting Nancy. If it was a boy, her husband wanted to name it, John Pierre. Her father preferred Petra John. Nancy did not interfere, but every time they settled on "John" it brought up memories she was trying to suppress. Thinking of John now induced melancholy and was not healthy for her.

Once the boy was born, the two Pierres settled on Pierre John as a compromise for his name. Nancy only cared that he was healthy. Raising him became her occupation and reality; nothing else mattered to her. She could lose herself in his needs and never worry about her own. She wondered how John would react to him being so tiny. She spent quiet moments thinking how John would have taught him to grow as a man, teaching him the things a man needs to know. But it was a fantasy because John was dead. Her wish was only in her mind as her son would never know his real father; and that made her all the sadder. The deep regret of not marrying John before he left for the frontier would haunt her for many years to come.

The things she wished she had done filled her day, but for the sake of her son and his well-being, she had to do things correctly. She missed John dearly and prayed nightly that his soul had gone to heaven. She implored God constantly for His blessing for her and her son. Now, she had only constant heartache where John's love should have been.

Within a year of Pierre John's birth Nancy's father passed away. The doctors never diagnosed the cause of his death, but surmised it was simply old age. Her father had protected her since her mother's passing in Jamaica. In fact, a large part of her father's success was due to Nancy's being at his side and representing him at official functions when he could not attend. She had gained a reputation as a valued asset to his position of charge de affaires. His death was a severe blow to her.

Within six months of her father's death her husband also

passed away. He had a severe bout of pneumonia and did not survive, succumbing after just two nights. His advanced age and the cooler climate of Paris played a role in his demise.

Nancy was now alone in a foreign land, without a male protector or any family members. Both her father and husband had left her some money to survive on, but it would not last long. At the time, in societies around the world, widows were treated differently after the proper mourning period. They were often dropped from the social rolls and were expected to just fade away.

That cultural practice worked for the widow if there was a family support subsystem, but Nancy did not have that; she was a widow with a child. Although a very good-looking, cultured woman with much to offer suitors, she was considered an American, and in France Americans were not well received because of the international political climate over slavery.

Despite the hardship of social stigma and financial constraints, Nancy was determined to raise her son properly and give him the best start in life she could manage on her own. As for her own future, she was plagued by a recurring thought. Within a two year span she had lost three of the most important men in her life. She was a widow, but was she a black widow? A haunting thought for such a young person, but the facts were there to see. Every man she loved had died. The conclusion seemed to be obvious: could the remaining man in her life, her son, be in jeopardy? She worried constantly.

Her early job searches were fruitless. Many thought it unmotherly for her to utilize a nanny while searching for employment. This distanced her further from social contact with her husband's and father's friends. But she was caught in a situation where she had to do something; her meager funds would not last long.

One day, her landlord told her of an opportunity with a Hanoverian newspaper trying to expand into the French marketplace. They were looking for someone who could translate American newspaper articles and wire messages into French. Parisians had an insatiable desire for news, particularly from abroad.

When she applied to the editor, he was taken aback that a woman would be so audacious as to even think she had a chance, much less a right, to hold such a position. The long pause before he addressed her showed that his mind was working overtime to find a way to deny her this opportunity.

He was aware that being a German paper in France was not the most enviable position, and he did, after all, need a translator. None had come forward so far because the parent company was located in Berlin. Parochialism at its finest.

The editor contemplated the situation and upon reflection said, "If I employ you, I'll be taking a risk as your abilities are unproven, and your status here would be unconventional. However, I will offer you the position with the understanding that you must use a nom de plume, madam. My readers would not understand a lady author."

Nancy needed the job and couldn't afford to stand on any principle that would interfere with her goal. She had to compromise. "Well, sir, then I will henceforth be John Alvarado for your purposes," she said confidently. In the end, they both got what they needed, not what they wanted, and they both compromised.

Privately, Nancy was thankful for the employment. She also found the requirement to use the nom de plume, "John Alvarado" ironic as she had lately been saying John's name out loud on occasion; even to the point of calling her son by his middle name and not his given name, Pierre. She missed John, but now when she inadvertently blurted out his name, she could coyly say that it was simply her nom de plume; and not what she was subconsciously thinking about.

Once she secured a daytime babysitter for Pierre, Nancy's adjustment to a work environment was quick. The fiscal situation remained tight as the rent went up and nannies were not cheap. But there was a certain satisfaction of earning a living and supporting herself and her son, albeit in a foreign country which was becoming more and more hostile to Americans. She initially enjoyed what many others would consider drudgery, translating foreign American newspaper articles into French. It was a much-needed distraction for her.

After three months, the editor called her into his office. She was ready for the worst, thinking someone had discovered she was the 'he' of the article translations. She needed this job badly. Her editor, Herr Schmidt, had a frown on his face and was in deep thought before he finally spoke.

"Madame Tillie, you lived in Jamaica and in New Orleans, didn't you?"

"Yes," she said, very confused now.

"Well, then, I have a proposal."

Intrigued that she wasn't going to be released from her job, but rather asked to do more writing, she leaned forward intently looking at her boss. "Madame Tillie, could you add anecdotal stories to the articles you translate about the slavery issue in the American States? I think it would be of human interest to our readers and capture their attention. The challenging part will be offering something different than the other papers in Paris."

"How so, sir?"

"Well, the other papers seem to always write about the abuse of the slaves in the American South. I want a different angle. I want the perspective from that of the plantation owner and the slaves themselves. I know you have not been a slave, but surely you can write some anecdotes that would pique our readers' interest. If you would, please add those anecdotes to the end of the article translations you do." Seeing the look on Nancy's face he quickly added, "By the way, the extra work comes with a pay raise."

She rose from her chair, said "yes" to Herr Schmidt, curtsied, and turned to leave the room. She was both elated and scared; how was she going to do her new task? The idea of a pay raise was buzzing in her head! Just as she reached for the door handle an inspiration came to her. She turned to Herr Schmidt and announced, "I have the perfect avenue to do as you wish, sir." With that, Nancy left the editor's office.

She had kept John's college letters and knew they contained the stories and information she needed to produce the anecdotal stories for the translated articles. John had written her a number of times about the northern attitudes toward slavery and his personal observations during his time in Michigan. Even in death John had come to her aid; those letters were to be her salvation.

Nancy's new work came easily to her. John's letters were indeed the boon she needed to add insight to the slavery question in America. It was the different perspective she provided that both chagrined and enlightened the newspapers' readers. The one anecdotal story that got the most reviews was the story about John's best friend's father being a freed black man and himself owning slaves. Parisians could not believe the hideous crime of slavery would be committed by a black on a black. Paris was buzzing and accusations of fraud abounded. But the circulation of the paper climbed.

"Well, Madame Tillie, or Mr. Alvarado I should say, we are selling papers like crazy after your last article. I assume it is true, is it not?" asked Mr. Schmidt. "Quite so, sir. The names are accurate and can be easily verified," she said. "And the next installment will be even more revealing, sir," teased Nancy.

"How so, madam?"

"Simply that slavery is no longer economically viable, and will collapse of its own volition. Currently, it is no longer expanding in the states. The reality is this--a plantation owner must house, clothe and feed a slave. If that same plantation owner hires a former slave to do the work for wages, that slave will have to be responsible for caring for his own needs. This is a much more logical economic situation for the land owner."

Nancy continued, "That leaves the Muslim world as the last bastion of slavery."

There was a long pause before Herr Schmidt spoke. He crossed his arms, looked at the floor and thought deeply.

"Madame Tillie, listen very carefully to what I am about to say. I am nervous and not altogether sure it will work. What I would like you to do, if you agree, is to move to Atlanta, Georgia, and from there travel throughout the South. Find these anecdotal stories and relay them back to the 'St. Germaine Recorder' newspaper here in Paris. I have not thought this through completely to be sure, but first-hand reporting on the slavery issue, in the manner you have done so far, would give our readers a perspective no other paper in Paris can supply. Traveling incognito would also be to our mutual advantage so no one would suspect you of working for a French newspaper. I am most eager to provide the French consumer with a balanced view of this most volatile topic of our time."

Nancy bristled internally about having to work undercover again; first with a nom de plume and now incognito reporting, but she also understood that it might give her access to things in the South she might not otherwise be privy too. She also knew anti-American sentiment was growing in France against the South's insistence on maintaining slavery. Although French by birth, her years growing up in the United States had given her an appearance of being American, and because of that, she felt a possibility that she might be in danger. Just the other day a demonstration within a block of her apartment caused her some concern.

Nancy's pause and reflection were equally as long as Herr Schmidt's. "I shall do it, sir, but remuneration will have to be adequate." Her boss easily acquiesced. In less than two years Nancy had been given two pay raises and now a promotion for her earned work. She could not have been prouder of herself, nor of her love for John's letters which had given her the needed boost in a fledgling career. She still missed him.

"Madame Tillie," Herr Schmitt said as he kissed her gloved hand in the French way. "It has been a pleasure working with you these last years. Your anecdotal stories have increased the newspaper circulation threefold, thank you." Nancy could see in his eyes this farewell was more than just an employer saying goodbye to an employee. Though she found Herr Schmidt to be a genuine friend, Nancy was emotionally void of any romantic feelings. She could not imagine falling in love again, not yet anyway. The only man she wanted in her life now was the young boy clutching at her skirt.

"Thank you for the opportunity, sir. I shall do you the greatest service while I am in Atlanta."

"If you would send as many stories as soon as possible, so as to keep the articles fresh and current in the newspaper, I would be grateful," he said.

"I will, Herr Schmidt. Be well." And with that, and a feeling of déjà vu, she turned to board the all-too-familiar ship with her son. Surprisingly, she was greeted by the same captain that had performed her marriage ceremony during the trip from New Orleans to France several years earlier. He did not seem to remember her until she mentioned her name and the details of the onboard wedding.

The passage to Jamaica was pleasant and the winds were fair, but after unloading some cargo and taking on new cargo in the Caribbean port, a change in plans by the captain raised the ire of several passengers.

"But I don't want to go to New Orleans, Captain, do you understand?"

"I am sorry, Madame, but I am charged with making a profit for my ship's owners and this run is bound for New Orleans. Don't worry, I'll have you in Savannah by the seventh as promised. With the weather being so fair the delay will be minimal and you need not disembark, just stay onboard till we conduct our business in the port of New Orleans. We will be underway soon."

With that, Nancy turned her back on him and gripped the ship's railing. She knew it was imperative that her articles begin immediately and she just knew there would be a significant delay. Little John clutched her skirt, trying to figure out what he had done to make his mother feel so sad.

The captain advanced down the deck, shrugging his shoulders and murmuring, "Shipping that caters to passengers? How absurd; will never happen."

Chapter 11
"Ducking and Dodging"

No sooner had Napoleon left, did Gunter suggest John and he head out of Ft. Worth in the other direction. The morning was still young and the sun had yet to show its rays in the eastern sky. Shuffling along the road south, the two of them considered their options.

They had to find Stephanie Dawn Bossar, but how were they to do that without alerting the thugs Sheriff Knapp would send after them? It would have to be surreptitiously done. The only way to gather information on someone out West was to frequent the places people generally gathered on the frontier. They had absolutely no idea where the Bossar family had immigrated to. They could not be too forward inquiring about the family's whereabouts without alerting all the ne'er-do-wells in the state of Texas. The bounty of $126 in silver pieces would lure all the ugliest of humanity out of the woodwork to collect it.

Clearly, the mercantile stores, forts and saloons were the best places to gather information. Encounters with wagon trains might also yield them some leads. The search would be long and hard, but it had to be done to clear John's name in a federal court, not in a corrupt county court.

John had several advantages in his search for the Bossar family. First, no one knew he was traveling with a partner. Secondly, he had held back some of the money from the merchandise sale in Fort Worth with the intention of repaying his father once this matter was resolved. Lastly, Gunter knew the country.

Gunter's friendship would be invaluable. With winter coming

on, they needed to make some decisions about the immediate future; possibly postponing their search and the inevitable confrontations he knew were coming when people recognized him.

No one knew what the French Vaquero looked like; it was just his name and description on the wanted poster. On the other hand, some people knew about his unique saddle and that he rode a fine horse that had two blue eyes and was stone deaf. That might be a bit of a problem.

With the death of Saand, John had become a giant slayer with all the accolades and expectations that come with that. He did not want to be a celebrity for killing people and refused to recount the tale of the encounter. If he could wish away the incident he would surely do so as it was responsible for his current circumstances.

Had he not killed the renegade, the incident with Willoughby, and by extension the encounter with Stephanie Bossar, would likely not have happened. And now John was being hunted for the death of Willoughby, a death that he never intended.

After killing Sannd he had been sickened at the thought of taking a life. That evening he needed to talk to someone about killing the renegade, but Napoleon was otherwise occupied and John was left to his own devices. It would be an understatement to say he was confused and miserable. Further complicating matters, seeking comfort that night had changed the future not only for John, but Nancy as well. John missed Nancy dearly. He wanted to marry and settle down, but now life had dealt them a significantly changed course. Hopefully his letters that Napoleon would deliver to her would help her understand what had happened.

There was a loud and joyous knock at Joanna and Pique Alvarado's front door. Pique thought it too early for anyone to drop by, but he was eager to greet any well-wishers who might want to visit.

"Joanna, come quick, we have visitors and you will be delighted!" shouted Pique.

Joanna came into the sitting room with several dishes in her hands, a bit angry at her husband for being so demanding. Then she saw their guests. She dropped the dishes, breaking all of them, and flew into the arms of her nephew, Napoleon. She immediately knew her son, John, was alive too. Her motherly embrace was genuine and Napoleon understood her joy. As she continued to hug her nephew she peered over his shoulder and glared at Big Dallas. He sheepishly lowered his gaze and stepped back. He knew he was in trouble with Joanna.

"Come sit down boys, tell us everything. You obviously were not massacred. Where is John?" Though overjoyed, Pique and Joanna had so many questions.

Napoleon filled his relatives in with all he knew. Using a chronological timeline, everyone was able to understand how the perception of Napoleon and John being massacred was concluded. But the fact that John was now a fugitive from the law dimmed the elation of his survival for his parents.

"We can only hope more letters make it back here, so we can keep in touch. I understand we cannot go to him as he has to find this Bossar family. We will have to be patient," a relieved Joanna murmured.

John's first attempt at gathering information about the Bossar family went seriously wrong. The crossroads burg of Williams Wells was just south of Ft. Worth. It was a total of five buildings on either side of an "X" road where people bartered goods. John had just come out of the saloon after drawing a blank for information from the bartender when he saw Gunter come out of the local mercantile store across the street. Gunter gave a thumbs down and proceeded to walk into the street toward John.

They both saw the threat at the same time. While Gunter altered his path and returned to his side of the street, John took the leather tong off his Colt '51. Coming down the muddy road was a freight wagon with a single team of draft horses. The driver of the wagon was staring cold as ice directly at John—his intuition shouted danger. Both John and Gunter saw a double barrel shotgun standing straight up in the bed of the wagon above its side wall. Clearly someone was lying in the bed below the side walls ready to spring up and blast someone at the signal of the wagon driver.

The driver never took his eyes off John. As the wagon got closer the driver said something inaudible and drew his pistol from under his coat, and the man in the back of the wagon rose to fire his shotgun. With the speed of the wagon John led his target too much and hit the driver in the leg. Gunter likewise missed a fatal shot, only wounding the shotgun shooter. The wagon horses panicked at the report of the four gunshots and stampeded down the street. The wounded driver was unable to slow them down because he could not apply the wagon brakes with his wounded leg.

Apparently, the town folk were used to gunfire in the streets because they did not react to the fight with panic. Instead, they were more interested in the runaway wagon headed toward the small school house at the other end of the street. John and Gunter simply mounted their horses and rode south quickly out of town.

"Well, that was interesting!" said Gunter.

"Yes, sir, it was. If this is going to be what life is like until we find the Bossar family, we'll have to sleep with one eye open. We need a better plan on how to get information next time."

"That's true, but with winter comin' we also need a plan to avoid the weather. I don't wanna be caught in the open when one of them Texas blue northern blizzards comes blowin' in," said Gunter.

Tinkle Creek, Texas, was an interesting town. It was a larger burg than Williams Wells and the only thing permanent about it was the buildings stuck above ground level taller than the surrounding sage brush. The lumber the buildings were constructed of was hauled in from some miles away if you could call them buildings. None of them had ever felt a needed paintbrush to protect them from the elements. Drab must have been beautiful to its inhabitants; otherwise they would have left long ago. Because of its location, the town had plenty of wagon traffic, both freight and immigrant. Coming by information might be a little less conspicuous here once they settled in.

Again, John and Gunter found themselves in the saloon asking questions about recent travelers. The saloon was even worse inside than the building itself was on the outside. One door, no windows, a board across two barrels for the bar and a foul smell permeating. The cuspidor needed emptying and several patrons needed to be thrown into the water trough outside for a good scrubbing.

One patron, fortified with liquor as anti-freeze for the winter, was boisterously bragging about how many buffalo he had shot to date. He drunkenly bumped into Gunter causing him to lose his balance. John instinctively punched the foul-smelling man on the point of his nose, sending him backward onto his backside. The cowboy grabbed at his nose as it gushed bright red blood. He did not look up at John but rather sat on his backside nursing his nose.

One of the other patrons of the bar got up and came over to John and Gunter. "Howdy, gentlemen. I'm Mayor Berwyn Palmer, but most folk around here call me 'Rusty.' How would you boys like a job?" Perplexed, John and Gunter moved closer to the mayor to hear what he had to say.

"I need a town sheriff and a deputy. Pay is ten dollars and six dollars a month respectively. I need some help to keep the peace, able to curb violence yet not overly reliant on gun play. I need all these folks to spend money in Tinkle without killin' each other." John looked at Gunter, Gunter looked at John and then they both said "yes" to the mayor. "I'm John Berquist and this is my cousin, Gunter Berquist." The mayor looked back and forth between John and Gunter and remarked, "Same Viking father but different mothers I'd say–you're hired."

"The army will clear the Comanche out of the Ilana Estacado next year and this will become a boom town for the settlers looking for all that free land to occupy. So, make sure we're a friendly town till then," directed the mayor. John and Gunter knew, as undermanned as the army was, it might be quite a few years before the Comanche were dislodged from the Comancheria. Those were some mean Indians out there on the staked plains.

The winter for Gunter and John went well. The jailhouse was warm and there was plenty of fodder for their horses. Law enforcement became a drudgery of stopping occasional knife fights and drunken brawls, but nothing major came about. John would often practice with his Colt '51 behind the jail. All in town knew the sheriff was willing, ready and capable of stopping any major crime, should it occur.

There was one occasion toward spring that unnerved John. He met a farmer and they struck up a casual conversation. John was all too willing to talk about anything besides his search and hiding. The farmer mentioned toward the end of the conversation that he liked John's horse. John thanked him and proceeded to talk about Patch's virtues and loyalty. The farmer asked where he had purchased him and before John thought about it, he made the mistake of saying New Orleans.

John's guard was up now, regretting what he had just said. Then the farmer said something unusual that scared John slightly, "I'll bet that horse likes carrots, big juicy carrots."

"Why yes, he does," said John.

The farmer continued, "I have a nickel in my vest pocket says that if you snap a carrot in half, your horse would not hear it." John made his second mistake. "Why, no, he wouldn't."

"Thought so," said the farmer. The farmer tipped his hat and disappeared around the corner of the building.

John was disconcerted by the conversation with the farmer. He had revealed two secrets about himself. He didn't know if the farmer was a spy for Sheriff Knapp and would come back to capture him and Gunter for the reward.

It was two full days before John figured out that the farmer could possibly be Patch's previous owner who lost him out on the prairie before the horse was found by Big Dallas for the New Orleans market. John breathed a sigh of relief upon reaching his deduction and was thankful the farmer did not make a big fuss about recovering his property.

The subterfuge John and Gunter were forced to perpetrate on the town in order to conceal their true identities was a heavy burden. John thought he could see a few hairs turning grey and he was just past twenty-one years old.

Once spring arrived, Gunter and John said their final good-byes to Mayor Palmer and headed south toward San Antonio. It was frustrating not to have developed any leads about the Bossar family, but San Antonio was a larger transient point for immigrants and might be more fruitful.

"I stuck ma fork in the ocean and came up with a notion," sang Gunter. His crooning was the only sound that helped pass the time during their journey between towns.

"You know, Gunter, your tunes never have a conclusion. What purpose, or meaning, do they serve?"

"Well, ya see friend, it ain't the words that matter it's the singin'. It lulls them prairie dogs into a false sense a security, so when we need some quick victuals they don't move so much when I draw down on em," joked Gunter.

"Indeed, if you hit one with that buffalo Sharps, we'll need a dozen pieced together to cook up enough for a meal, marksman Berquist," said John sarcastically.

"Not to worry, there's no fear a runnin' out of prairie dogs in these parts," mused Gunter.

Gunter sang on, "*Do ya ears hang low, do they wobble to and fro, can ya tie em in a knot, can ya tie em in a bow. Can ya throw em o'er ya shoulder like a continental soldier, do ya ears hang low?*"

John chuckled as they rode on.

The days were nice, and the nights were still cool, but the prospect of finding something about the Bossar family in San Antonio was the only thing motivating them. That is until a loud crack of a rifle ball passing over their heads made them duck for cover in a nearby grove of trees.

"Can you see where the shot came from, Gunter?" said John.

"Nope, but the only cover's 'bout seventy-five yards away in that grove of trees to the east. Gimme 'bout fifteen minutes to circle round an maybe I can get behind the trees and see who's shooting at us."

John stayed with the horses and Gunter maneuvered to the other grove of trees. Presently, John saw Gunter come out of the eastern grove of trees holding two rifles. Gunter signaled John to come up.

"You ain't gonna believe this!" Gunter said, "But when this here feller tried to ambush us, he fell off the log he was standin' on and broke his leg." John looked down at the disheveled man who was groaning in pain, the bone in his leg poking through his pant leg. It looked awfully painful, but John did not care.

"Why did you try to ambush us?" John inquired of the man as he lay moaning on the ground.

"Well, that sorrel looks a whole lot like a poster I seen. I was just trying to improve my life by cashing in on you two. Hundred twenty-six pieces of silver would change my life."

John went into a rage at the thought of the man trying to improve his life by killing another man. It was a tirade only John's parents and his best friend, Pasqual, had ever seen. The cursing and denigrating comments about the man went on for several minutes with some words Gunter had never heard spoken before on the prairie. As crusty as Gunter was, he was taken aback at the intensity of John's rant. John finally expended his diatribe by throwing his hat in the man's face.

"What're ya gonna to do with me?" pleaded the defeated man.

John did not answer, but walked over to the man's horse, unsaddled it, and turned it out on the plains. John and Gunter mounted up and rode off toward San Antonio with the man imploring them not to leave him.

"That was interestin'," said Gunter. John did not reply.

When approaching San Antonio from the north there is a small rise of land that overlooks the city, providing travelers with a picturesque view of the growing town. John could barely see the old Alamo ruins where the state gained its freedom from Mexico so many decades ago. He wanted to visit the historic place, but knew his time would have to be better spent in search of the Bossar family. He thought of Nancy again as San Antonio was the city to which they planned to elope if her father objected to their marriage.

"Well, ma whistle needs to be wetted right 'bout now," said Gunter.

"I hear you, but this time we should go into a saloon together just in case something goes wrong," said John. "I'm not in need of whiskey, only information."

The Black Cat Saloon was one of the better-established watering holes in San Antonio; even though their prices were a little loftier than others. It was well furnished, clean, had fresh saw dust on the floor, and the cuspidors were empty. Over the bar was an average size mirror with several rows of whiskey bottles staked to each side of it. The long bar even had a brass foot stoop to rest your boot on while sipping your libation.

"Barkeep, three fingers of your best whiskey, if you please, sir, and a tall glass of sherry for my friend here."

"You're in luck, sir. We do, in fact, have sherry; though not much call for it on the frontier. We had eight wagons come in from the east last year and they brought in some finer spirits. One tall glass of sherry and three fingers of whiskey, the best of course, coming right up."

"Excuse me, Senor, did you order a glass of sherry?"

Both John and Gunter turned to see a finely dressed Mexican gentleman standing behind them with a pleasant smile.

"Not many men out here are *cultured* enough to order the finer spirits. I commend you for your choice. If I might, I am Pedro Osorio at your service. I have a hacienda just east of town. It is hard to find the finer things these days in San Antonio, but I would like to buy you that glass of sherry and invite you to my table over by the window."

John and Gunter were pleased to have the chance to relax and possibly gain some intelligence about the city of San Antonio; and see if their reputations had reached this far. They accepted Pedro's invitation.

Soon the three men were seated around the table, sunlight shining on them, as they engaged in lively conversation. Suddenly, a dark figure blocked the sun that shone through the window. Outside the saloon, standing on the boardwalk, was a large man holding a double barrel shotgun pointed right at the three of them. Simultaneously, all three men pushed away from the table, diving for the floor just as the shotgun blast shattered the window.

Due to the closeness of the shot, the pattern was quite small and hit the center of the table, shattering it. The assassin took off running down the boardwalk and around the corner of the building. Pedro was able to struggle to his knees and managed to get a shot off through the far glass window of the saloon. It was an accurate shot and the assailant hit the boardwalk with such force that two of the pieces of boardwalk lumber broke.

Just as Pedro fired his shot, in through the swinging doors burst a bearded man without a hat. He had a yoke, a wooden beam that held two suspended buckets of buttermilk at each end, resting on his shoulders. John was still struggling to get up and was the only one in a position to defend them. He hesitated until the "milkman" pulled a flint lock pistol from under his coat, then John drew, center aimed the man, and fired. The man fell, spilling his blood and both buckets of buttermilk. Some of the patrons of the saloon who had hit the floor at the first shotgun blast, scrambled to roll out of the puddle of buttermilk and blood so as not to stain their clothes.

As the smoke started to clear from the gun blasts, the barkeeper peeked over the top of the counter surveying the last few minutes of action. He hated to see the mess of blood and buttermilk as the stain spread across his floor and shouted for the cleanup boy to fetch a mop and pail to scrub it. The barkeeper then directed a couple patrons to remove the body in an effort to minimize the mess and enable clean up.

But Pedro immediately took charge of the situation and told everyone in the room to stay put; including the men who were about to remove the dead man. He ordered one of the saloon patrons to get the sheriff and be quick about it. "NO one moves till the sheriff gets here and questions everyone."

Turning to his new friends, Pedro quietly said, "My apologies, Gunter and John. This sort of thing has happened all too often in San Antonio since the war with the Mexican President several years ago. Some Anglos around here want to rid Texas of all Mexicans, and assassination seems to be the order of the day."

It never occurred to Pedro that he might not have been the target of the assassination attempt.

Sheriff James, "Toots" Morgan, interviewed all concerned and determined this was certainly a case of self-defense. Since Pedro Osorio was one of the upstanding citizens of San Antonio, his word carried a lot of weight. No one knew anything about the two assailants and no further legal action would be taken. Sheriff Morgan gave a long look at John and Gunter, not buying that they were cousins, but Pedro had vouched for them and that was enough for the sheriff.

"I insist you two rest at my hacienda until you find the person you seek. It is the least I can do for you. San Antonio is a large city and your search could take a while." John and Gunter agreed since the ride into town was relatively short and they had so many places to make inquiries.

After about two weeks, Gunter ran across a blacksmith who

said Franklin Bossar had worked for him for six months. But he had quit the trade because he inherited some land up in north Texas and was going there to ranch it. The blacksmith could not remember where the ranch was. The pair figured they'd sidle north.

Chapter 12
"The Big Fight"

After leaving San Antonio they headed north, and the conversation focused on the question of what to do, and which northern town might be the jackpot.

"Texas is still as big a state as it was when we started this search, Gunter." John was dispirited thinking about the difficulties they faced in continuing to search.

"I know t'is, but if it weren't for your southern honor 'bout clearin' your name you could've jest gone back to New Orleans and been done with this whole mess. And I'd have the money for my buffalo hides by now. It's a fulltime job keepin' you alive so I can git paid, ya know!"

"But they're after both of us now since we killed several of those scoundrels who ambushed us. They want you as well."

"Yeah, well, let' em come!" Gunter remarked with bravado. "If they get in front of this here buffalo gun they'll receive all they can handle from me, I tell ya. Don't give a damn anymore. Let's find the Bossar family, get you outta this pickle and let me visit New Orleans. Might find a fine lady there and settle down," said Gunter with a wink.

There was a long pause then Gunter spoke up again. "I'm guessin' you're missin' your lady lots about now, friend."

"Yes, I am," said John with a note of sadness. "She's a wonderful, beautiful woman, Gunter."

"Don't s'pose she might know a friend or two that might be unattached and interested in a good buffalo hunter, do ya?"

"Well, there's the rub, Gunter. Young beautiful women look

for young handsome men. They have standards too, you know." John reached over and poked the man in the arm.

Gunter simply grimaced and made a barely audible grunt.

"You know, if you'd take an occasional bath and douse some toilet water on yourself, and maybe change out of those buckskins, you might make a reasonable example of a presentable.... something."

Not appreciating John's teasing, Gunter grunted again, glowered at him and dropped the subject.

Ever since John had dropped Sannd he'd been troubled by the experience. He liked the word dropped instead of killed, it seemed more palatable to him, but he inwardly knew it didn't matter what word he used, the result was the same. John had not had a full night's sleep in over a year and half since he had defended the wagon train from Sannd's final raid. He had nightmares and anxiety attacks that denied him rest.

John often woke in the night swinging his fist trying to fight those men who had tried to harm him, but he did not want to kill them. Every night before he closed his eyes, he looked skyward and prayed to God; always asking that He protect his beloved Nancy from harm as he could not be there to do so. The fatigue of this way of life was catching up to him and he was leaning on Gunter more and more to be alert to dangerous situations. Tonight, would be no different.

John's nightmares came and went, but he consistently woke by 1:00 or 2:00 in the morning unable to go back to sleep. One dawn, as he listened to the early morning sounds, he distinctly heard Patch's nicker and whinny and then a sudden loud "thwack" coming from the picket line. John was up in an instant, grabbing his rifle and running to where the three horses were hobbled. They were alert and looking downstream; obviously, something disturbed them from that direction.

In the early morning light John could see the fading boot prints stamped in the dew on the grass. He followed the drag marks downstream, his socks soaking in the morning dew. At twenty paces he found a rifle lying in the grass. Another twenty paces and he came upon a man retching in pain, rolling in the grass unable to speak. He was holding his midsection obviously out of breath.

"Come up here, Gunter, I have him!" yelled John.

As Gunter approached, he cocked the hammer on his buffalo rifle.

"No, Gunter, we're not going to shoot him. Not this time. No more killings."

"John, he'd have no problem killin' you, not one bit. Horse broke some ribs—we might as well finish it here and now."

"No, no more. I'm not going to do it." John was adamant. "We can't just leave a trail of bodies."

Gunter was agitated. "He'll tell all his stinkin' friends where we are. He needs to be dispatched now! He ain't no better than a piece of vermin. I say dispatch him now, and be done with it, friend!"

"No, just lower the hammer on your rifle and let's leave him where he is; he's punished enough. Come saddle up and let's go, Gunter."

Reluctantly, they gathered their things, broke camp without having breakfast, and headed northeast.

About a half mile from camp Gunter suddenly reined his horse up and stated, "DAMN it all to hell! I left ma pocket watch on the stump back at camp. Wait here, John, and I'll go git it. Be right back."

John flinched slightly at the report of a rifle shot back at the old camp. Presently, Gunter came riding back to him.

"What did you do, Gunter, what did you just do?" asked John incredulously.

"Nothin' friend, jus what ya did at Ft. Jessup. I shot a rattlesnake."

John eyed Gunter with suspicion and asked, "Well, did you find your pocket watch?"

Challenging the question, Gunter looked John right in the eye and said, "Don't own no pocket watch."

John closed his eyes and lowered his chin into his bandana and thought of the life he was leading. He hated it with a passion. He clenched his fist, raised his head to the sky and screamed, "No more killing, no more!"

"I wonder, Gunter, if any of my letters are getting back to New Orleans. You sent your friend to St. Louis with one to give to a friend of my uncle and he should have been able to forward it to New Orleans. I'd like to know if anyone knows what we're up to."

"Probably everyone, not includin' Sheriff Knapp, right? If Rod Willeford's given a task he sure would try to git it done. But remember, when he left for St. Louis, the Osage in Kansas were on the war path; he may not have got through."

After a minute, Gunter looked at John and said, "I'd like to talk 'bout your letters, John. I know you can't live without that girl in New Orleans, but tryin' to send them letters might be givin' our position away. Somethin' postmarked New Orleans from out here on the prairie might be a bit suspicious, specially since the transit point for all Texas mail goes through Crocket. As crooked as Sheriff Knapp is, he could be doin' some fake official business and lookin' at the postmarks, then sendin' his henchmen back after us. Kinda odd how some of these guys are findin' us, ain't it?"

John was forced to admit that the coincidence of how suddenly they had been set upon by thugs was unlikely. Seems like out of the blue they would be in a shootout with someone. Gunter may have a point. But John desperately wanted to let Nancy know he wasn't a murderer randomly killing people for no reason as rumors might have it. And he did miss her terribly.

"I see your point, Gunter, but that girl is worth everything to me. I guess those letters might be setting us up. Like you say, they may not even be getting to her. I pray Napoleon made it through; he can set the record straight for everyone back home. I just can't stand it if Nancy thinks ill of me because of the killings. I'd hate that."

"Good, then hold off on them letters. I'll give you even odds she's waitin' with open arms for you to return." Gunter looked at John with a snide grin, "sides, you're so cute anyway, Johnny!"

John reached over and almost knocked him out of the saddle, but Gunter was laughing so hard he might have fallen on his own accord.

The plains were a lonely and dangerous place to be, even when you had a purpose to be there. When traveling the prairie, people were always glad to encounter others who were eager to stop and talk about their journey.

Such was the case when Gunter and John happened on a cavalry patrol. The squadron leader was a Lt. Colonel, Robert E. Lee. John knew of his exploits in the war with Mexico, which made their conversation easy, as well as interesting.

While John and the colonel chatted, Gunter was busy observing the pitiful rations the troops were eating. He was so flabbergasted that they could subsist on so few provisions that he offered his service, at a dollar a day, as a scout and hunter in order to provide better food for them. He later commented to the colonel that he could cut down on desertions by feeding the boys properly.

The chance meeting became a mutually satisfying experience for the men. Unfortunately, no one in the patrol seemed to know anything about the Bossar family. Although one of the company sergeants had been involved in the cleanup of the Buerke wagon train massacre a year and half earlier, not much else was garnered from the army.

Having learned all they could, John and Gunter eventually had to part ways with the patrol. Lt. Colonel Lee had been amiable, and would have enjoyed a longer visit with Gunter and John, but he had to continue his pursuit of raiding Indians.

"Gunter, if you don't mind, since we're headed north, would it be okay with you if we paid homage to the Buerke massacre site? The captain was an exceptional leader and he took care of Napoleon and me from Ft. Jessup till we departed just after passing Crocket."

"No problem, John. It's on our way and I hear tell Captain Buerke's reputation as a wagon train master was the finest. Hard ta believe he succumbed to a raid the way he did."

"You know, Gunter, a lot of things about that raid sure don't add up. Like how did the Indians know where the Buerke train was going to encamp? And how did they know where the Bossar family wagon train was going to be the next day?"

"I kin see your point, John. You have lots of coincidences that don't add up; I cain't make sense of it either. Pretty soon them coincidences will add up to facts, then you'll have evidence and it'll all connect at some point," Gunter remarked feeling less certain than he sounded.

The trail toward the massacre site was uneventful and dreary. By the time they were within striking distance of Crocket, they were getting low on food and tired to the bone from their long journey.

"Gunter, do you see that line of smoke over there to the east? Might be a small settlement where I can purchase some foodstuffs for us. Do you mind setting up camp and I'll ride in and see if I can get us some beans and potatoes for supper, and maybe some directions to the massacre site?"

"Don't mind a tall. Gimme the pack horse and I'll have a roarin' fire and your coffee ready when ya git back. See that grove of trees there? You won't hav'ta look too hard to find me over there, but I'll likely be asleep when you get back. I'm tuckered, friend."

As John rode toward the smoke he kept hearing the sound of wild cackling geese, but he could not seem to locate them no matter where he looked. The closer he approached the smoke, the more frequent and louder the cackling.

When John broke out of the tree line and happened on the road leading to the small settlement, the goose conversation became more intense. Once John happened to look up on top of the building with a green roof, belching out smoke from the chimney, he noted that there were two geese making a great commotion and walking back and forth on the roof of the main building in town. Its roof was no doubt green because of the goose droppings.

The sign on the front of the slowly crumbling building said, "Duce Goose Inn - Niggers, Catholics and Comanche not welcome." John chuckled at the moniker, bristled at the admonition, but considered the probability that 99 percent of the patrons probably could not read anyway. Oh well.

As John approached the small town, something about it just

didn't feel right. Although the feeling made the hair stand up on the back of his neck, he needed supplies and information so he rode on. He shrugged his shoulders, then checked his guns.

He spied the local saloon, a run-down affair barely standing of its own accord, and headed for it. It looked like a place where a prairie princess could make your dreams come true or a bottle of whiskey could drown all your misery.

John tied Patch to the hitching rail nearest to the saloon door. He purposefully tied him very loosely, knowing that Patch was as tired as John and wasn't going anywhere. As he always did, John paused at the door and peered in, letting his eyes adjust to the dim lighting and surveying the customers. The interior was a pigsty, sour smelling and looked like a dark death trap to him.

As he pushed past the swinging doors, he noted the barkeep was at the far end of the bar. The customers were in a stupor, several were draped over the card tables appearing to be asleep, but more likely drunk and numb to the world. Glancing around the room, John could not see another way in or out of the place besides the single entry.

The barkeep saw John approach and reflexively poured a shot glass of whiskey and pushed it toward him as John leaned on the dust-covered bar. John looked at him, shook his head and said, "information" in a low tone, not wanting to compromise the barkeeper's tateltelling. John placed a dollar on the counter and the barkeep poured the shot glass contents back into the bottle and said, "Sure, what are you are looking for?"

"Last year there was a massacre near here. Wonder if you could give me directions to the burial grounds?"

"Easy to do, it was a hellava massacre. Never figured out what happened. I'd guess your camp ain't a stone's throw from the bloody site."

Just then the barkeep looked up and over John's shoulder at

someone standing in the door. He was more than a casual cus-
tomer judging from the rigid stance that the barkeeper assumed.
John concluded his business with the barkeep and slowly turned
to exit the saloon. The figure that captured the bar-keeper's attention was still standing in the door, pressing his arm against
one of the swinging doors and holding it open.

As John approached the exit, he noted that the figure had an
eerie resemblance to someone he knew, but he could not place.
His long beard, the shape of his nose, the frown on his lips and
his right eye cocked off to the side giving him an evil look, but
John still didn't recognize him.

Drawing closer, John could just make out two points of a
sheriff's star peeking out from under the man's vest. As the distance to the saloon doors shortened, the more uncomfortable
John felt in approaching the sheriff. The man was half blocking John's exit and wasn't budging. Just as John tried to pass
through the other half of the swinging saloon door the sheriff
spoke up.

"Nice horse you tied up to the hitching post, son," the sheriff
said sarcastically. "I heard about a horse like that in these parts
from some friends of mine."

John calmly replied, "Thanks, he's the best friend a man
could have."

John was face to face with the man when he heard him speak
and John instantly knew who the man resembled. He was none
other than Sheriff Kalvin T. Knapp, cousin of Hatten Willoughby
and the man who put out the warrant and reward of 126 pieces
of silver for John's arrest.

Their eyes locked as recognition dawned. They were less
than an arm's length from each other making it impossible for
John to draw his knife or his pistol. Knapp also knew that drawing his gun at such close quarters wasn't an option; however, he

did have his buffalo knife in a cross draw on his belt.

Although no signal was given, both adversaries knew simultaneously that the fight was on. John shoved the sheriff hard against the hinges of the open swinging saloon door as the sheriff grabbed his knife. They struggled for it, but Knapp had a firm grip. He tried to maneuver the knife to stab John in the stomach, but the blade point was at a disadvantageous angle for him.

John caught the sheriff's wrist, and using the door frame at his back as leverage, directed the blade upward toward the sheriff's chest. It went home with a quick slice and a soft grunt from Knapp. The sound was inaudible to the patrons of the saloon, but they could see the sheriff's face pale as he grabbed the blade with both hands and pulled it out of his deflating chest. He did not fall to the floor but remained standing struggling for breath.

The back of his vest had hung up on the hinge of the swinging door, holding Knapp in a semi standing position. Knapp let the knife fall with a clanging thud. Only then did the lazy and sleepy patrons of the saloon start to rouse out of their stupors and come to the defense of the sheriff. That gave John just enough time to bolt from the saloon and vault onto Patch's back.

As John wheeled Patch south to retrace the way he'd come in, he knew he had made a mistake. A wagon loaded with freight was backed up to the mercantile store completely blocking the road and his escape. Now the patrons from the Duce Goose saloon were beginning to pour into the street looking for John's scalp.

John could hear the shots ring out behind him as he heard someone yelling, "The sheriff's been stabbed to death!" Another voice hollered, "Shoot that French Vaquero, he done the sheriff in, knifed him through!"

John could see men stepping into the street and onto the boardwalk; others standing up in the freight wagon at the call to arms. He suspected that most of the mob weren't going to be very good shots as they held their shotguns and rifles to their shoulders, but kept their heads high to see what was going on. But it didn't matter how skilled the men were, a lucky hit to Patch or John was just as good as a well-placed shot.

John drew his first pistol from his cross-draw holster on his left hip. His only redemption would be with the help of Colonel Colt. As a load of buckshot tickled John's hat, he cringed slightly. His first attempt at returning the fuselage of fire was comical. One of the thugs who shot at John turned tail, dropped his shotgun, and dove through a store window head first, catching his boot toes on the lower window sill. John's shot went wild, hitting the window glass above the diving shooter, showering him with additional glass shards.

With bullets still chasing John down the street, he was getting closer to the wagon and could see no way around the blockade. He was going to have to turn Patch around and head out of town to the north through a gauntlet of mad men trying to send him to parts unknown. Bullets and shot were passing all around John and Patch but were missing their mark. It was obvious that a moving target was more difficult to hit for these boys, and Patch was moving with speed. John was thankful for the men's lack of accuracy as he would never forgive himself if Patch got hurt in this melee.

As John approached the wagon the driver stood up and cocked and pointed a shotgun. John made an amazing pistol shot at full gallop and hit the driver in the stomach crumpling him to the floor of the wagon. As John approached, he sat back in his saddle, threw his stirrups forward signaling Patch to slide. He slightly touched Patch on the right flank and, at the apex of the slide, Patch turned left picking up speed and heading north down the street. At the height of the turn the freighter on the back of the wagon stood up and pointed a pistol at John, but misjudging Patch's momentum, the man fired and missed. John did not miss, and the freighter fell off the wagon to the ground, moaning in agony.

John thought the sheriff's friends were good at ambushing someone, but in a stand-up fight they did not fare too well. On his way out of town the cacophony of gunfire was growing in intensity. Shots were ringing out all around him and to his right was a bearded man cocking his shotgun and holding it at waist level. John knew he had to take the man out before he fired, otherwise Patch would go down. But the excitement of the gunfight must have gotten the better of the bearded man for when he tried to pull the trigger his finger was on the front of the trigger guard and nothing happened. It was then that John put a bullet into his chest.

The man's friend was standing next to him as the bullet struck. Seeing his buddy go down, he realized that life was a little more precious now and turned, firing his pistol over his shoulder at John and retreated to some cover. John shot him in the back where his suspenders crossed and the man didn't move once he hit the ground. John knew he only had one round left in his Colt and would have to affect a pistol swap soon to get out of town alive.

The next adversary was trying to hide behind an oak barrel near the boardwalk. He was left-handed and must have been acquainted with firing a flintlock. He had a bead on John, but just as he pulled the trigger, he turned his face away and closed his eyes to avoid the flashing black powder from the frizzen and pan that did not exist on a cap and ball rifle. He missed as his shot went wide. John's pistol ball hit the rim of the oak barrel splintering wood into the eye of the man and causing grievous damage to his face.

Things were moving fast and Patch was giving John all he had in their escape out of town. John could not believe that the shooting games in the woods of Michigan during his college days would pay dividends now, but they most definitely were.

John quickly holstered the now empty Colt '51 into his cross-draw holster on his hip. He reached down to the flapped holster on the saddle, dangling just past the swell of his saddle, and unbuttoned the latch. He deftly grabbed his second Colt '51 and brought it to bear. It was the one he had taken from Hatten Willoughby over a year ago. This '51 was now going to be his salvation in his race out of town.

Just as John grabbed the grip on the second Colt a shot clipped Patch's mane throwing a hunk of it into the air. It was deep enough on his neck that Patch stumbled slightly, but regained his feet and resumed his race to the north end of town. The main street in town was now lined on both sides by all sorts of armed men trying to earn their 126 pieces of silver.

Stumbling out of the saloon, over Sheriffs Knapp's collapsed body, was the barkeep with a cocked double-barreled shotgun. He hesitatingly aimed at John and at the last second raised the gun into the air, discharging both barrels missing John by a mile. John wondered if it was because of their momentary friendly words earlier as they had talked at the bar. John refrained from doing battle with him.

The gauntlet was getting more vicious and difficult to navigate as men were determined to take down John and his speeding horse and earn the lifesaving silver coins offered on reward posters. It was a very powerful motivator to these otherwise unsuccessful men.

John knew he'd been lucky so far. Most people found it difficult to hit a moving target, and even more difficult when that target shot back. John hated what he had done to the first six men, but their lust for the reward silver was their own undoing. He was scared now, but the men lining the street were equally focused.

John kept looking for a side street, anything he could find to head out of town, anything to avoid the gauntlet laid before him. With only a fraction of an instant to think, John realized there was no way out, except to plunge down the street as fast as Patch could run.

He was ducking and diving through the fuselage of gunfire as his life flashed before him. He wanted to be miles away from here in the arms of Nancy, but he had business to complete. He had to get Patch out of this fight alive; he owed that to the horse that was doing his best to get to the end of the gauntlet.

A pale, baldheaded man holding a Mississippi musket tried to get the measure of Patch and his rider, but the speed of the action and his relative naivety about combat worked against him. They both fired simultaneously, the double cloud of black powder smoke obscuring each man's view of the other. Neither could see if they had struck their mark. Patch kept moving forward unfazed. John heard a loud thud, a groan and a plea for help come from behind him.

John could not aim his revolver, he had to relax and point it, letting his eyes control his body. Wherever his eyes went his body followed, if he didn't freeze. That was hard to do when he was a target, but at this speed it was crucial to let his eyes lead everything.

Up till now all of John's shots had been strong side for a right-handed shooter. As he sped down the street of the gauntlet, he noticed that his adversaries were lining up on both sides of the street. One even crossed over to the other side to make it harder for John to engage him, but John had practiced both off side and strong side shots in the Michigan woods during his college days. The numbers still against him were probably eight or nine men, and John had only five shots left in his lone revolver. He had to select the most threatening shooters and take them out as he raced out of town. They seemed to be spaced about thirty to forty feet apart on either side of the twenty-yard-wide street.

John elected to ride right down the middle of the road. Patch knew his job, and needed no guidance. He had to run straight, steady, and fast with his head down to give John the best chance to sweep left or right, shooting either an off side or strong side shot.

Just as the fusillade started anew a round hit John's right stirrup passing through the leather and under Patch's belly, doing no harm. John could not detect the source of the shot but did notice two men lining up their sights on him on his off side. It would be a tricky shot for him, but if John hit the closer of the two men, he might be able to drop him into the other guy, fouling his aim.

It worked. John's shot managed to hit the near rifleman in the head just above the eye spinning him sideways colliding with his comrade and spoiling that man's aim. The second man involuntarily fired his single shot rifle and the round impacted mere feet in front of Patch as he sped forward. The geyser of dust of the impacting bullet did not faze Patch and he continued to race to the edge of town.

John's luck was holding, but just barely. As that thought passed through his mind a shotgun blast of buckshot took John's hat off. It was a nice hat and John could only imagine how mangled it was now. But luckily, he did not have it tied to his head with a wahoo string or the departing hat might have choked him to death.

The edge of town was in sight but there were still a few adversaries to deal with. John looked to his right as a shabbily dressed buffalo hunter lobbed a bowie knife at him. Although it missed by inches, had John been going slower it would have easily sliced into the arm holding the reins. John ignored the man as he was no longer a threat, but the man next to him most definitely was.

The ponytailed man appeared to be an Indian who could use a rifle. He held it correctly, face on stock, rifle butt into his shoulder, lining up the sights. John raised his pistol, arm straight out and locked, cocked his piece and pointed directly at the man. John fired first, hitting the man in the stomach causing him to crumple to his knees as John and Patch sped by.

In quick succession there were two more riflemen to his left. They were standing next to each other with pistols at the ready. John turned slightly in the saddle to engage them, but it was unnecessary. Due to their demeanor and body language, it did not appear to John that either were competent shots. He suspected one was more than drunk and was out on the street because his fellow drunks were hooting and hollering. But the other one was a little more sober, and John focused on him.

When John pointed his Colt' 51 at the sober one, he elected to hastily retreat rather than shoot it out with John. But the drunker of the two seemed to think the whiskey he had been drinking gave him more fortitude and decided to gamble on shooting John out of the saddle. He lost, never to imbibe again.

John's options were becoming even more limited now with just two shots left and no idea how many additional shooters were still trying to take him out. How long had this fight lasted? It seemed like an eternity, but at the same time it buzzed by in his head in a flash.

John had to concentrate like he had never concentrated before. It was imperative to race to the edge of town and into the woods for cover in order to affect his escape. But the mob wasn't going to let him go that easily; he would have to fight like he had never fought before.

Just then John saw a vagabond sling a bucket into Patch's path. Neither John nor Patch were fazed by the obstacle, as they had practiced numerous times jumping bales of hay. If the design was to trip Patch as he was running full tilt, or spoil John's aim, it failed miserably. Patch easily jumped over the rolling bucket without breaking stride. That surprised two of the men who were ready to pounce on John as he should have fallen off Patch.

Regaining his seat after Patch vaulted over the bucket, John took deliberate aim at a rotund well-dressed merchant who was all too eager to add the reward money to his wealth. The size of the man, made John's targeting much easier. The merchant leveled two dueling pistols at John intending to bracket him by discharging one, allowing John to duck to one side on Patch's back, then engaging John with the other pistol as John tried to recover. But John sought to best him and shot first, hitting the obese man in his vested pocket watch. One of the dueling pistols discharged at the impact of John's round on the pocket watch, and ricocheted to the other side of the street laying another man out cold. If there was humor to be had in a deadly situation that was going to be it. John suppressed a smile and looked for one more shooter to deal with before he exited the gauntlet.

That sorry individual presented himself on John's left side in an upper story window. He was holding a Sharps' carbine much like John's own and had John dead to right in his sights. But when aiming from an elevated position one must aim low to hit the target. This fellow forgot that rule of thumb and instead his bullet went high hitting John's own aimed pistol, dislodging it from his hand just as John fired at the man.

After the Sharp's bullet struck John's revolver, the numbness in his hand was nothing like he had felt before. John tucked his hand into his belt to keep it from flopping around and hunkered down close to Patch's neck making as small a target as he could. The edge of town and the end of the gauntlet was just feet away.

Why John assumed the edge of town was going to be his salvation he did not know. Just as he crossed the boundary a rifle ball came within an inch of his left ear. The concussion numbed John's hearing and shook his balance, disorienting him for several minutes. Patch kept running for all he was worth, saving them both.

Though reaching the cover of the woods, and despite the hearing loss in his left ear, John could still hear the men of the town ordering others to mount up and pursue him. The cacophony of the thundering hooves of at least three horses chasing him was unmistakable.

John had to do something, but Patch was asking John to slow down, as he was getting winded and John could hear and feel Patch's labored breathing. John could see that the road ahead took a sharp left hairpin, slightly descending turn, and after making the almost one hundred eighty-degree turn, he reined in Patch and put him into an extended trot. Over his shoulder he could see through the trees that, indeed, three horsemen were pursuing him and would soon make the hairpin turn in the road. He had only one choice now.

John slowly reined in Patch, stopped him and turned him around facing the direction of the approaching men. Patch and John stood perfectly still in the middle of the road awaiting the approach of the riders. Patch needed the respite and was quickly recovering from the long gauntlet run. John noticed the blood coming from Patch's wound on the crest of his neck where the chunk of mane was missing. It did not look serious, and John thanked God for that.

He was slowly regaining his senses from the concussion of the last rifle shot that had caused his left ear to ring unmercifully. Pausing and regaining his strength in the middle of the road, John was going to have to do something that he would regret the rest of his life.

He drew his Sharps rifle from the scabbard, loaded a paper cartridge, closed the action, sheering the end off. He blew away the excess powder from the breech and deftly capped the piece. He and Patch stood ready as the three riders rounded the bend.

They were packed tightly together with one rider slightly in the lead of the other two. Once they saw John, they spurred their horses in unison toward him and began firing their pistols. John stood in his saddle, leaning forward supporting himself on the swells and cocked his rifle aiming between Patch's ears. At thirty yards he took careful aim at the lead horse's chest... he fired.

The billowing smoke cloud obscured John's view of what happened and he did not stay to see the calamity he had unleashed. He immediately turned Patch back down the road and put him into a trot. What he had done was the stuff nightmares were made of for lovers of horses. He never looked back, but he could hear the cursing of men, screaming horses and breaking of bones.

Some yards down the road John saw two men on horseback approaching him. One looked familiar but the other was a total stranger. In the fading light he was leery of both until they got closer. John was out of bullets and figured to bluff his way out of this situation. He put the Sharps in the crook of his arm and rode right up to the two men.

To his surprise the man on the right was none other than Gunter. John did not recognize the one on the left, and did not take his eyes off him.

Gunter spoke up first. "Looks like ya been bowlin' today, John!"

John, still focusing on the other man, answered Gunter wearily, "Those boys were after my skin."

Gunter noticed John's focus was on his companion and thought he better introduce him.

"John, this here is Franklin Bossar, of Crocket, Texas. Come across 'im 'bout an hour ago. He invited us to eat sup at his daughter's place mile or two from here."

It took several seconds for the name to sink in to John's buzzing brain. He had killed a lot of men and horses to meet this man.

"I understand you want to speak to my daughter, sir."

John haltingly replied. "I do sir. I do indeed."

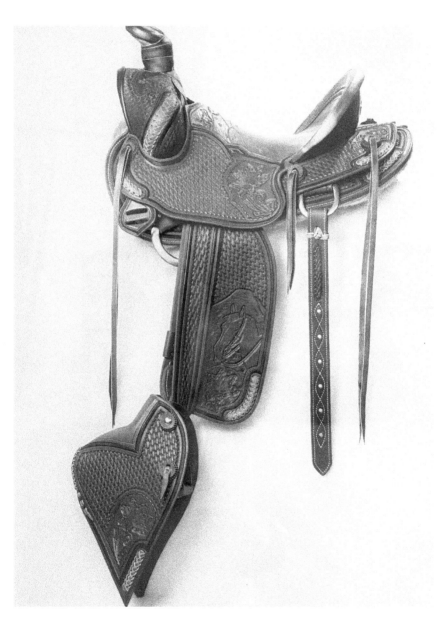

Quewannoceii Saddle

Six up Mule freight Wagon

Going Home

Chapter 13
"It's Over"

Joanna was aware of John's constant nightmares. She could not imagine what her son was going through, but his nightly screams and insomnia were of tremendous concern to her. He always seemed to dread going to bed at night. She'd become aware that he often awoke early in the night to some frightening thoughts that seemed to keep him awake. He often took lengthy naps in the middle of the day to recover some of the much-needed sleep he lost to whatever demons invaded his dreams. She felt for her son, but she could not help him. It was something he must work out for himself.

This had been going on ever since he came back from the frontier; the last six months seemed like an eternity to her. For Joanna, the revelation that John had killed so many men was shattering. It was hard for her to believe, even after these long months. Her only solace was the Texas Rangers' report stating that all the killings had been justified. She never thought her son could do such a thing, but the evidence was there. She had to accept that John could, and would, be a dangerous man when he needed to be.

Since the fight with him about going to college, John no longer confided in Joanna about the most intimate things in his life. It was natural for males to outgrow the need of parental guidance and seek their own counsel. Joanna felt a loss as her boy made the transition to manhood and left her behind.

But hope lived in Joanna that maybe John would open up to his father and at least talk about what had happened in East

Texas. Maybe Pique could help John sort out the overwhelming issues confronting him. But for now, John kept his thoughts private. All his parents knew about the big fight in Crocket was the public accounts that were recorded in the newspapers. At least when Gunter was in town, he and John would take long rides and John seemed to come back refreshed. She wished he would find a nice woman with whom to share his life and perhaps be able to find peace from his obvious pain and anguish. Joanna would love to be a grandmother.

"Come, Son, your lunch pail is ready, and I have fresh water too, you'll be late," said Joanna.

"Thanks, Mother, I'll be there in a moment."

"I don't understand why you feel the need to be the night watchman anymore. You seem to enjoy it though."

"I don't particularly enjoy it, Mother, but if I'm to run the family business then I want to understand all of the issues and problems that go with being the head of the freighting and mercantile store. That means pulling the night watchman duties at the wharf for our three warehouses. Remember, it's a unique service the Alvarado's have done for our customers that no one else in New Orleans provides. It gives us an advantage in the warehouse storage business on the wharf."

The walk on Canal Street to the warehouse on the wharf was going to be a pleasant one this evening. John reminisced that it was a similarly peaceful evening when he escorted Nancy back to her apartment some three years ago. The breeze was cooling the day down and the task of guarding the warehouses was very simple for John. The Alvarado's always had a family member protect the goods stored in their warehouses awaiting shipment. The threat of fire and theft had caused insurance rates to climb, but it was this simple task of posting a night watchman that many of the Alvarado customers appreciated the most. They were also willing to pay for the service.

John had been back from east Texas for almost six months. Things in his life had been hectic since the trial at which Stephanie Dawn Bossar's testimony had assured his acquittal for the murder of Hatten Willoughby. The Texas Rangers tried to recruit him, the New Orleans city fathers urged him to run for the state legislature and the Army wanted him to sign up as an officer in the militia. He declined the Rangers invitation and hesitated on running for the state legislature. But he did sign on with a support logistics battalion as a second lieutenant in the militia.

John's biggest regret of all his experiences for the eighteen months he spent on the frontier is that he lost Nancy. He was unable to find any trace of her. He did not even know the name of the ship she left on. That alone would have been a boon in his search for her; it would have been the best way to trace her. His contact with the French Foreign Service turned up nothing. They informed him that once her father died, they did not keep track of any relatives. He wished he had married Nancy before he had left for damned Texas...!

He could not explain to anyone the feeling he had every morning when he awoke. It was like losing a loved one and you had to grieve all over again. That was the constant pain he suffered for the decision not to marry Nancy when he had the opportunity. At least he could have had the alcalde, the local magistrate, perform a ceremony and then they could have had a more formal wedding when he returned. The thing he missed most about Nancy was her voice. It was so melodic and soothing, exuding a lullaby effect on him. He could listen to her talk all day. John was glad he had at least told her *that* before he departed for Texas.

Anxiety and grief hung over him. Although he could do nothing about it, the thought that someone else might be sharing her love both angered and saddened him. He still loved her deeply and his arms ached to hold her again. He knew only those who had experienced such a deep loss of love could understand his anguish–knowing she was out there somewhere, but not with him. Unable to find her, he could only pray she was happy. Having abandoned God momentarily for not answering his prayers, he still prayed to Him to keep her safe. John knew killing was an ultimate sin and his eternal redemption would be limited, but he still found some comfort in his hope that God would at least look after Nancy.

The family had taken John's advice and invested in local railroad projects. Two of his cousins were on the boards of several rail lines running throughout the South. However, they hesitated investing in the Trans American Railway that would connect the East with California because of all the corruption. John's father had also taken his advice and started to import the exquisite cheeses from Michigan; they were best sellers.

Gunter had taken over the Alvarado's freight line terminus in Ft. Worth and it was prospering quite well. He was the only non-Alvarado to be employed by the family business. Gunter met a widow whose first husband had been murdered by the notorious renegade, Sannd, and John served as best man at their wedding. Gunter's new bride asked John about the deportment of Napoleon several times.

John was constantly greeted by passersby, both well-to-do and not so well-to-do, on his walk to the docks and he treated them equally with a gracious greeting and a firm handshake. He knew he could probably be a good politician, but felt politicians often lied to secure votes and that was something he refused to do. He suspected that honesty might keep him from ever getting elected to anything.

John could be brutally honest about any subject, using logic, not emotion, to reach a solution. If people could accept that, he would consider a candidacy; otherwise he wished they would not bother him about politics. However, an encounter with one William Tecumseh Sherman gave him pause to consider a seat in the state legislature.

Mr. Sherman, a West Point graduate, was an educator at heart. He thought John's reputation could win a seat in the state legislature where John would be in a position to lobby for funding of a state university system. Since John agreed with Sherman on the subject of higher education he was tempted; however, he didn't like the idea of using his fame as a gunfighter to elevate such a noble cause.

John decided against a run at the time, but supported Sherman when he became the Superintendent of Louisiana State Seminary of Learning and Military Academy; later known as Louisiana State University. John would wait and see if any future opportunities for public service came his way.

The walk to the docks was reminiscent of the promenade he and Nancy shared the night before he left for Texas and it filled him with wistful memories. John was completely engulfed in one of these memories when he was slapped on the back by his best friend Pasqual. Still not emotionally healed from his combat in Texas, John was startled at the friendly attack and nearly jumped off the sidewalk.

"How are you this fine day, friend?" Pasqual playfully nudged John.

"I'm good, I guess. Thinking about the best times and escaping the worst times, you know?"

Pasqual wanted to support his friend, but found it difficult as John seemed to guard his feelings about all the death he had caused. Having been best friends for most of their lives Pasqual felt slight resentment that John didn't confide in him about things that were obviously troubling him.

"I'll tell you what, tomorrow morning when you no longer feel the need to be a guard dog at the warehouses come out to the farm and we'll go deer hunting, what do you say?"

John paused for a long moment, looked at Pasqual and nodded his head. "A good hunt would do me good right about now, see you on the morrow."

The docks were as busy as ever; particularly when a new ship had just docked. The workmen were excitedly unloading casks of Jamaican rum, many of them headed toward the Alvarado warehouses. As John watched the cranes lift the loads from the hold of the ship, he noted a young boy, no more than three years old standing at the railing thoroughly enthralled with the mechanical apparatus; mesmerized by the pulleys and ropes. He was a good-looking child with very blue eyes.

Just as John started to turn toward his appointed night watchman duties, he felt a tremendous blow land on his left shoulder and the back of his head. Staggering forward and then stumbling to one knee he started to black out. As he looked up toward his left side, he saw a well-dressed man with a raised broken cane sword in both hands about to deliver a death blow. The man was yelling something that John, in his debilitated state, could barely make out.

"You killed my cousin and I'm going to do the same to you, you, you…FRENCH…VAQUERO SCUM!

As John faded and before he completely collapsed, he saw

a shower of wood splinters cascading all around him. Some minutes later John had the distinct feeling of some large fingers pinching his cheeks.

"Come now boy, you've been clobbered harder than that and shook it off. Wake up, John!"

The throbbing in John's head and the ache in his shoulder were very noticeable now. He had the feeling that he was weak from loss of blood too. "What the hell happened?" John said to no one in particular. As his eyes began to focus, he looked up at Pasqual's toothy grin.

"You were hit in the back of the head by that fine Texas gentleman lying prostrate over there. He was about to decapitate you with his broken cane sword when I took the liberty to bust a clerk's stool over his head," said Pasqual proudly. Pasqual assisted John to his feet and steadied him as he was still very dizzy from the encounter. As John surveyed the unconscious attacker, he could not place him and could not fathom the unwarranted attack.

Still shaky, John looked up to the ships railing where the young boy had been standing. By this time, his mother had come forward and was standing next to him. There was a lady standing there with hands crossed, holding a purse below her waist, a look of terror on her face gradually turning to a glow as tears ran down her cheeks. She raised one hand and waved at John.

The wedding was the social event for New Orleans society that year. Joanna and Pique spared no expense for the gala event. The entire extended Alvarado families were all invited. This was to be a ceremony uniting all the namesakes of the famous explorer.

Nancy received the most unique and satisfying gift from

an Alvarado family member. At the reception, Raul Alvarado, the assistant postmaster, presented Nancy a stained wax paper package with a blue ribbon binding it together. As she opened it, she could not believe its contents. As Raul made his presentation, Nancy was overcome with emotion. Disregarding decorum, she embraced the postmaster and kissing him on the cheek, declared, "Thank you, sir!" Adding with glistening eyes, "This is the best, best gift possible." On their honeymoon Nancy read the letters John had written to her from the frontier. As she read them aloud John enjoyed, once again, the beautiful melody of her voice that he had so missed.

John immediately adopted Perrier for social reasons. Most people noted the resemblance to John and thought it just a nice coincidence, giving it little further thought. However, John knew the truth and was totally enamored with his son. He loved the opportunity to teach him how to shoot a bow and arrow, a rifle, how to ride and care for a horse, and all the ideas and knowledge that would assure his son would grow into a man of strength and integrity.

Hatten Willoughby's cousin, Ozias, was extradited to Texas to face his crimes. Ranger Irwin was charged with escorting him back to Crocket for trial, but it is said that he tried to escape and didn't make it.

BOOK 2

Chapter 14
Crossed Sabers

John sat in a chair on the New Orleans shipping dock, looking out across the Mississippi River utterly dismayed. He could not believe the article in the New Orleans Picayune newspaper. The headline screamed in bold letters, *South Carolina Secedes from the Union, War Imminent*!

Pondering this development, John muttered, "What a stupid thing to do! How hot-headed the legislators must have been! How easily led by the nose they must be by the elites of our grand state to think that war was going to solve anything!"

Lincoln had his hands full if the state acted on its war threat. But if they refrained from any overt action, peace may still prevail. South Carolina did not want to be told by the federal government how to handle its affairs. State's rights had festered for several decades on the national scene, but the underlying culprit was slavery, and everyone knew it. Only 10,000 families in the South owned more than fifty slaves, about 25,000 families owned less than thirty and fully three fourths of all households did not own any slaves at all. Yet the elite democrats were dragging down the South and for what? For a system that was dying out anyway!

John knew that if war came and Louisiana seceded, New Orleans was vulnerable. The war of 1812 with the British proved that. John would have to make plans to protect his family. The north would have to shut off the Mississippi to throttle the South's economy and would have to occupy the leading port city, his home, New Orleans.

John had only served one term in the Louisiana legislature, but he still might have some influence. Although his goal in those two years was to get legislation passed to start a university system in Louisiana, people still might listen to him about not seceding from the union. That was the worst idea he could think of right now for the South.

He knew some of his adversaries in the legislature may not listen to him because of his past--a past filled with gun-fighting in east Texas. But he had to speak up. During his college years in Michigan John became aware of the economic advantage the North had and the population to fill their army ranks. Unless the South fought a quick war, it was going to be doomed to a catastrophic loss.

Damn South Carolina all to hell!

John rose up from his seat in the Louisiana legislature to address the assembled lawmakers. It was the finest building in all Louisiana. The cigar smoke was strong, men were sweating because of the humid afternoon and the ladies fanned themselves vigorously to cool down. Undoubtedly, the

temperature was also up because everyone's emotions about the day's vote had caught citizens by surprise.

"Gentlepersons..., South Carolina was rash in its rush to vote for secession. We are not militarily prepared now, nor will we be in five years, to confront an organized Union army bent on occupying New Orleans and controlling the Mississippi."

In the gallery behind him a voice rang out, "Sit down you half breed or go home!"

John ignored the harangue. The rest of the assembly was stunned at the outburst, but they eventually turned their attention back to John.

"South Carolina voted to secede with emotional fervor and not logic. They were prodded by elitists who are motivated for their own self-interest." A hush fell over the assembly. John continued, "We all know that slavery is dying of its own volition and can't be sustained." Uneasiness stirred in the crowd. "We can't be led by those who want to keep slavery when the majority of Louisianan's don't own slaves. We can't be led by a few to our destruction!"

Again, the single voice rang out in the gallery. "Traitor to New Orleans, leave us if you don't want to help keep our self-respect and independence! You're a half breed and a coward!"

John was unable to locate the source of the derision, but he recognized the voice.

"I hear your coarse obtuse voice, Mr. Grout. Show yourself and argue the merits, but dare call me a half breed again and I will see you outside this assembly!" John shouted back.

David Grout had migrated from Cincinnati, Ohio, over ten years ago. He was the assistant editor of the New Orleans Picayune Newspaper. A scandal artist rather than a reporter, he published sensational articles more than factual ones. John had refused to give him any exclusive reportage on the 'Big Fight in Crocket, Texas', and Mr. Grout resented John for that umbrage.

Mr. Grout then proceeded to manufacture stories about John's gun fighting days, embellishing what few facts he could garner with outlandish lies. John never paid any attention to the newspaper but Napoleon, John's cousin, did. On one occasion Napoleon and Mr. Grout crossed paths at a fine restaurant in New Orleans and got into a heated argument; resulting in Napoleon beating David about his head and shoulders with a cane. That didn't seem to dissuade Mr. Grout. He continued his rough treatment of John Alvarado in the Picayune until one evening when David was on his front door stoop struggling to find his door key. A musket ball extinguished the porch light, missing Mr. Grout's head by inches. The adverse treatment of John in the Picayune ceased.

As John continued his address, he could see by the body language of the audience that his position was unpopular. Many were angry at him and very displeased that he had even broached the subject. But to secede from the Union in John's educated opinion was pure folly, and John had a stake in the legislature's vote.

"Gentlemen, I implore you to think, for God sakes, think! Do not let your emotion ruin your lives. It is time you engage with facts. Use your minds and not your heart! If it is to be war the consequences will be grave. New Orleans will be the first city the north will attack as it is key to the South's economy. We will feel the wrath of righteousness of their cause first. This war of liberation, or Civil War, will be a battle of ideas interrupted by artillery. Think gentlemen, think," pleaded an impassioned John.

John knew this assembly had no concept of what war was; what killing was. They couldn't see the North's position, and they couldn't understand that the North was unable to fully see the position of the South. Someone had to peer around the corner of emotion and appeal to sanity. Someone had to do something.

His plea did not make a dent in the audience's demeanor. The rumblings and undercurrent of hidden conversation were rising against John. But no one would confront him directly.

One gentleman stood up and patiently waited to be recognized.

"The Chair recognizes the gentleman from Baton Rouge, Mr. Tieg."

"Mr. Chairman I wish to raise a point of order."

"Go ahead with your point of order, sir."

"Thank you, sir. Mr. Alvarado is no longer a member of this assembly and therefore has no privilege to speak to this assembly during the session. We only extended the courtesy because he had been a past member of the legislature. Therefore, he should be excused while we debate our vote."

"Quite right, sir… Mr. Alvarado, you will refrain from speaking and remove yourself from this assembly."

There was a general approval from the floor that Mr. Alvarado was out of order and should depart to the gallery. John took his rebuke with dignity, but left with a parting shot.

"*etre sage*, Gentleman… be wise. Be wise."

John tapped the podium twice with his sword cane and walked off the floor of the legislature toward the gallery.

The displeasure of the audience with John's speech was palpable. As John approached the gallery searching for Mr. Grout to deal with his unwarranted comment, a tall, well-dressed, bearded gentleman approached him. The man had a large chew of tobacco in his mouth and it appeared to John that he was working up to spit on him as soon as he got close enough. John casually put his hand under his coat where he would ordinarily carry his side arm but grabbed his pocket watch instead. The bearded man saw John's motion, thought better of his potential action, blanched and swallowed hard. He then turned and left the gallery not daring to approach John any closer.

John smiled to himself. The power of a gunfighter's reputation had its advantages'."

"How long has it been since we climbed up this cypress tree, Pasqual? Remember, we used to come up here to solve the mysteries of the world; maybe admonish a dictator, or even a king, or tell each other secrets."

"Maybe thirty years, Johnny. I know things about you, you know things about me and nobody listens to our solution to the world's problems. But it does us both good to talk about everything anyway, friend."

"I fear the war that's coming is going to test our souls, Pasqual. This war between the north and the south is going to set brothers apart. Families will divide, and friends will feud. I worry about the safety of my children and wife. I know New Orleans will be the first to be attacked by the Union navy. General Scott will listen to General 'Old Brains' Halleck and try to strangle the South's economy. He has to do that to bring the hot heads to their knees, make them think of their action as being too rash. Without the profits from the cotton sales around the world, the South will be significantly crippled. But your dad's farm will be profitable, raising food stuffs as it does."

"What will you do, Johnny? Your family business of freighting is as vulnerable as anything else. By the way, how's the rest of your family, your sister too?"

John missed the intensity in Pasqual's question about his sister.

"My father and uncle are preparing themselves for the worst. War can be good for some and devastating for others. But my three cousins seem eager to defend New Orleans, maybe too eager." With a strain in his voice John continued, "My sister is still recovering from the loss of her husband from the last yellow fever epidemic."

"Things are changing fast, friend. I've just accepted my promotion to captain in the militia and can't get out of it. If war comes, I go where I am told to go. Fortunately, I'm in the quartermaster corps, moving freight."

After a long pause, John continued reflecting on the direction his life must soon go.

"I've never been in favor of slavery, Pasqual—you know that. My family only employs family members, and has never used slaves. In fact, Gunter Berquist, who runs the Ft. Worth terminus of our freighting outfit, is the only non-Alvarado in the family business. I won't fight for slavery...don't believe in it."

Pasqual could see John's quandary. "You're going to be called up if those South Carolinians do something rash; you know that, don't you?"

"Yes, I do. But I'll have to do what Lieutenant Colonel Robert Lee of Virginia did. He could not fight against his home and his state. New Orleans is my everything, my family, my friends, my life. I will not fight against her."

"You made that plain with your rhetoric in your legislature speech, Johnny. Seems no one listened to what you had to say. I can see what you were trying to do. But I fear as you do, that emotion will carry the day. Louisiana is bound to secede and go to its doom. At least I am not part of all this coming madness."

"No, you're not, Pasqual. The calamity that's coming should not affect you, your family, or your farm. But invading forces sometimes don't discriminate friend or foe, they just conquer. My caution to you, friend, is to beware of all strangers. They may try to corrupt you to maintain a hold on this country. And Lord knows, Cajuns and creoles don't like to be controlled by outsiders."

"No, they don't. We might fight someone that tried to force us to do anything. Yankees and all their self-righteous crap!" Pasqual's blood was getting up.

"Calm down, 'P.' I need you do something for me."

"Name it, Johnny."

"Colonel Braxton Bragg will be organizing the Louisiana militia soon and I'll be going places as directed. Would you look after my family while I'm gone?"

Without hesitation Pasqual replied, "Yes, of course! That is what best friends are for."

"It's secession, boys! We're going to form a new country!" shouted Dufilho at the top of his voice.

John could hardly hear himself think with all the celebration around him. It was noisier than any New Orleans celebration ever had been. His cousin was delirious with joy about the forthcoming war. The exuberance was contagious with the rest of the younger men in his family, none of whom had ever killed anybody. But John had. He had killed, was famous for it, and didn't like it. He tried to hide his fame, never talking about the numbers of men he had killed. Ten years later he could still not get a full night's sleep because of the nightmares about all the men he had killed. He would give anything to have never been a killer. And now he was in the Louisiana militia, getting ready to witness more killing. He hated it, but could not avoid it. He wanted to slap some reality into his younger cousin, but in his heightened excitement Dufilho would not understand. The whole thing was madness.

John could well remember his own excitement when Sergeant Thompson wanted him to join the Second Dragoons and go fight the dictator Santa Anna in old Mexico. But John did not have responsibilities then. He was seventeen and eager to serve. But now he wanted to discipline his younger cousin for something he himself was once ready to do. It was all incomprehensible madness to John.

"Hey Johnny, I'm to join the Louisiana Legion enlisting on the morrow. What do you say to that, cousin?" an elated Dufilho shouted.

A dismayed John shouted back over the din of celebration,

"Your eagerness is too much for me, Cousin. Harness it! War will not be so delightful once you get into it."

"Nonsense, Cousin, those 'blue bullies' will pay a price if they come to take New Orleans. They'll pay a price for their self-righteousness. It'll cost them dearly. Remember General Jackson taught those English redcoats a lesson. We'll teach these northerners the same lesson."

John's blood was up now; his cousin was not thinking this through. "Don't you know that the northern generals learned the same lessons that Jackson taught the British, and might have a different plan to take New Orleans? Don't you think they learned a thing or two in the last fifty years? Think! Use your brain besides something to keep your ears apart for God sakes!"

Just as John was trying to talk some sense into one cousin another cousin walked up behind him and slapped him on the back. "John, I'm to join Dufilho in the Louisiana Legion on the morrow too. We'll serve together defending Ol' New Orleans. Can you beat that? This is a good day to get 'owly' and party!"

John slowly turned to Quinin, glaring at him and said as he walked away, "I'll pray for all of us."

Quinin looked at Dufilho and asked, "What bee got up his bonnet?"

John and Nancy did not participate in the general revelry of the 'secession party' that was enveloping New Orleans. They preferred to keep their own company and enjoy what little time they had left together before John was called up with the rest of his regiment. Nancy saw the brooding look on John's face and could guess at what was on his mind. She sat watching him, not wanting to interrupt his thinking. In any event, she liked just looking at his pleasant features.

"Well, Lady, it's done. We're to be in a war that will not bode well for anyone. I fear the worst for everyone. I worry about you and the children. Pasqual will always look after you and I want you to put your faith in him should things go wrong. He'll see to your safety, as well as that of mother and father. I suspect if we're invaded, he'll move the lot of you to his farm outside of town. If you can remain in the quadrangle here in town try to do so. If you must move, father will tell you why someone must remain in the house at all cost."

It seemed to John that Nancy was aware of the coming dark clouds, but as he gazed into her eyes, he could tell that she was thinking of something else rather than what he'd just told her. He wasn't going to question her; he just wanted some peace and quiet right now. Then through the sitting room door burst his eleven-year-old son.

"*In Dixie Land I'll take my stand...*" Little John Pierre never got to finish the verse. John was up in an instant, grabbing his son by the arm, swinging him around and giving him a single swat on his bottom.

John bent down and put his face into the boy's face and sternly admonished him for being so joyous on such a solemn occasion. Little John was totally perplexed, everyone around him was in a party mood but he was being berated for the same by his father. The boy stepped back, pausing for a moment knowing he shouldn't say anything, turned on his heels and ran up to his room.

Nancy sat still. She knew now was not the time to say anything either. She was aware of John's quick temper and it would pass just as quickly as it had erupted.

After a few minutes Nancy spoke up. "Not the boy, John, he doesn't understand any of this, particularly why you disciplined him."

John was still simmering and knew he shouldn't say anything to Nancy at this moment as it would only make things worse. But his emotion, something that he always tried to control, got the better of him. He needed a release and Nancy was prepared for it.

By this time, Nancy had worked for Herr Schmidt's Paris newspaper for over ten years as an incognito reporter. She had reported on slavery in the southern United Sates providing antidotal stories that Parisians absorbed with intensity. The world political situation was intensifying now that South Carolina had formally seceded from the Union. The world, Paris in particular, was engrossed in the internal turmoil of the now fractured United States. Nancy's reporting, albeit disguised, was read lustily by Europeans.

Herr Schmidt,

Find enclosed the latest installments of my stories about the South and slavery. I think they will be most enlightening to your readers. The turmoil that secession has created is turning New Orleans upside down. I fear that violence will ensue and even a civil war will break out very soon. I can see the fracture in my own family.

I am advised that if war does break out, New Orleans will be one of the first casualties, maybe even conquered by Union forces. Therefore, in that event, we must make arrangements to send my correspondence to you by French packet shipping, which would be immune to seizure by the Union navy. In addition, your forethought to change my nom de plume to J.A. from John Alvarado would also be crucial to be maintained.

Kind regards, Sir
Nancy Alvarado

P.S. If there is a way you can put me in touch with a Mr. Le Matt of Paris it would be very helpful. Thank you again for all your kindness.

Herr Schmidt was thankful to receive Nancy's latest installment of articles. His Paris newspaper had been very successful publishing them. It gave the average Parisian a personal view of life in the southern United States as it related to slavery. He was as concerned as Nancy that he might lose a crucial source of detailed information about the looming civil war. The *ST. Germaine Recorder* was a standout in Parisian society because of Nancy's reporting and he didn't want to lose her. But why did she want to be put in touch with an arms manufacturer like Mr. Le Matt?

While walking on the New Orleans shipping docks John approached a man shrouded in the fog and slowly recognized him as his cousin, Napoleon.

"What are you doing up so early on such a dismal morning, Cousin?"

"I'll ask you the same question. Damp and cool, but still a time to get in a brisk walk before the day's business begins," replied Napoleon.

"Indeed, Cousin. A constitutional is healthy this time of the morning," John said.

There was a pause and John was prepared to hear his cousin say that he had joined the Louisiana Legion and was off to train for the coming war. That would leave no one at home to help either set of parents run the family business. Cezanne and his father were getting on in years, but might be able to struggle by without the youth in the family.

"Johnny, I hope you don't find any cowardice in my decision to stay with the company and not join the army with you boys in the family. We need someone that can stay involved with the business to see it through these coming hard times."

John was ecstatic that his cousin was willing to continue the family business. His younger cousins were already enlisted, and John was part of the militia. At least one vigorous Alvarado would stay behind to take care of both families.

John didn't hide his surprise. "You must also count on Pasqual to help out should you need him. I'm sure he'll be an asset to you. Besides, I don't think the ladies of New Orleans could live without your presence for any length of time." With a playful smile, John winked at his cousin.

Napoleon retorted, "I'm not sure I could live without the ladies of New Orleans for any length of time, is more like it.

"You know, Johnny, this war is the right thing to do. We're a different culture than those Yankees. We should be an independent country. We don't understand them, and they don't understand us. I'm like you. Slavery is driving all this, but even without that issue we still aren't like them northerners. They're plain different."

"Yes, they are, Napoleon. But they think they're righteous to impose their way on us because of the slavery issue. That will make demons of them."

"Good morning, sir. I'm Sergeant Alvarado, your company first sergeant."

John stepped back a pace, returned the sergeant's salute and sized up the man. He was obviously a professional non-commissioned officer who had been drilled properly and had a commanding presence.

John paused for a moment collecting his thoughts.

"Sergeant Alvarado, are you from the New Orleans area? Are you related to the original Alvarado of the De Soto expedition in any way?"

"Yes sir. Just like your family, my ancestry goes back to the twenty-one peasants deposited by Moscoso Alvarado on the banks of the Mississippi to survive on their own. Just like your family, we took the general's last name to garner respectability. All twenty surviving branches of that expedition did the same."

"I see, Sergeant," said John, worried that he might have a political type on his hands. "What experience do you have?"

"Joined the Army in '57, sir. Worked mostly in coastal artillery in Mobile, Alabama. Figured I'd come home to help the Louisiana militia."

"How is a stint in coastal artillery going to help this company of the quartermaster corps? Seems you're misplaced, Sergeant."

"Got an injury, sir, not much good to the artillery right now. Still want to help the cause."

John thought he'd tease the sergeant and blurted out, "What did you do? Drop a cannon ball on your foot?"

There was an embarrassed pause from Sergeant Alvarado. "Not quite that simple, sir, but essentially yes I did."

John appreciated the honesty of the sergeant and was himself embarrassed that his attempt at a joke made the sergeant uncomfortable.

"Well then, Sergeant, I suspect we'll be recruiting soldiers that have similar maladies, not quite good enough for the infantry, but still capable of some good service. We need to be on the lookout for good teamsters and bull whackers; men that have done some substantial freighting. We'll need about one hundred twenty-five to one hundred and fifty for the company."

"Yes sir. I have twenty-seven on the muster roll right now that fit the bill. Some have been in the army awhile and all of them wanted to trade the blue uniform in for the grey of the southern army."

"Any good sergeants and corporals in the batch, Sergeant Alvarado?"

"Yes sir. I served with a couple of them before. But any experience would be an advantage for us as a unit."

"Yes, it would, but I want to meet all the ranked ones, to see if they're fit to hold respective stripes in this new company."

"Yes sir, I'll arrange it. Meanwhile, a new batch of recruits is assembling in the market, the old slave auction in the center of town. We might want to get there and get the rest of the company signed up."

John inwardly blanched at going to the slave auction, but he needed to fill out the roster for his company. The irony bothered him immensely. Furthermore, he knew that his speech in the legislature was not well received by many New Orleans residents. He had created enemies; like the tobacco chewing man who wanted to spit on him. John knew those types would also be at the auction center.

"Beg your pardon, sir. We have an enlisting station over by General Jackson's statue. It seems there are numbers of men that want to join your company. I don't know why the rush, is there something you should tell me, sir?"

John was amazed at the line that had formed at the table in front of his company flag. He didn't recognize any of the men standing there. As John approached the front of the line there was a general murmur of approval by the assembly and several sought to shake John's hand. A slender boy probably eighteen or so, asked John for a small speech of encouragement. Slightly embarrassed, but aware that such men needed direction and encouragement, John reverted to his campaign days when he had run for the legislature. He had no idea if these men were pro slavery, or against it. Or if they were like him, against it, but would fight for the South because it was their home.

"Boys, I need your help! I need bull whackers and teamsters; this company will be moving the Army's freight. I'll work you sun up till past sunset, life in the quartermaster corps will not be a picnic. The sergeant has the muster roll; he'll be ready for your signatures." John paused, and then thought for a moment. He needed a rally cry for these men so attentively listening to him. "Boys, we'll not be bullied by those blue bellies!"

There was a cheer for John's modest speech and Sergeant Alvarado herded the elated men toward the table, so the corporals could get them signed up. Later that evening, John swore them into the Southern Army and gave them instruction for the next assembly date.

Sergeant Alvarado approached John with the muster roll and informed his captain that he had 135 men enlisted. Several were infirm and might be forced out after the first drill. Some were too old, but moving freight would be just the business for them instead of the infantry. The tally included eight corporals with prior U.S. Army experience as well as three sergeants.

"Well, sir, at least we have the makings of a good company with experienced leadership. We'll whip them boys into shape in the coming drills," crowed Sergeant Alvarado, extremely pleased with himself.

"Sergeant, I also want our boys drilled in small unit tactics."

There was a pause as Sergeant Alvarado was taken aback for a moment by the captain's directive.

"Sir, I don't understand at all."

"Sergeant, we may be a freighting outfit, but we won't always be escorted by infantry or cavalry. We may have to defend the wagons with what men we have. I want the company drilled in small unit tactics. Send for a couple of infantry non-commissioned officers after we get them some basic training."

"See your point, sir. I'll get on it," Sergeant Alvarado replied.

"Sir, the three sergeants and eight corporals are waiting for you over at General Jackson's statue. Thought you might want to meet them. All have prior service in the Union army."

John approached the assembled men. "Men, listen up. I am your company commander. We have one hundred and thirty-five raw recruits to whip into shape before we receive our wagons and horses. It will be up to you to get them into Army shape. You have the experience, but I don't want you to abuse them, but rather teach them. With drill and discipline, we'll be the best company in the Southern army. You will be the leadership of the company. Everything it does reflects on you. I want these men to be good marksmen. That falls on you. We will draw all the equipment for an infantry company and carry it in the wagons. I require efficiency from everyone. We must move supplies for a moving Army, no ifs ands or buts."

The non-commissioned officers seemed to understand John's emphasis and appreciated their respective roles in organizing the company. They appreciated that their first sergeant was also one of them. However, they reserved judgment about their captain. He would have to earn their respect since he was a militia captain and not a professional officer. Collectively they were mystified about the need to train the recruits in marksmanship since they were a quartermaster unit. Sergeant Alvarado answered that question later that evening to their satisfaction.

That afternoon John left further instruction with Sergeant

Alvarado. He would soon receive a Second Lieutenant Wilkerson as the new company adjutant and he was to make him comfortable. There would be a brigade parade in three weeks and the company needed to be ready for that excursion. Meanwhile, John had to travel to Baton Rouge for a staff meeting with Colonel Braxton Bragg and draw their wagons and mules from deserted Union equipment.

Upon John's return he received disheartening news from Lieutenant Wilkerson and Sergeant Alvarado.

"Beg to report, Sir, a Captain Sherer, brigade adjutant, came by last week and took thirty five of our hundred and thirty- five men and posted them to the infantry. He checked them over and said they were fit for such duty. He said he knew you back in your college days, sir."

John indeed knew James Sherer of Maryland. He was a cohort at Hillsdale College and he was a slaver through and through. John also remembered they had had a confrontation which resulted in John punching that southern gentleman in the nose and setting him on his butt.

"Not much can be done about it now, boys. I need to go into New Orleans and do some more recruiting for the company. Have the three sergeants and you accompany me to the docks this evening. See if we can't get the company numbers back up," directed John.

It was almost a circus atmosphere when John Alvarado showed up on the New Orleans shipping docks. The enjoyment at seeing a local hero brought out the whiskey glasses and merriment from most of the laborers. There was back slapping and old tall tales to be heard as the men surrounded John, excited to see him. Lieutenant Wilkerson and the four sergeants were totally mystified at the popularity of their captain.

Someone found an old wooden round tub, turned it upside

down and beseeched John to climb up on the top and address the crowd.

"Gentlemen, and I use the term very loosely," there was laughter in the crowd as John continued. "I do not ask for your vote this time, but rather that you join the cause. Join my company in the quartermaster corps, avoid being shot at and deliver the goods to our troops."

To Lieutenant Wilkerson's and Sergeant Alvarado's surprise, that was all the convincing these men needed. They were all too eager, and all were ready to join up. The sergeants inspected the recruits' health and had the thirty-five replacements in less than twenty minutes. Lieutenant Wilkerson and Sergeant Alvarado were dumbfounded at what had transpired and agreed to talk to Captain Alvarado about his popularity.

"Sir, that was amazing! How did you do it? I've never seen so many flock so quickly to a recruiting table," an amazed Lieutenant Wilkerson said.

Sergeant Alvarado chimed in too. "Sir, is there something you need to tell us?"

"All in due time boys, all in due time."

Sergeant Alvarado approached John and whispered in his ear. "Sir, I can't have the boys being too familiar with the company commander. They must respect you. You can't lead by being popular, you have to command them, not be friends with them."

John knew Sergeant Alvarado was right. He had been caught up in the moment, acting like it was a political rally instead of a recruiting campaign. The accolades of the men had been exciting--reminding him of his earlier run for the state legislature. John gave a sigh and paused for a long moment.

"You're right, Sergeant. We're going to war and many of these boys will be in harm's way. I owe them my best decisions. I'll do better in the future. Meanwhile, organize them and get them to the camping grounds with the rest of the company."

"Yes, sir," replied Sergeant Alvarado. But as the two parted, Sergeant Alvarado shook his head. What kind of officer did he have on his hands? Extremely popular, slightly unconventional, and from what he had heard, not all that involved in the 'cause.' He would have to be patient with Captain Alvarado, but the interests of the company would come first for him. The boys needed *his* best to take care of their respective jobs, mused Sergeant Alvarado, and he would do all he could for the company's well-being.

Just as the sergeant was about out of ear shot, John called to him. "Have all the sergeants available when I get back to camp. I want to assign them their duties."

"Mr. Q, are you about?"

Phinacensit Quenelionous was an immigrant from the Basque country bordering Spain and France. He came to Louisiana because of the cultural persecution that both nations pressed on his countrymen. He had heard of the freedom he could have in the new world, particularly in America. He was getting up in age now, estimating that he was about eighty, but could not prove it. He still was spry, but bent over at the shoulders from working in his saddle shop. He never drank, he enjoyed good conversation, and went to church every Sunday. Mr. Q had lost both his sons and wife in the frequent yellow fever epidemics that New Orleans was infamous for. He spoke with a slight lisp and had an accent that most people could not place. His wit and memory, however, were extraordinary.

"Well, Johnny, how are you? How are the children? They're such a joy to me when you bring them around. Haven't seen you in quite a while, what are you in need of?" a surprised Phinacensit said.

Before John could answer, Mr. Q quickly changed his greeting. "Sorry, sir. I ought to address you as captain, not Johnny, my apologies."

John chuckled, "We've known each other for how long, sir? I'm still Johnny to you and you're Mr. Q to me."

With a big grin on his face, Mr. Q extended his hand, knowing his social faux pas was forgiven.

"Mr. Q, these army '59 McCellean saddles are hard on a man's posterior. I need modification to this army saddle, so I can maintain my seat under all conditions. The big thing for me is the stirrups. The hood on them won't let me shove my foot in all the way to the heel of the boot. You know I've ridden ox bow stirrups all my life. These give me a cramp in my arch. I need an ox bow stirrup substituted for the army one, while keeping the hood intact."

"Cramp in the arch of your foot? That has to be an uncomfortable feeling, Johnny. I see your point. I certainly can install an ox bow instead of the army stirrup if you need me to. What else?"

"Take the stirrup leather fenders off and build me a substantially larger set of saddle bags. The army ones are so small. I also need a good-sized valise for the back of the saddle."

As Mr. Q wrote out John's order with his quill pen, John could tell there was something on the old saddle maker's mind. But it would be up to Mr. Q to broach the subject if he chose to do so.

"Here's your receipt, Johnny. It'll be about a two-week project. I need to get about twelve dollars for all the aggravation this will cause me," a slightly irritated Mr. Q retorted.

John knew he was going to be there for a while as Mr. Q was in a mood to unload about some topic that was important to him. But that was alright; listening to the old man was a joy for

John. He had relished the stories about the Basque country that Mr. Q shared when John hung around the saddle shop as a boy. Hearing about historical places was always a mind teaser for John. He loved first hand history from a primary source.

"Can't believe all this talk about the coming war, Johnny. I wish everyone would stop and think. War ain't as fun as it's cracked up to be. When I was a young man, I put a lot of Frenchman and Spaniards in the ground. They all wanted to subdue us Basque. I still to this day don't know why they wanted what we had, which wasn't much. They both thought that they were superior to any Basque, and we had to fight them both. And for what? Lost a lot of my family killing Frenchies and Spaniards" Mr. Q sat down in an old rickety chair, put his head in his hands and tried to weep, but he couldn't. "This is going to be the same, Johnny. Them northerners are coming, and for what? Can't they just leave New Orleans alone?"

John put his hand on Mr. Q's shoulder and said, "I'm afraid they can't. They're full of self-righteousness and are on a mission to master the South, Mr. Q."

Chapter 15
War!

The day after the vote to secede was dismal, uncertain, and sobering for John. He was experiencing an agony of body and spirit. He knew that the war was going to end in sorrow, consternation and confusion. Everyone's world would be turned upside down. But many could still not see that fact.

"Pasqual, what's the matter?" John inquired of his best friend.

"Nothing, Johnny, just all this war talk has me down a little."

John knew something else was wrong, Pasqual did not meet John's eyes and he never did that.

"I'll wait as long as you please until you're ready to talk, Pasqual, but something is bothering you."

From out of the blue Pasqual blurted out, "How's your sister?"

John was taken aback and held his response for the longest time, gazing intently at his best friend.

"That's the second time you've asked me about my sister, Pasqual. Is there something that I should know?"

Pasqual wasn't ready to broach the subject yet, but his intemperate blunder moved the timetable up.

"Well, with the war coming on, and she being a recent widow, and Ms. Nancy traveling to Paris... uhmmm!"

"Pasqual, what is it? We've been best of friends too long for you to beat around the bush. In fact, you're hiding behind the bush, what is it?" an impatient John anxiously asked Pasqual.

"I would, um, I would like permission to see your sister, John."

John was struck dumb. He could not believe his ears. His sister had lost her husband in the last yellow fever epidemic to hit New Orleans and his best friend wanted consent to visit with her. But the war was on the horizon and change was coming to the South. What Pasqual wanted was not socially acceptable, not even in New Orleans. As forward thinking as New Orleans was, an interracial relationship would be hazardous to the parties concerned. John had to think this through. His sister, his best friend in life, he loved them both but…

"Pasqual, do you have any idea the problems you'll have even in New Orleans?"

"I have somewhat, but I've also talked to Nancy a bit about it, John."

"What does Nancy have to do with your relationship with my sister?" John was more annoyed than ever since he had not detected any of this in his own house. He was completely blindsided.

"Nancy said that inter-racial relationships were more relaxed in Paris, more accepted," a very nervous Pasqual lamely responded.

"Even so, Pasqual, how would you make a living? You're a very good farmer, but my family couldn't support you."

A slightly irritated Pasqual retorted, "I would not expect the family to support us, John. Nancy would give up her translation and story writing at the *St. Germain Recorder* and I would assume the role of J.A. in her stead. I would write the anecdotal articles for the paper."

John had been conspired against by the people he loved the most. What was he going to do? He knew he could not say no. But how was he going to protect them? That was his life's role, protecting the ones he loved and the innocent. John was completely confounded by this family conspiracy. How could he protect them, particularly since his regiment was being called up, and they were likely to leave the New Orleans district to fight the coming war elsewhere? John could feel his hair turning gray again, he wanted to yell at someone, or something, but he had to remain restrained. The family's future was in his hands.

The White House

"Mr. President, good morning, how are you, sir?"

"General Scott, the question is how are you today?"

General Scott was the hero of the war with Mexico some twenty-five years earlier. He was a bold general, innovative and aggressive and tended to be apolitical. He focused solely on the needs of the army. He constantly fought with Congress to fund the small professional army that he felt the young nation needed, but Congress never wanted a professional army, always looking to what had succeeded in the past. The volunteers had always served American martial interest ably up till now.

"My health is not the best, sir, rheumatism and gout keep me grounded most days. But my mind is clear, sir."

"Then you will not be able to take the field, to bring the seceding states back into the Union, General Scott?"

"I have capable officers, Mr. President, that will do the necessary work, although about half of the army officer corps and non-commissioned officers have elected to fight for their respective states rather than the Union."

"I am aware of the leadership issues, General Scott. I have governors and senators who keep pushing political generals off on me who may not be that capable. But I need their votes and their state militia volunteers to fill the ranks of the army. My initial call for seventy-five thousand men in ninety days was challenging."

"General, do you have a plan to bring the seceding states back to the Union? That is my whole purpose, to preserve the union."

"I do, sir. It's called the Anaconda Plan." General Scott pushed the document across the map table toward the president. "The South's sole source of international income is 'King Cotton'. This plan will strangle the South's external trade with the outside world allowing us to subdue them economically into submission. They have far fewer miles of railroad track, fewer army age males and fewer manufacturing complexes. The plan will work. But it will take time to employ, Mr. President."

Mr. Lincoln scooped up the paper and began reading it. General Scott remained patient and mum as the President absorbed its' content. Presently, the old general noticed the President raise his eyebrow and hesitate. He raised his head from reading the document and queried the general.

"General Scott, this section about subjugation of New Orleans, do you think you can do it? Remember, General Peckham of the British Army in 1814 with the best troops in the world did not take New Orleans."

"Yes, sir, we can. The United States Army learned from his mistakes and we can take New Orleans."

Chapter 16
"The Bad Gets Worse"

"Boy, it's cold tonight, Quinin. Didn't know standing guard duty along the "big muddy' could be such a bone-chilling experience," a frozen Dufilho chattered, as he added another log to the small campfire. He also thought to himself how the glitter of secession was dimming now on this dreary, wearisome night.

"General Moulton sure has a strange way of fighting those Yankees. Guarding a chain across the Mississippi is not what I signed up for. What's it been, a year and all we have done, brother, is march back and forth from the fort to this guard post, raise and lower the chain for friendly traffic on the river then make sure it's up at night."

"I know, the chain is supposed to stop and then slow down the sailing vessels at this bend in the Mississippi. The hundred and seventy-seven guns of Ft. Jackson and Ft. St. Philip will blast them to kingdom come."

"I'm with you, brother. I thought the Louisiana Legion would be defending the ramparts against an all-out invasion by the blues by now. You know, something like General Jackson did to the lobster backs in '14. Remember how grandfather used to talk about making them lobster backs run down the delta?"

"Hush, Dufilho." What's that noise? Put the fire out...."

"Halt! Who goes there?"

"It's Sergeant Roberts, boys... let us pass."

Quinin stood down and rested his rifle while Dufilho restarted the campfire.

"Listen up, boys. The blues are up to something, so the

general wants to reinforce all the post. I brought the whole platoon with me to share in your guard duties. We'll do some scouting and reporting. General wants no surprises. Four-hour shifts, fifty percent alert. You Alvarado boys got the second shift; go get some sleep right now."

Two days of fifty percent alert was wearing the platoon down. But if the word was that the blues were up to something, then all the boys had to be primed for anything. Tonight, was especially hard for guard duty. Visibility with the low evening fog and no moon meant it could be anyone's guess who might be out there. The bull frogs were in full throat tonight and the alligators were starting their mating calls. Maybe those eerie sounds would keep the 'yanks' at bay for another night till the platoon rotated back to the fort...

"Halt, who goes there?"

The fight for the western end of the chain that blocked the Mississippi River approach to New Orleans lasted only twenty minutes. Of the forty-seven Louisiana Legion soldiers under Sergeant Robert's command, twenty-seven were killed outright. The remainder were all wounded, some severely. They were now prisoners of war and were taken back to the surrendered Confederate Fort Jackson. Admiral Farragut's flotilla rushed past the fort toward New Orleans, guns blazing.

Quinn never saw the blue soldier who bayoneted him. It was a quick thrust from behind, through a lung and into his heart. He was impaled on the bayonet and dead before he hit the ground. Dufilho had a severe head wound from a stroke of a rifle butt stock; unable to walk he was carried by his friends into imprisonment.

Once the old hulks and the chain barricade were breached, Admiral Farragut's large fleet pushed past the two forts. It only took General Butler and his seventeen thousand troops three days to capture the city of New Orleans. Resistance was nominal, mostly relegated to an ineffectual attempt at burning the docks. However, the population of the city would resist in many other ways over the next three years. The seizure of the city effectively shut off any commercial traffic up and down the Mississippi. It was the first stage in General Scott's anaconda plan to strangle the South and it was working. The precipitous fall of the 'King Cotton' economy started with the control of New Orleans. The slave trade also faltered with the major ports' capture.

Captain John Alvarado's regiment left New Orleans four days before the Yankees' invasion. They were headed to the Missouri theater to counter an incursion by Union forces there. All the men in John's company were devastated when they heard that New Orleans had fallen. The problem with recruiting a regiment from one location was that they now all had relatives behind enemy lines. Morale was at an all-time low in John's company. John now faced a long separation from his family that would rival the one that he experienced in his gunfighter days. At least his best friend would look after his family; that was the only comfort he had.

The trek toward Missouri was arduous both for the men and animals. Once they left the true southern states for the border ones, procuring supplies became harder for the regiment. John oversaw transporting those supplies, not acquiring them. In enemy country the southern army simply requisitioned them from the local population, who resented it, as the Confederate dollar was not worth much. Sometimes the locals would try to reacquire their prized animals or fodder by using force to raid the unprotected supply trains. They also assisted the Union Army to track down any Confederate unit that might be unguarded. Given the situation, John's forward thinking about training his transportation company in small unit tactics paid off several times. Just three weeks after New Orleans fell, John's leadership would be tested in action.

John had directed several small wagon trains as a civilian, but this time he commanded sixty military supply wagons and he had to get the supplies to the depot in order that the regiment could continue its march and engage the enemy. He employed many of the same organizational techniques he had used on the Texas frontier: up and moving before first light, noon for cooking and grazing the teams, and guards to the four points of the compass. All that had served him well in Texas; today was no exception.

Again, the higher command did not see fit to provide any escort for the rations and ammunition that he was transporting. He was told to send for help should he need it, but hurry forward.

The company was camped by a small stream with plentiful grazing for the animals, plentiful firewood and some cover within easy reach in the rolling hills nearby. The night was balmy, and the men did not pitch any tents, but slept on the wagons and made hasty meals at the small camp fires. Before the crack of dawn, Sergeant Alvarado had the company harnessed up and ready to march.

"Captain, southern scout coming in, he's coming up fast, sir!"

As the rider approached his company commander, he put his horse into a slide, almost hitting Sergeant Alvarado with the full force of the animal. The sergeant was not amused at all.

"Save your horse, son, you have to ride him the rest of the day! Report!"

The private, after leaping from the horse's back, breathlessly pointed to the road behind him and said, "Union cavalry coming up fast, platoon at least!"

In the increasing morning light John peered through his binoculars down the road. He paused, and Sergeant Alvarado could see John's lips moving as he was counting the approach-ing enemy.

"Bugler, Lieutenant Wilkerson to me. Sergeant Alvarado, dismount the men from the last ten wagons and prepare to de-fend the hub!"

Protesting, Sergeant Alvarado responded, "Sir, we are not an artillery outfit."

John angrily shot the sergeant a glance and calmly told him to form a skirmish line: half the men on one side of the last wagon, the other half on the other side. "Have them load now, sergeant!"

"Lieutenant Wilkerson reporting, sir."

"Jim, get the first fifty wagons going to the depot. Send a rider for help. I don't know how many more Union cavalry we might have on our hands. I'll fight a rear-guard action. Get moving."

"Sir!"

John could see that his boys weren't going to be ready to fight before the Union cavalry was upon them. He took another look through his binoculars.

"Sergeant Alvarado, they're not cavalry, they're Union mounted infantry. They have shoes on, not boots. Bring my horse up. Get the boys ready!"

As his teamsters were fumblingly loading their rifles and pistols, John knew he had to do something quickly. He needed to delay the fast-approaching enemy long enough so that his partial company could prepare a defense. He could only think of one thing. He acted.

As he mounted Patch, he pointed the horse down the road directly at the oncoming Union patrol. They were fast approach-ing his unit in a column of twos, apparently thinking the cap-ture of the wagons was going to be an easy endeavor. Because of that misjudgment, many of the Union infantry still had their rifles slung over their backs, and with the rising sun off to their right, slightly blinding them, the Union troops did not detect John charging at them at full speed.

John did have an advantage over the 'Blue Patrol', as they were unlikely to be very good equestrians and would not be expecting him to be coming right at them. He kept Patch on the grass-covered center of the road, avoiding the hardened road wheel tracks that would make maneuvering dicey at best.

The patrol belatedly started to unlimber their 'long tom' single shot rifles at about a hundred yards from the wagons when they saw the sole attacking rider heading right for them. The combined closure speed would be forty miles an hour.

Patch always ran with his head down giving John an ability to swing his pistol left and right, side to side, without having to raise his arm up and over Patch's elevated head to engage the combatants on either side. Another advantage for him in close quarters fighting, John was going to ride between the advancing patrol of twos, down the grass strip and shoot them as he passed, making him too close for them to use their rifles. John had twelve rounds in his two Colt's model 1851s to take down seventeen 'blue bellies'. What the hell was he thinking?

There was really no time to think. All that time he spent in the north woods with his friends playing a game of mounted target shooting, and the gun fights in the streets of Crocket, Texas all those years ago, were his inspiration as to what to do. John and Patch were coming on fast. Patch was steady and John was sure he could inflict casualties. He had the advantage. He would be deadly.

As the range between the two charging adversaries evaporated, John noticed that the oncoming cavalry was mounted on horses a full hand taller than Patch, allowing them to shoot down at him from their perch on taller horses. This put John at the advantage as he'd end up shooting even with the bellies of the clavaryman as he passed them.

John's charge at the Union cavalry was working. Their formation was starting to break up. They were splaying out from the road letting John ride right between them. He started to engage them with his Model '51 colt at twenty yards. Just as John thought, he was able to shoot level at the first "blue" soldier, hitting him in the chest; the soldier slumped in the saddle moving off to John's right. Just as quickly, aiming across his body, John shot the soldier to his left hitting him in the stomach. That "blue" fell to the ground in a thunderous heap as his horse stumbled over his body and fell too. The third soldier was coming on too fast, so John did not engage him, but focused instead on the fourth soldier on his left. That "blue" boy's eyes were so wide open, and the fear on his face so pronounced, that John could tell he was going to be ineffective as a combatant and did not shoot him. From somewhere a shot passed over John's head.

Time seemed to stand still while John fought for his life at forty miles an hour. The fifth soldier was moving too fast also, but John chanced a shot and missed. That "blue" boy was visibly angered at John and tried to turn his horse back too quickly to engage him. However, the maneuver was harsh, and his horse swerved and stumbled, falling to the ground and breaking its neck instantly, pinning the rider's leg down in the fall. More shots flew past John and Patch, but none struck home. John had three more rounds left; he would need them.

The oncoming cavalry had spread from the road now, but the closure speed was still the same. John's shots would be at a greater distance. He still had to give his boys time to load and set up a defense. John took deliberate aim at a Union corporal and hit him in the throat. The soldier's head dropped, chin resting on his chest, and the horse continued to charge forward without guidance. Because of the closure speed several more "blues" passed John by, but tried to turn their mounts to take a second chance at him. The next soldier sought to collide with John and dismount him forcing John to shoot that soldier's horse in the head to avoid the collision and injury to Patch. John was sure that soldier was critically injured when his horse collapsed from under him. John's final shot went haywire when the soldier that John took aim at ducked just as John fired, returning a pistol ball in John's direction grazing his collar and drawing blood.

John had to be careful now. He had to execute a maneuver that would get him back into the fight and not cause Patch to fall. The grass in the center of the road between the wagon ruts was still wet from the morning dew so John slowed Patch gently to a stop. He shoved the empty '51 into his belt and reached down to the pistol in the pommel holster on Patch's right shoulder. As he did, two rifle balls just missed John's head. John noticed blood dripping from this neck wound onto his shell jacket sleeve; but did not feel any pain. Once he had the second pistol in hand, he wheeled Patch around and faced the "blue" boys, proceeding to attack them again as he headed back toward his own skirmish line. They were scattered now, but still full of fight at what John's singular surprise attack had done to their platoon. They were determined to kill John and his bald-faced horse.

The Union troops were flabbergasted that John was coming at them again. They never expected that and the surprise gave John another advantage as he pressed Patch forward in a faster charge. The Union troops were slower now after turning their mounts trying to get at John. He was much faster, but the timing still had to be precise. He saw his first chance at inflicting more damage on these "blue bellies." A private tried to swing wide of John, but John's advance was too swift, and the bark of John's pistol was sharp and final. The boy fell mortally wounded from his horse. Two more troopers tried to get at John, but John was able to wound one who fell from his horse fouling the legs of his neighbor's horse, tripping the lot into a dusty tumble. John knew both troopers were out of the fight. He had four more shots left before he could gain the safety of his own skirmish line and there was still more than half a dozen enemy left. He would use Patch's speed as best he could.

The return fire from the "blue" boys was getting more accurate now, but they always misjudged John's faster pace and seemed to shoot behind him. The melee was getting intense and he dared not slow down. John's next shot went wide when the soldier he tried to kill dodged it by ducking down to the right of his own horse's neck, trying to return John's fire by shooting under the galloping horse's jaw. He missed John and rode past him trying to rein in his own mount and come back at John from the rear. John had to ignore him for now because two other "blue" soldiers were headed right for him, intending to collide with Patch. John had to shoot fast, first left then right hitting both soldiers in the chest. He lowered his profile as bullets rang out around him and headed for Sergeant Alvarado and the safety of his own skirmish line.

As John passed through his kneeling gray soldiers skirmish line he yelled over his shoulder, "Sergeant Alvarado, if you please!"

"Ok, boys… ready… aim…fire!"

John still had his back to the fight when the fusillade enveloped the remainder of the oncoming federal troopers. By the sound of the bullets crashing into the men, their yells and the horses' screams he knew the battle was over for the "blues."

As John wheeled Patch around he saw what his "grays" had done, and it was devastating. Not a single trooper was up, nor any of their horses.

"Sergeant Alvarado, reload, then advance. Put any wounded horse out of its misery. Arrest any walking wounded and post all the dead under the apple tree by the creek. I want all the Union weapons and cartridge boxes. Be quick, we may have more "blues" about. Post one guard on the prisoners and tend their wounds."

"Sir!"

John was sick to his stomach at what he had seen--the horses, the brave men, it was all a waste. He had done his military duty, but for what? Such a damn shame. He just shook his head and looked to reload his pistols and hear the sergeant's report.

Susan, Dufilho's and Quinin's mother, totally broke down when she was informed about the fate of her two sons. Her wailing and crying could be heard a block away from their home. Joanna could not console her. The only thing she could do was be patient until the tears dried and some semblance of coherence returned to her. Nancy, like the rest of New Orleans, knew that the city was conquered but not subdued. The invaders were despoilers of homes and would be resisted.

"Susan, we must trek the seventy miles to Fort Jackson to see to the proper burial of Quinn and attend to Dufilho in the prison. He is alive and may need our nurturing." That idea of healing the one remaining son gave a purpose to Susan Alvarado that she would cling to in her desperation and loss of her youngest.

"Yes, Joanna, Dufilho is alive and he needs me. I shall go to him."

John had a very serious problem now. He had several wounded enemies for which he was responsible and he had limited resources to deal with them. Hopefully, the other fifty wagons of his company made it to the depot safely, but no word on that yet. Just as John needed to decide on his next move, his northern scout was coming in at a trot.

"Sir, beg to report Confederate infantry company coming up at the double quick."

"Have their company commander report to me. Post yourself to the north again and keep a sharp eye out. Got to be more Union boys out there somewhere."

"Sir!"

"Lieutenant Smith reporting, 1st Mississippi Company A."

John returned the lieutenant's salute and put him at ease. "Post your men in the shade by the creek. Take a rest. How many in your company?"

"Yes, sir. Forty-seven effectives, sir. Could we get some rations? Boys haven't eaten in a day since we marched to your aid. We were guarding a bridge crossing three miles north of here when your lead wagon alerted us."

John was somewhat relieved that his fifty wagons were at least three miles away from him and well on their way to the army depot. He ordered Sergeant Alvarado to break out all the rations that Lieutenant Smith needed. Now was not the time to relax. He needed to deal with the wounded Union boys and get the rest of his unit to the depot and their freight unloaded. The wagon animals had been standing in their harnesses too long and needed to be watered and grassed. He ordered them unhitched and hobbled.

Sergeant Alvarado alerted John in a loud voice, "Northern scout coming in at a trot, sir!" John turned to see the same private hustling into camp. He was red-faced but otherwise not alarmed.

"Beg to report, squadron of Confederate cavalry coming up,

sir. Be here in about ten minutes."

John smiled at the scout, returned his salute and motioned him to go back to his post up the north road. Just as the north scout wheeled about, a voice from the guard on the prisoners shouted out loudly that the eastern scout was coming in at a gallop just over the rise to the right of his command. John went from relieved to alarmed in the space of a second. He received the scout's report of a battalion of Union infantry deploying to the east, no supporting artillery or cavalry. Where did three hundred infantrymen come from… where?

"Sergeant Alvarado, every available man to the crest of the east hill at the double quick. Lieutenant Smith, form your men on the military crest of the east hill. Move!"

John's only option now was to fight a holding action till he could get his teams hitched again. Hopefully the Confederate cavalry would get here in time to facilitate his meager battle plan.

As John peeked above the crest of the east hill with his binoculars, he could tell the opposing infantry was about to advance on his position in three companies, ranks of two's, with one company in reserve. They were tightly packed to give max effect to their massed rifle fire. They had dropped their back packs, and were determined to fight; maneuvering exceptionally well. He heard the Confederate cavalry come into camp and retreated down the hill to address their commander.

"Captain Alvarado, sir, three hundred Union infantrymen about to attack from the east."

Major Timpson returned John's salute, looked up the east hill and saw the small band of defenders ready to defend its crest from three times their number. He noticed that all the teams were unhitched and there were wounded soldiers under the apple tree.

"What might you suggest, captain, since I have only just arrived."

"Major, we might pull it off if you can take your squadron to the south of this east hill, up into the draw that leads east and flank the Union infantry. They won't see you and they don't know you're here. I'll grab a flag, put all my men on the crest of the east hill, and demonstrate to hold the deployed Union infantry. I'll start firing immediately to disguise your move till you're in position. We might be able to cross the blue's T'."

"You West Point, captain?"

There was a long pause and John shook his head no.

"No matter. I can maneuver as you suggest and make a revolver charge. I need your bugler to sound the charge when I'm in position. I don't want to peek over any hills and give away our position. Crossing the T might work if we move fast enough."

As they parted, each wished the other good luck. It was crazy, but it just might work. John gained the east hill crest and ordered Lieutenant Smith and Sergeant Alvarado to commence firing at the Union battalion. He knew that Lieutenant Smith's infantry would be more effective at the greater range, but John needed all guns to report to give the impression of a larger force. John kept constant tab on the Union formation with his binoculars.

John always ordered his bugler to stay with him. As a backup he told his eastern scout to be ready to ride to the Confederate cavalry and order the charge if they did not hear the trumpet call.

"Bugler, have your canteen ready. I want your whistle to be wet, no dry mouth when I need you to trumpet on the bugle." The bugler acknowledged John's order.

John judged that the cavalry should be in position now, but the Union infantry was still too far away for the crossing the 'T' flanking maneuver to be effective. He had to draw the Union formation toward him to set the trap. He ordered the unit standard bearer to stand and wave the stars and bars vigorously.

"Lieutenant Smith, have your men stand and deliver a volley at the Union battalion, reload then fix bayonets!"

Lieutenant Smith looked at John with incredulity as he knew that would invite a return volley from the "blues" that would surely cause casualties to his men. John returned the lieutenant's gaze with authority.

"Do it, Lieutenant. I need the Union boys to come at us another fifty yards. Do it!"

"Sergeant Alvarado, hold your fire momentarily."

The massed fire of Lieutenant Smith's infantry billowing white smoke obscured the view of the field momentarily for John. Under its cloud, the "grey" infantry fixed bayonets. As the smoke was slowly dissipating in the slight breeze, John could see that the Union infantry front rank had knelt and was preparing to fire.

"Sergeant Alvarado, fire!"

As the Union volley of smoke and lead engulfed the battlefield, mixed with that of Sergeant Alvarado's return fire, there was the staggering sound of the dull thud of impacting bullets hitting men, breaking limbs and ending lives. Two of Lieutenant Smith's men fell, one rolling all the way down the east hill landing against one of the parked wagon wheels. John could see the Confederates' fire was effective as several of the blues fell within their formation. He could also see that the Union commander was elevating his sword hand. Above the din and the roar, and the pulse of rifle fire, he ordered, "Forward, Forward!"

They were attacking John as he had hoped. Timing would be critical. He had to let them advance fifty yards before he ordered the hidden cavalry to charge out of the shallow ravine into the left flank of the unsuspecting Union battalion. John could see the blues were well disciplined and very well trained. They would fight to the end.

With dismay, John saw that the Union infantry had stopped after only twenty-five yards. But then he saw they had charged bayonets and continued their approach directly toward John. John's anticipation was unbearable. He had to order the bugler at the exact moment to make this action work… Just a few yards more and the trap would be sprung…

"Bugler, sound the charge! Scout, ride to the cavalry now!"

"Lieutenant Smith, up and fire into them! Sergeant Alvarado, the same. Get into it boys, keep them busy!"

The cloud of white smoke obscured John's vision again. He could not see his formation's volley affect, but he could hear it. It was a sickening sound as the lead bullets found their mark. Men screamed and died, including his own troops. Just as the smoke was clearing, he could see the grey cavalry top the crest of the southern ravine and charge into the flank of the Union infantry. The pistol charge was devastating. All the cavalry fire concentrated on the two files of forward charging infantry. Unfortunately, the Union infantry was at ninety degrees and they could not bring their rifles around quick enough to bear against the cavalry lightning assault. The infantry rifles were empty, so all they could do was parry with their bayonets, while the grey cavalry fired into the Union ranks with six shot revolvers.

The fight was sharp, violent and swift with the grey cavalry firing into the blue infantry's faces not more than a dozen feet away. There were bayonet thrusts, saber strokes and pistol shots…men going down to their knees, spinning around like tornados, flinging out their arms, spitting out blood, falling, dying, headless, disemboweled and limbs hacked off. The blue men lay in heaps that would make a sane person think that this was hell on earth. John gazed at the debacle It was the most terrible day of his life.

The cavalry envelopment was complete. The assault from the front by his company, and the riding around the back and sides by the two hundred mounted soldiers, made resistance by the Union battalion a waste of lives. It was as if heaven and earth had collided down onto the Union infantry battalion. They started to invert their rifles, putting the butt stocks in the air in a sign of surrender. Presently, the Union battalion commander bugler blew the surrender and struck his colors.

The Confederate cavalry had all but surrounded the Union battalion. John's company approached from the front at a walk with bayonets fixed. As he approached the shattered blues, they slowly dropped their rifles and cartridge boxes. John halted his formation and noticed that Major Timpson and the Union commander were already negotiating the complete surrender of the rest of the battalion. Major Timpson signaled John to come up. As he side-stepped through the piles of the wounded and dead, he thought that he recognized the Union commander.

"Captain Alvarado, this is Major Edward Windsor, 1st Wisconsin 2nd battalion," said Major Timpson.

John immediately recognized Edward from his college days at Hillsdale. He gave up any military protocol and extended his hand in friendship. Major Windsor took a moment then realized that this was his collegial pal from so many years ago. In the middle of the carnage the old friends embraced.

Edward Windsor was almost in tears as he surveyed what remained of his command. Too many of his men were hurt and dying. The major thought that this small battle was hell for his men, or at least as good an imitation as is produced in the 'upper world'. He needed to get them help as soon as he could. He was at Major Timpson's mercy now. He hoped that John would mitigate any harshness that the Confederacy might impose on his battered troops. He turned to Major Timpson and asked to the deportment of his battalion. It didn't help his composure when the Confederate major said, "I will volunteer to say I am very glad at what has happened here today; but there is a great deal still to be done tomorrow."

The Union first sergeant came up and reported to Edward that there were 27 dead and twice that many wounded; and that they were being cared for. Edward asked if Major Timpson had a surgeon that could lend a hand with the survivors. "No, sergeant major, no medical staff at all," was Major Timpson's reply.

Just as Major Timpson replied to the Union sergeant major, Sergeant Alvarado gave his unit's casualty report. "Three grey infantry dead, five wounded and two cavalrymen wounded." The numbers were staggering for such a small engagement, but in the years to come it would be insignificant compared to the casualty list that would be reported in newspapers in the eastern theater.

The debate now was what to do with all the prisoners. If John and Major Timpson took them back to headquarters they would have to look to the men's care and daily living. John's rations were for the Confederacy, who sorely needed them. To care for some 250 sick and wounded prisoners was more than Major Timpson could handle. Transporting them was more than John could handle. They both hoped that their superiors would condone their action.

Major Timpson finally spoke after he consulted with John. "Major Windsor, have your men stack arms. Take a squad down to the stream west of here, retrieve all the wounded mounted infantry and bring them here. Bury your dead, pick up your packs and march back to your headquarters."

Major Windsor could not believe his ears. His whole battalion was to be paroled and not imprisoned. He looked at John and said, "Thank you, friend. Amid all this blood, sanity exists."

He shook John's hand vigorously and ordered his men to complete their task. "We will march back to our boats on the river forthwith. Thank you again, John."

That last statement piqued John's interest. He did not say anything at present, but mulled it over in his head. It took a moment, but he realized he was just given some valuable military intelligence.

Chapter 17
"The Best"

The travel back to the Confederate depot was arduous for the shorthanded wagon train that John commanded. They had to transport over three hundred stands of Union army small arms, and several wounded soldiers. They slowed the travel to ease the pain of the injured and make them comfortable. John worried that there were still Union army formations that might harass him, but to his relief none showed.

It was late when the remainder of John's command pulled into the Confederate depot. He saw to it that the animals were fed, the men bedded down, and the wounded hospitalized. He then reported to general headquarters, weary and tired to the bone; his neck wound sapping most of his strength.

Major Timpson was waiting for John outside of General Taylor's command tent. He wanted to make a joint report with John to the commanding officer. General Taylor was the son of a former president, who like General Lee, chose to fight for his state not because of the slavery issue, but because of his loyalty to his birth place above any politics. A short man, but a commanding figure nevertheless. He was an able commander who was never given the manpower to carry out his mission west of the Mississippi. Brigades were siphoned off from his army to fill out eastern commands, leaving General Taylor to scratch an Army together as well as fight a better equipped adversary.

"Well, Captain, we will soon find out what kind of general commands us this evening," said Major Timpson.

With a quizzical look on John's face, he asked the major what he meant.

"If General Taylor invites us to remain at attention while we give our report then he is a rank general. If he asks us to take our ease, then he is a man to follow to the gates of hell!" John did not comprehend the idiom the major postulated, he just knew he wanted to make his report and then get some rest. He was feeling somewhat nauseous now and his right leg felt like it was going to buckle at any moment. John stiffened as he entered the command tent, presented his military courtesies and heard General Taylor say, "At ease, boys."

Major Timpson reported on the fight on the east hill: How the combined forces of the squadron of cavalry and the infantry company, plus the quartermaster troops, had crossed the 'T' of a Union infantry battalion at John's suggestion. They had surrounded the battalion and defeated it, collecting three hundred stands of arms in the process. He also related how John, only moments before the east hill fight, had single-handedly defeated some seventeen mounted infantry troops to avoid his supply train being captured.

General Taylor turned to John, "You okay, Captain? You look a little pale even under these candles…You West Point, son?"

"I'm fine, sir, and not West Point. There's some intelligence about the fight that's relevant, sir."

"One moment, Captain. Whose idea was it to release all those prisoners?"

Major Timpson took full responsibility for that decision, never letting the general question John any further about the issue. The general then inquired of John as to the military intelligence that he thought was important.

"Sir, two times the blues showed interest in my wagon supply train. Their major said he was going to retire back to the river and the supply boats on the Red. My guess is they don't have a way to supply their infantry. They don't have mule teams and wagons. They're completely tied to the supply river craft. That means their forces can never be more than a day's march from the river."

It did not take General Taylor long to absorb the information, but as he did so, he looked at John directly and in a single breath said, "Are you sure you're okay? Captain...ORDERLY! ... get the chief of staff ...NOW!"

John collapsed on the command tent floor; he had completely blacked out.

The thirty-four ladies of the South had gathered at the loading ramp of the side paddle steamer Chattanooga, tied up to the New Orleans dock. They all had a relative that was being held prisoner at Ft. Jackson, seventy miles downriver, and they were determined to see to their relative's deportment. As they faced off with a burly, tall and unmovable Union sergeant, no was an answer they weren't ready to accept.

"Sorry, ladies, not accepting passengers today. We're going to Ft. Jackson and there's no room."

Susanna interrupted the sergeant with urgency in her voice, "We will go with you to the very same fort to tend to our loved ones. We hear they are not being treated as good Christian men should be!"

Shaking his head, no, the sergeant liberally put his hand into the picnic basket Susanna was holding, retrieving an apple. He was about to take a bite when Susanna took a full-handed swipe at the taller sergeant's face, staggering him sidewise. He barely recovered from the blow before Susanna brushed him aside and approached the private guarding the gang plank, who quickly sidestepped her, as all 34 women boarded the steamer. Everyone found a place to be seated and waited for the paddler to depart. The captain of the boat did not come forward to collect the dollar a person passage from the ladies. Just how brave did everyone think he was?

The reception at Ft. Jackson was bland and non-ceremonial too. The army private at the landing was confused as to what to do with the 34 disembarked ladies. The blank look on his face when Susanna confronted him surprised even her.

"Where is your officer?" Susanna demanded.

"Ma'am, he's billeted in New Orleans. Only comes here once or so a week to check on things, ah… ah," stuttered the private.

"Where are the prisoners, young man? We want to see our men," demanded several of the ladies in unison.

"They're locked up in the powder magazine down in the lower galley of the fort," responded an utterly dismayed soldier. "Ladies. I can take you to them if you wish!" He tipped his kepi to them and beseeched them to follow him to the inner cavity of the makeshift, run down, prisoner of war installation.

The stench was more than the southern ladies could bear. They put their delicate perfumed hankies to their noses and mouths in order to deflect the foul air in the dungeon where their boys were housed. It was disgusting how their loved ones were being treated. A hundred men in a space built for no more than fifty should be billeted.

Susanna almost screamed her demands. "This place needs a good Christian cleaning! Ladies, we must complete it before the paddle wheeler departs. Scrub this place top to bottom and attend to your men." Susanna then shouted, "Private, we need fresh water and a lot of hot boiling water. We are going to make this place habitable for Christian men. Be quick about it!" The army private pivoted on his heels as if his Union general had given him a direct order under battlefield conditions.

The ladies dove into the task at hand, even the three who could not find their son, husband or brother among the one hundred prisoners. But some of the medical needs were beyond their capabilities, so they helped as best they could. The meals they brought to the prisoners were the first truly decent food that they'd had in over nine months. The prisoners, their bodies underweight, begged for more. Their condition was a disgrace to the care the Union army was giving them.

It was a difficult task, but the southern ladies made it happen before the paddle wheeler blew its steam whistle to re-board for the trip back to New Orleans. Susanna made sure all the Louisiana Legion men knew that the southern ladies would be back next week with fresh clothing and much more food. They would also bring Dr. Peters with them. The one hundred prisoners saw a ray of hope in what Susanna was doing to alleviate their suffering.

She found Dufilho's grave as she departed the fort and made a mental note to take care of it properly. She would beseech the commanding general to let Quinin be paroled because of his severe head wound that still had not healed. Susanna left Ft. Jackson exhausted, but with a new mission in life that would only slightly replace the loss of her oldest son. Her grief was replaced with hope that she might rescue her youngest from this hell hole of a prison.

John had been unconscious for over 72 hours, having been deposited in a local church being used as a makeshift hospital. Over three hundred other wounded men had been crammed into the small white rectory. The church pew that John's bed was made on was not wide enough for a man to sleep, and sometimes in John's bouts of fever and coughing, he would roll off it and fall onto the floor, landing in his own vomit. A kind medical steward would clean him up and put him back on the pew only to have to repeat the task an hour or two later when John convulsed again. John's delirium lasted a full week before he could gain any sense about himself. Meanwhile, he was at the mercy of the army medical stewards. Many of the men would die there, never recovering from even the slightest wounds. Infection was widespread due to the contaminated well water and other unsanitary conditions.

John was slowly recovering, but he did not understand from what exactly. The one doctor that he had any discussion with said John had some sort of blood infection, but could not explain the numbness he had from his neck down through his right shoulder to the elbow. John could feel and move his hand but above the elbow was numb and tingly. The doctor would only say, "That's interesting."

General Taylor's army was re-deploying after several battles along the Red River. The medical stewards were packing up and leaving the care of the wounded soldiers to the local population. John still could not move from his bed and continued to have bouts of coughing and fever. It was up to the generosity of the St. Michael's church pastor and parishioners to continue to care for the three hundred wounded. The number dwindled daily and many of the soldiers were buried in the local cemetery. Major Timpson happened to drop by and visit his wounded troopers and saw John still convalescing.

"How are you, captain?"

"Not well, sir. Sorry for not standing."

"No problem. I'm happy I happened onto you before my cavalry unit left for Pea Ridge, Missouri. I have a citation and a medal to be awarded to you from a grateful General Taylor.

Your intelligence has helped him keep the Union army off balance, so he can pressure them up into Missouri. He has forwarded a copy to Richmond. You did well at the East Ridge battle, John. That was a pretty mean fight we were in!"

John, still weak from his blood infection, lay prostrate on his bed trying to comprehend what the major was saying. Without thinking he blurted out, "Where is my horse, Patch?"

Major Timpson, realizing that John was still in some sort of delirium, just shrugged his shoulder, bent down and patting John on his elbow, wished him good luck with his recovery. He left the citation and medal with a parishioner and was gone. John collapsed, not knowing how Patch was doing or even if he was still alive. He dreaded that some army trooper might have confiscated him. It pained John to think that Patch might be abused by someone who did not know he was deaf. The weeks would drag on.

"Morning, sir," said a hobbling Corporal Scott, as he dragged himself across the aisle of the church toward John's bunk in the pew. "Remember me… your northern scout, sir? Took a rifle ball in the meaty part of my right leg. Hurts like hell, but they didn't have to amputate it. Doc said I might make a full recovery."

John was totally surprised to see Corporal Scott, since the army had been gone for weeks. John's mind was clearing after weeks in the hospital so he had no problem understanding the corporal.

"We've been mustered out of the army, sir. We're on the invalid roles and no longer any use to the military. I brought your papers with me."

John blinked several times at the news that the corporal gave him. He could not believe that his military service was over. He had been away from the army for almost two months, and although not yet fit, he still wanted to get back to his command.

With this news, he could now go home to his family… or could he? New Orleans was an occupied city. He had written to Nancy several times, but he never received any replies. The Union army was choking the Mississippi and blockading all river traffic. It was possible that Nancy might not even know he had been wounded.

In a way, John was sad that his troops were without him. Most were from New Orleans just like him and he hoped the best for them. Now Lieutenant Wilkerson would be making the life and death decisions for his old company. Good luck to all of them.

The only sane plan that John could come up with now was to navigate his way to Fort Worth, Texas, where the terminuses of the Alvarado freighting business were located. Gunter Berquist was still the head of operations there and would put him up till he could figure a way to get back into the city of his birth and back to his family. But John was still weak and without any method of transportation. He would have to solve those two problems before he could move. Maybe 'Scotty' could help.

"Well, captain, we need to make some plans. I'm headed back to a little place called Waco, Texas. I figured we might travel together for a while, being crippled as we are," offered Private Scott.

"Scotty, if we're mustered out of the army there's no need to address me as captain anymore. John is just fine. We do need to get back home, but the Yankees have New Orleans bottled up. I need to get to Ft. Worth and hole up there for a while. But we need some transportation to do it and maybe some new clothes, too."

"Well, sir, you have your horse and I have an old mule that ought to work. I can go into town and buy some clothes and sell our uniforms, but will need the balance somehow."

John looked Scotty in the eye with an intense look and said, "What do you mean, my horse?"

"Had him boarded at the livery since you were sick. I think he is a little portly now since he hasn't been exercised for a couple months. Got to pay that bill too."

The wave of relief that came over John was immeasurable. He had assumed Patch had been killed, or confiscated and was headed north into Missouri with the army. Hearing one of his troopers had thought to care for his horse in his wounded state filled him with overwhelming gratitude.

"Had to take care of your pony, sir. After what the two of you done at the Battle of the 'East Ridge' charging at them 'blue bellies' like that! Never heard of or seen such a thing. Damned flat crazy!"

"Thank you, Scotty. You're the best! You have a guaranteed job with my freight company if you want it. Fort Worth is a growing place. Not bad to settle down in."

John wanted to leave in a couple of days so he directed Scotty to his army saddle bags, retrieving gold coin to pay for Patch's board and get both of them new clothes. Scotty had never owned store bought clothes before. He felt like a king in his new attire.

Leaving the makeshift hospital was an enormous boost for John's mind. He no longer had to listen to men cry out in the middle of the night as they died in their beds. He no longer had to see men sit up on those makeshift bunks, call out unintelligible words and fall to the floor dead. The relief from the foul smell of the hospital alone gave John the best present he could imagine. The church was now the dominion of the wolf and the vulture and his friends would sleep in their lonely graves with no relatives to attend them. All it came to was pain, death, wounds and minor glory for most of the slain.

The sun on John's face, the fresh breeze in the air, and the rhythmic pace of Patch's walk were all liberating. John would try to hide the horrible experiences of the last two months as much as he could. But they would follow him the rest of his life, just like the men's deaths that he had caused in his gunfights.

The weather was fair, there was plenty of game and Scotty was pleasant company on the trip to Ft. Worth. Hopefully, Gunter had news from New Orleans. Hopefully, the Union occupation was not too arduous for his family. Would the terminus of the Alvarado freight business be functioning when they got to Ft. Worth?

For now, John needed to relax, ride and enjoy the warming sun's rays. Scotty also seemed to relax. The short nine months in the Confederate army had affected Scotty as severely as John. Life was good right now. Travel was easy. Trouble had its own agenda. No sense in hurrying.

Chapter 18
"Dreams of Peace"

John's convalescence at Gunter's home in Ft. Worth lasted longer than he would have liked. He was sicker than he thought, but slowly, with the attendance of Gunter's wife and the fresh air, John slowly recuperated from his wound.

Scotty found ample employment with the Alvarado Freighting Company. With the Confederate's instituted draft, manpower was in short supply and Gunter was only too happy to have Scotty. Since he had been put on the invalid roles by the army, he would not be rushing off to war. The business was still thriving despite the war and Texas, as of now, was not tainted by the bloodshed.

John slowly gained his strength and was even helping drive a 'six up' when the freight business needed extra help. But he wanted to get back to New Orleans. Since the Yankee conquest he had not heard from anyone in the family. It seemed the blockade of the city was complete. The only news was about the explosion of two powder factories in the New Orleans area. The papers also carried news that General Butler was a total tyrant when it came to the military governance of the city. Hanging a citizen for taking the American flag down from the United States Mint building and destroying it was just one harsh example. The general had also ordered that all foreigners register with his occupation forces. He went so far as to confiscate $800,000 from the Netherland's consulate. Rumor had it that he'd also enlisted former slaves into the U.S Army to control the New Orleans population. Definitely the acts of a tyrant.

John always read the newspapers about the war. He tried to keep tabs on his boys and see where they might be fighting. One day, to John's dismay, the list of casualties at the battle of Wilson Creek, Missouri, listed Major Timpson as dead. John was saddened and deeply affected by the loss of his compatriot. That day John was determined to try to get back to New Orleans and see to the deportment of his own family before it might be too late. Prior to his departure, he had his discharge papers recorded by the county records office. It might become handy in these confused days and times.

At least John would be traveling during a fair time of the year. Several cavalry patrols were headed in the same direction as John and he simply tagged along. They were only too eager to have him accompany them. At night they would ask him about the East Ridge fight. None of his escort had been bloodied yet, and all were apprehensive about their future first martial engagement. John's quandary was how to slip into New Orleans undetected. He still had friends in his birth city and he thought Mr. Q. might help him.

There was a light knock on the Alvarado's front door; Joanna barely heard it. She thought whoever it was seemed very timid at trying to raise her attention. Besides, it was late at night. Who could it be?

Joanna slowly opened the door, and as she did, she backed away into the sitting room, put her hands over her mouth to stifle a scream, but managed to get out a muffled NO! Pique, standing behind her, also let out an alarmed NO.... not you... not you!

It was a full minute before Joanna and Pique could regain their senses and comprehend what they saw. But it was undeniable.

In front of them was Pasqual, John's best friend standing erect in the uniform of a Union Army Second Lieutenant. The pause between the three was interminable… it seemed to last forever. All three tried to find the words to say to each other and Pique finally broke the awkward silence.

"Come, sit," was all he could muster because of the shock at seeing John's best friend seemingly betray his adopted family. But Pique sensed that Pasqual wasn't finished surprising his adopted family.

"Momma, I can't stay long. I do need to inform you that the military governor has decided to enlist a black regiment for the protection of greater New Orleans. He's also elected to have us billeted in civilian quarters throughout the city. I thought it best I seek you out and stay with you instead of someone else." Pasqual was embarrassed at the excuse he just made.

Indeed, the 'beast' of New Orleans, as General Butler was known, had enlisted a full regiment of free negroes to help pacify the city. Of his original 17,000 troops, most were being drawn off toward the big fight at Baton Rouge and Port Hudson. There was a general unemployment problem in New Orleans since the successful blockade of the Mississippi, and there was no shortage of 'darkies' who were willing to sign up for the regiment.

The First Regiment Louisiana Native Guards, or as they preferred to call themselves, "Chasseurs d' Afrique," became a well-organized unit under mostly Union officers. However, those negroes who were literate were able to secure commissions for themselves. Pasqual had learned his letters with John and Joanna's assistance almost thirty years before. He was articulate and had a commanding presence in front of his platoon. His immediate supervisor was Capitan Sherer of Maryland, the same officer who only a short year before was a Confederate officer confiscating 35 men from John's enlisted quartermaster company. He was a former cohort of John's at Hillsdale College who had been captured at the battle of New Orleans, paroled and subsequently sworn allegiance to the Union rather than go to a prisoner of war camp.

Captain Sherer was no friend of New Orleans and took his duties seriously, enforcing the 'beastly' General Butler's directives. He was a Maryland man from that border state where loyalties vacillated with the wind. He looked out for himself, intending to profit from his position, and fanned the flames of discontent with the locals as much as he could. He remembered John Alvarado distinctly and would seek revenge for the bloody nose that John had given him way back in their collegial days. He thought billeting Lieutenant Pasqual Toussaint with the Alvarado family was a stroke of genius on his part. Captain Sherer was no southern gentleman.

Pasqual had a problem. He had sworn on a bible that he would protect and defend the constitution... but he did it with reservations. His primary loyalty was to his family and New Orleans. More importantly he had given his word to John, his lifelong best friend to watch over his family when he had gone north to fight. The conflict of swearing on a scared bible and deceiving others as to his real intention kept Pasqual up nights.

The shock of Pasqual standing in their house in a Union officer uniform had not worn off when in through the door barged Nancy. She seemed flush with excitement, but contained it when she saw the confrontation between Pasqual and her mother and father-in-law. She gave a curt 'good evening' to all and whisked herself up the staircase to her bedroom. As she did, Pasqual noticed that the hem of Nancy's skirt showed a very thin line of white powdered flour. Pasqual quickly averted his eyes so that Joanna and Pique would not notice what he had discovered.

Joanna, still startled by what John's best friend had done,

mustered the courage to invite him upstairs to his room. A room he had often stayed in over the years; not as a guest, but as a family member, as their son's best friend. Their house was made in the fashion of a quadrangle with a center courtyard and two stories above. It always had plenty of room for family and friends. The store front was on the street side and the three other sides flanking the small fountain/courtyard gave the family an inner sanctuary from the busy street that the house fronted.

At the same time, John was dodging several army patrols inside the city limits of New Orleans in his futile attempt to get to his parent's house. He decided to visit his saddle maker on the outskirts of town instead and hoped to have a place to stay that evening. He would attempt to contact Nancy by other means.

On this cool and rainy evening, as he approached Mr. Q's saddle shop, he noted the dim light coming from the small window. He peered in and saw Mr. Q hunched over his saddle stand apparently asleep at his work. John was about to tap on the windowpane when Patch nudged him from behind and chomped on his bit several times. John turned and placed his hand on Patch's head between his eyes, and whispered, "I know you're hungry, but give me a minute, boy."

Mr. Q aroused from his light stupor and instantly peered out the small window, trying to focus on the murky figure staring in at him. It took a moment, but Mr. Q motioned the figure outside to come in. John opened the door and shook the rain from his dark cavalry rain poncho and doffed his hat.

"Sorry to trouble you this late, Mr. Q…. Could I put Patch up for the night in your stable?"

"JOHNNY!… Johnny, how are you? I can't say I would mind one bit, help yourself. The Union boys have confiscated all my mounts and the stable is empty as of now. Help yourself, son."

Mr. Q was delighted to have John visit him. Not many folks

came by these days. The curfew that the 'Beast of New Orleans' imposed made it impossible to travel the city after the work day was done. But that is the kind of thing a tyrant does to control any population. Mr. Q saw to the feeding of Patch and John. He often spoke in a whisper so that strange ears did not report to the Union Army what John and he discussed.

"Have you heard what the blue boys have done to Pasqual, Johnny?" a disheartened Mr. Q inquired. John, sitting at the table enjoying the first decent meal in weeks, looked up and just stared at Mr. Q., but finally said, "I fear that this experiment of war is going badly for everyone."

"They've made him into the 'Baron Samedi' for sure; the keeper of the gates of hell. He's the instrument of the Union army enforcing all the tyrant's rules. He and that Captain Sherer run this city for their own purposes. You must pay up or you can't work around here. Corrupt for sure, Johnny!" Mr. Q kept shaking his head in shame. "Same thing happened in the Basque country. A Frenchman and a Spaniard always tried to get money from us. They tried to hijack us, but we fought them then, and we'll fight these blue bellies now. Shame, Johnny… They say Captain Sherer knows you?"

John stiffened in his chair at the mention of his old nemesis from his college days. He was aware that the Union army would parole southern officers and re-enlist them in the Union Army. Sherer would be a hindrance to John reuniting with his family, but he smiled inwardly at the prospect of Pasqual being the devil. He knew his best friend. He was just where he needed to be. John thought to himself that Pasqual was as clever now as he ever was.

Hailing from the southern state of Maryland, Captain Robert Whitney Sherer was a true slaver but he did not own any slaves. He believed that slavery was not forbidden in the Bible and therefore palatable to those who were willing to take care of a race not capable of caring for itself. He often cited the Romans, Incas, and Aztecs as cultures that sanctioned the practice. Even North American Indians had the habit. He was all too willing to be part of the Louisianan Chasseurs d' Afrique directing 'darkie' soldiers at his will. But he would have total control of his unit. Any who objected would be released into New Orleans where jobs were very difficult to find. One thing he always remembered about New Orleans, ever since his collegial days, is the one person who lived there that he hated with a passion.

Nancy enjoyed sitting on the small balcony overlooking the frontage street that approached the family quadrangle home. There was always something going on in front of the family store front entrance. It was natural for neighbors to gather at the small open-air market where Samson Toussaint farm produce was hawked to the public. She could also just see the docks and the family warehouses and where the shipping would tie up, and always paid attention to any French-flagged ship that arrived. She wished the children didn't play in the street, often scolding them that there was plenty of room in the quadrangle's interior garden. But kids were kids and defied their parents unnecessarily.

It was a surprise when she saw Mr. Q coming down the east street, hunched over, slow gaited and wearing a large sombrero. He never ventured into town, much less this close to the family home. John had always gone out to his saddle shop. Just as she was contemplating Mr. Q's approach to the house, and wondering what it could mean, she happened to spy Captain Sherer and Lt. Pasqual coming from the opposite direction. She immediately left her seat on the balcony and stepped inside the house, peering out carefully, keeping an eye on all three men as they approached the vegetable vender stand just below.

They all stopped at the fruit stand admiring Manuel's produce, fingering the best of them. Captain Sherer snapped up an apple and looked directly at Manuel while he took a bite.

"How's it like to be a freed man?" he pointedly asked Manuel.

Manuel was confounded by the question. Standing in front of him was the "Devil of New Orleans" Captain Sherer and his master's son, Lt. Toussaint. You could only be a freed man if the army enforced General Butler's rules and the blue army had not been to his farm yet. He was a slave owned by a former slave, but he didn't feel like a slave. His master, Samson, and the other bought slaves all shared the work equally on the farm. Samson even bought both his slaves' wives and allowed them to raise their own families. Manuel had been blissfully happy farming for Master Samson and Pasqual for over thirty years. But what irritated him the most was that Captain Sherer was not going to pay for the apple he was consuming right in front of him. Before Manuel could answer, Captain Sherer turned to Mr. Q.

"You're the noted saddle maker of New Orleans, aren't you? What brings you to town today?"

Mister Q.'s reply was short and curt, "Same as you, vegetables, but I intend to pay for them." With that he took his fruits and left the money with Manuel and entered the Alvarado Mercantile store.

Nancy was so nervous and anxious she could not stand it. Mr. Q simply told her to meet John at the east end of the Magnolia Bridge one hour before curfew started. She was totally blindsided. With the city being occupied by the enemy army, she understandably had not heard from her husband in over a year. He was alive, and she was going to see him, hold him and not let him go again!

The corporal of the bridge guard noticed Nancy and thought she had a remarkable resemblance to his fiancée back in Indiana. As he approached her, she noticed his motion and elevated her left hand to her mouth, feigning a slight cough, ensuring he would notice her wedding ring. The Union guard arrested his approach and averted his gaze. From across the bridge she saw a familiar silhouette in the dimming light. The clothing was not recognizable to her, but the sturdy erect gait of a determined man was; it was John.

Her John. She was beside herself, she wanted to run to him, but immediately thought better of it with so many Union army men around the bridge. John had to avoid a carriage on the narrow bridge by walking close to the railing, but he kept his pace steady as he walked directly toward Nancy. The anticipation was killing them both as the distance closed. They could not give way to their desire to rush into the other's arms. The "Beast of New Orleans" guards might interfere with them just to exercise some sort of morbid control over New Orleans citizens.

Neither could believe that after so long, their life's love was standing before them. The anticipation, the pulsing hearts and desire was undeniable. Then Nancy noticed the scar on John's neck. Sorrow filled her heart, and then rage that John had suffered injury in this terrible war. She wanted to hug her husband and soothe the trauma, both physical and emotional, that he must be feeling.

John could only stare at Nancy, fearful that she wasn't really there. It seemed like an eternity he had longed for, dreamed of… Nancy…the woman of his dreams, his lover, his friend and the mother of his children.

"Nice night for a promenade, you two," the young Union corporal blurted out from his post at the bridge.

Nancy gave the corporal who had gazed at her a slight curtsy, nodded her head politely, and then, with a sly smile, took John's hand. "A promenade, indeed, sir."

Pasqual doffed his hat before he entered his adopted home. He was in full uniform from his day's duties but did not relish this final appointment. He stood erect and faced his stepmother as she came into the dining room carrying a set of dishes for the evening meal. She promptly berated him.

"You know the rules, Pasqual; no Union uniform at the dinner table. Go upstairs to your room and change please."

Pasqual remained standing, firm and erect looking at his stepmother. She knew something was wrong.

"What is it, Pasqual? I can see it in your face." Before Joanna received an answer from her son's best friend, dread overcame her and tears started to well in her eyes. She set the dishes down on the table, clutching its edge to steady herself.

"Momma, Dufilho has died in the prisoner of war camp at Fort Jackson!"

Joanna was glad she had a steady grip on the dining table edge, otherwise she may have fainted. The news that her oldest nephew was dead was scary in itself, but simultaneously she was relieved that it was not her son that had died. She wanted to strike out at someone, but Pasqual was just delivering the news. She started to cry for her sister-in-law and rushed to Pasqual, throwing her arms around him. She was inconsolable. Joanna's sobbing brought Pique, Nancy and John's sister, Julia, to the dining room where Pasqual told the others the sad news. John's sister left the room and went upstairs, and Nancy just stood there twisting her handkerchief into knots. Nancy's jaw tightened and she, too, left the room and went upstairs to her room. Pasqual tried his best to comfort Joanna and Pique.

Tonight was the seventh time that Nancy and Manual had walked to the docks where a French flagged ship had tied up. Ever since John had ridden off to fight this war she had stayed in New Orleans and fought it her way. Manuel always brought the vegetable cart, drawn by a donkey, when the two of them went to the family warehouses to barter deals with various French sea captains. It was always the same, several barrels of white ground flour suitable for baking. It was worth its weight in gold, and she paid in gold. But caution was always the word. The Union army needed to control all commerce into, and out of, New Orleans and conducting unauthorized business with a flagged foreign ship was an international taboo, unless the "Beast of New Orleans" decided to change the rules. Nancy gave the sea captains a folder with her latest writings to be forwarded to Herr Schmidt in Paris. It was dangerous, but Nancy figured it was worth it for the life of her city.

Chapter 19
"Resistance"

New Orleans was a cosmopolitan and international city. It had a unique identity and generally was nonconforming to international standards, making it extremely hard to govern for the Union army. Once General Butler formed the Chasseurs d' Afrique, he stood a better chance of exerting a firmer hand over New Orleans' affairs. The enlisted local populace of freed black men was better equipped to arrest the normal functions of the city so that General Butler could use the city as a military base for operation up and down the Mississippi. The constant headache was the various battles that were fought outside the city limits to protect the Union supply lines. Sometimes these battles would rage for days and involve several thousand men. The Palmerston plantation was just one example where Confederate forces fought the Union army to a standstill until reinforcements arrived late in the day.

"Lieutenant Toussaint, call the men to attention," demanded Major Sherer.

The restless crowd of soldiers turned their heads toward their battalion commander.

"Pay attention, men. You are the protectors of the city of New Orleans. You are the sergeants and corporals of the first regiment of guards of New Orleans. We constantly have adversaries that try to undermine the authority of the federal government in this city. The Federal government has made you free men and Confederate forces continually try to re-enslave you. They go so far as to try to assassinate you while you go about your policing duties. Last week at Palmerston Meadows four of your cohorts were found shot to death, execution style. The murderer has been apprehended and hung, but we found this weapon in his possession. Lieutenant Toussaint, display it if you would."

The general mood of the noncommissioned officers of the regiment was increasingly agitated by the major's speech. But, the Le-Matt pistol that Lieutenant Toussaint was passing around showed the deadly nature of a new weapon compared to their own single shot rifles.

"It fires nine pistol rounds then has a twenty-gauge single barrel under the shroud to add more devastation. It's made in Paris, France. Note the date of manufacture, four March 1862--just last month. In short, men, this weapon is being smuggled into New Orleans and is being used to kill the men of this regiment. We must find the source and hang the culprits forthwith. Are you with me, men?"

Even Pasqual was mad that his men were being executed for trying to bring peace to his city. He felt responsible for them even though he was a New Orleans man first. Murder was not what he signed up for. The men's passion was up and he had to make sure they did not become avengers without a purpose and randomly kill. He had to control his men. Even now the talk was getting out of hand about what the boys were going to do to the general population. The grumbling was getting louder, satisfying the major, but frightening Pasqual. He finally called the men to attention and dismissed them to their daily duties.

Nancy loved her city as much as anyone. General Butler's infamous General Order number twenty-eight, was an affront to sensible residents. In addition, the "Beast of New Orleans" was not allowing any commerce to take place where he and Major

Sherer weren't getting a cut of the action, both enriching themselves. They had a whole army to use to do so, and that army was literally strangling New Orleans economically. Nancy did her best to help those that she could. Getting French sea captains to go along was the dangerous part.

Smuggling barrels of rich white baking flour would serve to feed several families, mostly the children. She used the proceeds from the secret news articles that she posted to Herr Schmidt's Paris newspaper to pay for the barrels of flour and more. It was the "more" part that would get her hung if she wasn't careful.

From her balcony perch of the quadrangle family home she could barely see when ships tied up to the family dock north of town. When a French flagged ship did so, she would make her way to visit the captain and close a nefarious deal. This day was clear, warm and the narrow street below her was lively and unusually active. Manual's vegetable stand was drawing several customers and the children were in the street playing their innocent games.

As with all wars recruiting and training suffered the urgency of the times. Not all recruits were thoroughly trained nor were their animals of burden. Accidents happened and some were deadly.

There was a loud banging and clattering coming from up the street. Nancy could not see what the matter was, but she instinctively rose from her chair and scanned the street below to find her daughter's whereabouts. She saw her on the other side of the street, playing with others her own age. The noise from up the street was getting louder with cursing men adding to the cacophony approaching the family residence. Unbelievably, she spied a runaway team of six horses towing a Napoleon caisson and twelve-pound bronze cannon. It was unattended by any soldiers and the horses were panicked and running wild-eyed at a frightening speed toward Nancy's little girl. The cannon pivoted back and forth careening and banking off the walls of the various houses on the narrow street. The steel wheels struck the stone bricks, giving off occasional sparks, which frightened the horses even more.

A young man dove at the lead horse's head harness in hopes of stopping the rampaging hitch, but he was shunted aside by the forward force of the speeding six horses. He was trampled by them unmercifully. It was then that Nancy realized her daughter and several other children were going to suffer the same fate as the young man. The mass of animals and several tons of cannon and caisson were going to wreak further havoc and there was nothing Nancy could possibly do about it. All she could do was scream!

Nancy just stood there looking down at her baby girl, a contorted smile on her little face, her mangled body dirty from the wagon wheel marks. She wept with rage and compassion at the same time. She dared not bend down and touch the child for a perceived fear that she might hurt her little girl even more. Nancy saw seven other children in various states of pain crying out for their parents. One elderly lady seemed to be dead as well as another young man. The devastation was total for the city block residents. Those unhurt tried to be of assistance. Three artillerymen ran past Nancy in a vain attempt to catch up to the runaway team of horses. None stopped to help the injured.

A crowd was gathering just as Major Sherer, with a squad of blue soldiers, approached the accident scene on his routine patrol from the opposite direction. He halted short of the mayhem and surveyed the mass of casualties. The crowd started to turn on him, seeing his ilk as the cause of the casualties that were still in need of assistance. The crowd of parents and bystanders were growing agitated as they formed a circle around their fallen. As they moved toward Major Sherer, he ordered the squad of Union soldiers to fix bayonets and form a picket line in front of him. That action cemented in the minds of New Orleans residents that Major Sherer was, indeed, the "Devil of New Orleans" working for the "Beast of New Orleans." For that he would be cursed till his dying day. As Major Sherer backed away from the tormented scene he glimpsed Nancy mourning her little girl. But his dark heart would not even consider consoling her. She was the French Vaqueros whore!

The tragedy outside the Alvarado family home was not going to put Pasqual in a particularly good light. Ever since he had been assigned billeting to the Alvarado house he had hoped to be able to steal some intimate moments with Julia. They needed to make plans, but his heavy-duty schedule put pressure on their secret relationship; a taboo affair for many in New Orleans.

Wearing a Union uniform was more debilitating than he had anticipated. Susanna insisted he dress for supper in civilian attire whenever he could. After all, she still had a son in the Confederate army. But the death of his adopted niece was the most difficult thing. The general population blamed the Union army for the tragedy and him by extension. He knew Julia hated the blues even more now. Her cousins were both dead, now her niece, and her brother hadn't been heard from in over a year. Pasqual was anxious to talk to his sweetheart, but was usually thwarted by events or the family. If only Nancy or John would speak to their parents, things might be easier.

"Nancy, a moment please," said a nervous Pasqual.

"Pasqual, what is it? I am in a hurry to go to the docks and then to the church to make the final funeral plans for the little one."

It was the way she said "the docks" that heightened Pasqual's interest. Something about it didn't seem right. Why go to the docks at all? The funeral was paramount. Pasqual's mind was working overtime; to the point that he forgot what he was going to ask Nancy.

Nancy was in deep conversation with a French sea captain and two of his sailors inside of the Alvarado Warehouse number one. The single candle lit only a modest portion of the center of the barn like structure. There were seven wooden barrels standing next to Nancy and the captain and the pair seemed to be haggling over the price of each barrel. Pasqual's approach was unnoticed by all gathered around the scattered barrels. The captain seemed to keep his hand on one barrel in particular as he fervently argued with Nancy. Pasqual thought he had enough evidence, but wanted Nancy to finish what she was doing and leave the scene so he could act. But when the corporal standing beside him stumbled on a wooden crate his stealthy observation was uncovered.

"Halt, raise your hands and don't move!" yelled Pasqual.

The French sailors, not understanding his commands and thinking they were about to be robbed, turned on Pasqual with their belt knives drawn. The Union corporal shot the nearest sailor in the leg knocking him to the ground. He then pressed his bayonet to the chest of the second sailor forcing him to drop his knife.

The look on Nancy's and the French sea captain's faces was stunned confusion.

Nancy tried to speak, but Pasqual raised his hand, stopping her. The French sea captain cursed at Pasqual and started to claim international exemption under some sort of French treaty, but Pasqual again raised his hand, stopping him from speaking further. He had to think. General Butler had gotten into a lot of

trouble harassing foreign nationals in New Orleans, even drawing a rebuke from the President of the United States. Pasqual
could not afford to be the source of an international incident.

"Corporal, is the warehouse completely surrounded?"

"Yes, sir, every window, every door."

Pasqual drew his pistol. "Good, assemble all your men here.
We have the smugglers."

"Yes, sir!"

Pasqual did not allow any conversation until the ten man
squad of blue soldiers surrounded the smugglers.

"Corporal, detach one private and escort this young lady
back to her residence. I have no idea what these French brigands
had in mind, but we will not let it pass in New Orleans."

"Sir!"

The French sea captain detected that something was up and
remained quiet, intently listening to Pasqual's instructions.

"Everyone here, start rolling these barrels back to the French
ship," commanded Pasqual.

Once the party arrived at the wharf where the ship was tied
up, Pasqual ordered the two sailors to board, but held the captain back. He could see the crew members on board were per-
turbed that one of their own was wounded in the leg and that
their captain was being held on the dock.

"Corporal, skirmish line facing the ship, fix bayonets."

"Sir!"

"Captain, start rolling all the barrels off the dock and into the
river," directed Pasqual.

The French sea captain did not argue, knowing this act would
snuff out an international incident that neither country wanted.
He pushed six of the barrels, one by one, off the wharf into the
Mississippi River; each one floating down river. After each barrel splashed into the water the French crewmen seemed to grow

more agitated, seeing profits floating away. The seventh barrel sank when it hit the river water.

Pasqual had his back to the ship's gunwale and did not see two of the ship's crew peek over it with pistols pointed at him, but the French captain did. It all happened in a blink of an eye.

"Arreter!" yelled the captain as both seamen fired at Pasqual. Simultaneously, the corporal ordered the picket line of blue soldiers to fire at the two pistol armed seamen. The noise was jarring. Pasqual turned in time to dodge the pistol balls, but the French captain was grazed in the leg by one of his own men's pistol shot. None of the volley of rifle balls from the army rifles scathed the seaman, but rather hit the rigging and gunwale of the ship.

"Reload!" shouted the corporal, "and prepare to board the ship."

"Belay that order, corporal!" demanded Pasqual as he assisted the wounded sea captain up the gang plank and flung him to the deck.

"Corporal, have your squad withdraw the gang plank, cast off the mooring lines."

"No, lieutenant, you cannot do this!" yelled the first mate. "We do not have any sails set and we will not have any steerage, we will drift in the river to who knows where. The sun is setting, we cannot navigate!"

"That's your problem, sir. Deal with it!"

The scramble to set sails was a blur of activity by the French seamen while the river turned the frigate this way and that. But Pasqual was relieved that they did get it under control.

"Corporal, form the squad and move at the double-quick back to the barracks."

Pasqual knew that the gunfire would attract attention. He didn't want another incident like the one that had happened to Major Sherer. He was determined to get his boys to cover. Maybe, just maybe, nobody would be the wiser.

However, Pasqual new he had one more thing to do. With the men on their way back to barracks, he dropped back and confiscated a tavern goers' horse and headed to the southern docks. The guards there belonged to a different regiment and he was not sure they would obey his orders.

As he rode up to the most southern of New Orleans docks both of the white solders came to attention "You boys keep an eye out. Six barrels of flour fell of the dock up stream and are floating our way. Recover them and a young lady will come here in the morning and give directions to send them on the St. Mary orphanage. Get to it".

Major Sherer did hear the volley of rifle fire and came running to the north docks as fast as he could. He was eager to avoid an army versus civilian incident like the one three days before. But when he arrived there was no one there. He thought that there had been a French frigate tied up to this dock only this morning, but it too was gone. Maybe he was mistaken. He was about to return to his headquarters to dispatch the patrols to enforce curfew when he felt like someone was staring at him from the shadows. He could not see anyone immediately, but he just felt it. He instinctively drew his saber.

To the side of the warehouse in a shadowy fold that could obscure a person, John Alvarado stepped forward. He was resolute in his approach toward his hated foe, never faltering in his march toward Major Sherer. John halted several feet from him so that he could see his eyes clearly in the fading sun light.

"I thought you were dead, you French Mexican whore!" exclaimed Major Sherer in a slightly high pitched voice.

"You killed my little girl!" John snarled and in a low, controlled voice said, "I will do to you the same."

Major Sherer did not blanch, but pivoted his saber in his hand, making ready for the fight.

"I owe you, too, John Alvarado. We will settle it here and now."

John knew that if he fought without emotion and thought clearly, he would be deadlier in combat. Sherer's face flushed red, and his neck muscles seemed to throb and pulse as his heartbeat increased. John also knew that a man with a saber was only good for four or five swings before his arm began slowing from fatigue. As long as he was quick and nimble, he would be able to press his small scrimshaw engraved handle knife home at the critical moment. Avoiding the crushing blows of a saber was not going to be easy though.

"I see you're weakened by your neck wound. I don't wish to take advantage of you, Mr. French Vaquero."

"Look to your last sunset, bastard!"

John was not ready for Sherer's first slash, but he reacted in time. The full cross cut at John's head was so swift it halved John's hat and caused Major Sherer to pirouette and spin three hundred sixty degrees. Their eyes met. The sun's retreating flame glowing in the major's deep-set eyes gave him an evil look. A forward thrust missed John entirely as he stepped lightly to his left. Major Sherer was putting all his force into his attack hoping to end the fight quickly. It was also the sign of a desperate man. John still hadn't slashed at his adversary. He needed to get in under the major's saber to be effective. Being patient was all John could do for now.

The major then forced a downward blow that caught John off guard. John tried to move to his right, but the saber came down on John's left leg catching the top edge of his boot, shaving away a good six inches of the leather. John could feel his own blood dripping down his leg onto his sock covered ankle. Still John did not parry. He could see beads of sweat forming on the major's brow. He was tiring from swinging the heavy blade of the saber. John turned so his back was to the mooring line post and he backed up to two of them till he felt them against his backside. He stood there inviting Major Sherer to strike. And strike he did, with a double handed grip on the saber, Sherer thought to cleave John in half. At the last possible moment John ducked and moved so that the downward force of the blade stuck itself into one of the mooring pylons.

Sherer, for a split second tried to dislodge his saber, giving John just enough time to move in and thrust his own small blade into Major Sherer's chest. It was a fluid motion taking a fraction of a second. John's blade went through the heavy blue jacket and into his nemesis's heart. Sherer hung on John's blade for a moment then collapsed to the dock floor, dead before he hit the ground.

There was no time to celebrate. John had to move fast. He rolled the dead major into the fast moving Mississippi River, threw the saber into the muddy water as well as his own scrimshaw knife that his uncle had given to him so many years before. Just as he tossed it away the last rays of the sun disappeared beyond the horizon. John knew he had killed his last man. But this time there was no regret.

EPILOGUE

General Butler, the "Beast of New Orleans," was relieved of command of the district by President Lincoln in December of 1862. The travesties of executing civilians, confiscating private property, and constantly enraging international powers were too much for the president. Butler was reassigned to the eastern theater of the war where he performed poorly as a field commander. He later was elected four times to Congress and once as governor of Massachusetts. He failed in his attempt to become president on the Democratic ticket.

Major Sherer failed to report for duty that following day and was considered absent without authorized leave. Three days later, a bloated body was noted floating down the Mississippi River that had a blue jacket on it with one majors' epaulet. It was assumed that the major was injured, slipped off the docks, and drowned in the swift waters of the' Big Muddy'. The City of New Orleans was obligated to bury him as it had done for countless other hapless men over the last century. Two days after his burial someone smashed his gravestone with a sledge hammer.

Napoleon Alvarado invested heavily in southern railroads and riverine barge traffic. The family fortune was assured with him at the helm of the business. He never married, preferring to play the field.

John's son, and Gunter's stepson, Stephen, had a high adventure in the gold fields of Alaska. Later in life they both enlisted in Teddy Roosevelt's Rough Riders and served with distinction in the Cuban war. An Alvarado served in every one of Americas' wars. Donald Alvarado rose to the rank of colonel and was the chief of logistics for the Big Red 1 division in the Vietnam War. But for the most part, the Alvarados found the National Guard enough military.

Unfortunately, Pasqual and Julia never married. If there was any city in the South that might have tolerated an interracial marriage it would have been New Orleans. But the general feeling in the city was that Pasqual had put on a blue uniform and for that, he could never be forgiven. They remained close for over twenty-five years, wondering if the day would ever come that they might consummate their relationship. No one ever knew that it was Pasqual who tried to mitigate the efforts of the "Beast of New Orleans" and the "Devil of New Orleans."

Nancy and John remained together into their eighties; never leaving each other's side for more than 24 hours. They became the leading family of that great, gracious, friendly, and cosmopolitan city.

Nancy continued to write under her nom de plume for the Paris newspaper. She constantly sent articles to the paper that dealt with the excesses of the new-found Jim Crow laws that were making their way through governments in the South. She always used the proceeds to help the less fortunate in the city. Her journal, from which this novel is derived, was rescued from her home's attic after Hurricane Katrina.

John successfully ran for the state legislature two more times. He was asked to run for governor but declined when he realized that he would have to enforce the Jim Crow laws. He was unsuccessful in getting the funding for any major university system for Louisiana.

Patch became a minor celebrity when, during one of John's campaigns, a northern carpet bagger tried to shout John down while he was giving a speech. Patch pinned his ears back, picked the carpet bagger up by the back of his coat collar, shook him and then dropped him to the ground. The crowd was delirious. Horses are smarter than we think.

"Well corporal Scott, that is the gospel about John Alvarado, the French Vaquero of New Orleans."

"Well sir, you do have a famous and notorious relative. Hell, of a story. Someone ought right a book about him."

After a very long pause Lt. Alvarado said, "I think I will Scotty."

THE END

CPSIA information can be obtained
at www.ICGtesting.com
Printed in the USA
BVHW030525310121
599043BV00001B/45

9 781977 233721